NOWHERE PEOPLE

NOWHERE PEOPLE

Paulo Scott

Translated by
Daniel Hahn

LONDON · NEW YORK

First published in English translation in 2014 by
And Other Stories
London – New York

www.andotherstories.org

First published as *Habitante Irreal* in 2011 by
Editora Objetiva, Rio de Janeiro, Brazil

ISBN 9781908276384
eBook ISBN 9781908276391

A catalogue record for this book is available from the British Library.

Supported by the National Lottery through Arts Council England.

Obra publicada com o apoio do Ministério da Cultura
do Brasil / Fundação Biblioteca Nacional. This work was
published with the support of the Brazilian Ministry
of Culture / National Library Foundation.

Supported using public funding by
**ARTS COUNCIL
ENGLAND**
LOTTERY FUNDED

MINISTÉRIO DA CULTURA
Fundação BIBLIOTECA NACIONAL

For Simone da Costa Carvalho

contents

whatever happens there's
always something left
over to happen again

nineteen eighty-nine

If he'd had to summarise his days as a political militant, Paulo would have said that he went from total idealism to unparalleled cynicism, then finally to the melancholy escapism of these last months. That's not how it should have been, just when the Workers' Party won the Town Hall elections in Porto Alegre and he became known up and down the country as a student leader, a key figure with a good chance to try for a seat on the City Council three years from now, and only twenty-one years old, about to graduate in law at the end of the year from the Federal University of Rio Grande do Sul, and for whom it took the whole of last year to realise this fact: that despite his *great potential*, he is no more than a minor foot-soldier, a pawn among the other pieces on the board, not greedy enough to challenge, equal to equal, the schemings of the gang on the second echelon, many of them creeps he had already hated even before he joined, back in eighty-four. His current difficulty in getting more deeply involved in political life, in making a career of it and fighting for it, would only end up in physical dependency, and its price already seems to him to be too high; and he knows that if he does not push himself forward and just allows himself to be carried along by the party's almost inevitable ascent he runs the risk of one day having to cling shamefully to the coat-tails of one of the creeps he so despises in order to get himself a place in the administrative machine and support himself financially. Just as hundreds of his fellow activists are doing, throwing themselves into the contest in the pursuit of positions in the state administrative departments, in the mayor's office, the deputy mayor's office, in foundations, public institutions and joint public-private enterprise; people who until recently, especially over a beer, would insist on beating their chests and declaring they were only there to rescue Brazil from exploitation by capital. In a way, he can understand: he is asking too much of himself and is unable to face up to the days that have finally arrived with any sense of calm, these days towards which his physical, mental and emotional energies have been channelled over the past four years. What is certain is that since the beginning, when he took part in that first local party meeting in Glória in eighty-three, he had promised himself he would not allow his theoretical unpreparedness and almost complete innocence in relation to politics to be transformed into mediocrity. Already he can't help seeing most of the leadership as members of a Machiavellian and tightly-knit little fraternity of opportunists carrying forward their own plans in order to attain power and, consequently, some money as quickly as possible. He has lost his capacity to assimilate contradictions. He has stopped believing. Which is why his focus on what needed to be done and the resulting calm of *belief* have disappeared. This anxiety remains. Less than a month ago at a consultation with Doctor Geraldo, who has been looking after his family for three generations, he heard: 'Paulo, this stress of yours is manifesting too severely in physical symptoms; it's all going to your stomach. It's not normal for a big lad of your age to have chronic gastritis as advanced as yours.' The doctor spoke with his measured border accent and looked at Paulo until he said yes, I know, doctor, I'll try and take care of myself. He left the surgery with a prescription for an acid blocker even stronger than the Cimetidina he was already taking and an absolute ban on consuming any kind of alcoholic drink or spicy food for a fortnight, at least. He doesn't feel comfortable. And even having decided to cut himself off from the party completely, Paulo still has not cancelled his membership and remains bound to the Trotskyite-based organisation with which he has been involved for three years, and last Saturday (despite being deliberately late and missing the ten-thirty bus that had left Porto Alegre the previous night for the city of Rio Grande, carrying another fifteen militants who were taking part in the year's first clandestine meeting of his organisation), he woke up before six, washed his face, packed his law-trainee rucksack with three changes of clothes and left the house in his Durepox-grey Beetle, an eighty-three model, to pull in half an hour later at pump number four at the Ipiranga petrol station on the corner of Santo Antônio and Voluntários da Pátria and ask the attendant to put in thirty litres of petrol which he would split with his two acquaintances from São Lourenço do Sul, Eduardo 'Blondie' Vanusa and 'Handlebar 'Tache' Nico, dressed up as the Beagle Boys, slumped in the passenger seat and the back seat respectively (and still drunk from the rounds of beer with Steinhäger they'd consumed at Bar Lola while they waited for a certain Neide from the Porto de Elis Cocktail Bar – who was going to show up dressed as Dr Frank-N-Furter, the cross-dressing Transylvanian from *The Rocky Horror Show* – to get them into the invitation-only fancy dress party taking place in the Bar Ocidente; Neide, as it turned out, never showed up), and at quarter to seven cross the Guaíba drawbridge and head towards the south of the state for what might be his last meeting as a member of the organisation, driving without worrying about his passengers, who had already given up and were drooling into the upholstery of the seats; driving without having to put up with three hundred kilometres' worth of feeble talk about revolution and the Fourth International, about which of the Workers' Party girls they'd had and, with the help of the most preposterous Reichian arguments, about the ones who might have started off stubborn but were now desperate to give up their pussies. Saturday passed slowly. He struggled to stay awake during the debates; he couldn't bear to look at those people any longer. It was not a coincidence that at night, as soon as the last panel discussion came to an end, he slipped away, got his car, went to Cassino Beach. There he came across the birthday party in the ballroom of the Hotel Atlântico where he happened to run into Manoela, a producer two years older than him, with whom he had fallen in love at the end of a summer on the Ilha do Mel three years back. She was the one who spotted him and came over delightedly and after the requisite where have you been what have you been up to how have we left it so long, and as soon as he said he'd driven down from Porto Alegre, told him she was working as a theatre producer and was currently touring with a group who were due to be on stage at the Sete de Abril Theatre in Pelotas on Sunday and she needed someone reliable to take the costumes for the play back to Novo Hamburgo, where they were based, bemoaning the fact that the original budget was inadequate and that no delivery company would do it quickly enough without charging an arm and a leg and, not letting him respond, said she would give him seven thousand *cruzados* if he would drop the clothes off at her assistant's house to be washed and mended in time for Friday's performance at the University of Vale do Rio dos Sinos; she said that she and the actors would be staying in Pelotas till Thursday night to see to certain commitments they were obliged to honour for the local town hall, and no sooner had she asked would you help me out on this one? than he accepted. It was then that, skilfully, she adjusted the details: the clothes would actually only be ready for him on Tuesday, late in the morning on Tuesday, as there was a workshop, and he knows what they're like, these things to do with didactic stimulation and learning strategies and all that. Paulo felt like he'd been duped. On Monday afternoon he had to be at the law firm where he was doing an internship. He considered for a few moments – there's nothing that needs doing that can't wait till Wednesday (he'll phone to let them know that he'll only come in to work on Wednesday). He let Manoela keep talking until he interrupted. 'I don't have anywhere to stay Sunday night or Monday night.' She smiled (smiling is part of the process by which she senses an opportunity appearing). 'We're in the best hotel in Pelotas,' she said snobbishly. 'Space won't be a problem. The lighting guy's room was vacated yesterday, the nights have already been paid for, it's all settled. You needn't worry, you can take his place . . . and I've got to say, you're in luck: the son of a bitch bagged himself the best room of all.' The truth was, he loved watching her in action, doing whatever she wanted to make her plans happen right away, even when he was the victim. They exchanged small talk, they joined the people shaking frantically on the dance floor. He considered making a move on her, putting his arms round her waist, pushing things a bit just to see where it might go, but there was no point. Manoela had always been out of his league, she always would be. And as a song came to an end, in a blasé tone of voice that made him feel confusingly mature, rather like Manoela herself, he said I'm going to go for that walk now, Manu, she stroked his face affectionately, and each went their own way. He got a beer from the pantry, struck up a conversation with a girl who looked just like the actress Malu Mader and who seemed to have had too much to drink. This pretend Malu, who was really Ana Cristina something-or-other, said some nonsense that really annoyed him; all the same they walked together to a party that was happening two blocks from the hotel and where to his misfortune they were only serving a sweet red wine. He lied about having already graduated and said that he was travelling to Cuba in a few weeks and then to Spain and Portugal to do a master's in comparative law at Coimbra. Lying, lying out of spite, was what the situation called for, it was the only way to be affectionate, responsive. Even though she was pretty out of it, she said that she so loved his *dynamism*, and he kissed her unenthusiastically (her resemblance to the goddess Malu Mader was not close enough). Then he listened to her country-girl inanities until he was convinced that it would be better to get back to his accommodation once and for all and make sure he was in a suitable physical condition for the following morning's debates. Contrary to his expectations, the Sunday debates were worse than Saturday's. He didn't stay for the end. He had no qualms about slipping away early, his fuck-it switch was activated; in his mess of a life nothing would go back to the way it used to be. He wanted madness, impetuosity – like he found in all those French writers he read, in the English bands from the sixties, Spanish comic books, the rhythmic ferocity of rap, the words and attitudes that should be current and brilliant, endless and impossible. He rushed to reach Pelotas before it got dark. The hotel and the room were indeed very nice, and on Monday – after finally managing to park his car in the guest car park which had, according to the manager, been full all weekend because of the National Festival of Desserts – spent his day wandering the city's streets and squares and around half past six in the evening went into Aquários, the café-diner on the corner of Quinze de Novembro and Sete de Setembro, for an espresso. The counter, the tables, all occupied. He thought about turning around, yet instinct made him walk over to the table by the side door, where a teenage girl with short black hair wearing glasses with funny white frames was busy reading an issue of *DUNDUM* magazine (what girl from the interior would be sitting blithely reading *DUNDUM* in this place, the absolute domain of middle-aged men?). He approached, asked if he might sit down, she threw him a suspicious glance, said nothing, he assured her he wouldn't take up more than a few inches of the table, explained that he had been walking all day and wouldn't be able to enjoy his coffee if he had to drink it standing up. She nodded, making no effort to hide her surprise at the sheer nerve of this guy, he thanked her and seeing that her cup was empty asked whether he could buy her a drink, she said she'd have a tea. It was easy enough for them to start up a conversation that would reveal her name, Angélica, and her odd, ironic, rude, dry sense of humour. They talked mainly about poetry (she was much more comfortable on this subject than he was). At a certain point in the conversation she took a spiral-bound exercise book from her bag, the kind that schoolchildren use. She didn't make any fuss, just opened it at a page near the middle and (after giving him a meaningful stare) began to draw him. Paulo didn't want to ask, didn't want to interfere, he kept talking. She finished the drawing, closed the exercise book, put it down on the table. Even after other tables had become free and the activity in the café had thinned out, they remained sitting there together till the place closed, at which point they paid the bill and left. The moment they set foot on the pavement, Angélica handed him the exercise book, said that he would be part of a new game which one of her school friends had made up and that she'd thought was really cool. 'You get an ordinary exercise book, like this one, you find someone you like a lot, you draw that person as best you can, then you give it to them, on condition that they'll write something on the following page and, without waiting too long, a week at most, they then pass it on to someone else, who passes it on to someone else and so on. I'm not sure I've explained it clearly. Have I?' He said it was a bit like a promissory note to the bearer, a promissory note that would never be paid and, as soon as she was done smiling, he asked whether he was allowed to believe that she liked him a lot. She took a cigarette out of her bag and shrugged just the way someone old and weary of life would shrug after revealing their affection for someone who wasn't expecting it (or who didn't deserve it, but it happened anyway). She changed the subject. 'There are some poems I wrote in the first dozen pages.' He didn't wait, he tried to give her the kind of hug a friend would give her but she moved away saying, frowning, that she was really late for a family engagement, before turning her back on him sharply and walking off towards Praça Coronel Osório. He went back to the hotel, opened a few cans of beer, and spent the rest of the night reading and re-reading what was written in the exercise book. Then on Tuesday morning (as soon as the actors had released the costumes) he took all the various bags they handed him, folded down the back seat of the Beetle, arranged the luggage, covered it with a dark grey cloth that Manoela had insisted on giving him, stressing how useful it would be in stopping all that gear from attracting the attention of the highway police, and, just minutes before it started raining, he, Paulo, turned right onto the BR-116 towards Porto Alegre. And at Cerro Grande, even with the limited visibility due to the rain that had now become a storm, he saw a shape, a person crouching by the side of the left-hand lane. He braked without stopping completely. It was a little Indian girl holding a pile of newspapers and magazines to her chest. Beside her, two white plastic bags on the ground. He lowered the car window and let his gaze rest on her, wondering, struck by the sight of her, how far she'd have to walk to find somewhere dry where she could take shelter (the closest indigenous villages were kilometres away). He looked in his rear-view mirror. Behind him: the deserted road. And, now looking back at her over his shoulder (the car moving at less than ten kilometres an hour), he thought about stopping, but he did not.

two

A few kilometres further down the road and refusing to admit that, for a moment, his nerve had failed him and that the sight of the girl had struck him like almost nothing else in his life, Paulo imagines that some lorry (even though not a single vehicle has passed him going in the opposite direction) must have stopped already and offered her a lift. He goes on for a few hundred metres, pulls over, turns off the engine. Takes a deep breath, twists round towards the back seat of the Beetle, pulls off the dark grey cloth covering the various bags holding the clothes from the theatre company, opens one, takes out a white face towel that looks unused, a sweater and a pair of tracksuit bottoms, size S. He also finds a little retractable umbrella in the worst sort of green, a luminous lime colour. He looks ahead, then again into the rearview mirror, starts the engine, switches the indicator left and gets back onto the southbound lane, keeping his speed slow because of the storm that is getting ever stronger and the worn-out tyres which threaten to send the vehicle skidding on the water. He feels put out, a feeling that gets worse as the number of kilometres increases: three hundred and sixty, three hundred and sixty-one, three hundred and sixty-two, sixty-three, four, five, six, three hundred and sixty-seven. (He hadn't realised he had driven so far.)

She is in the same place, in the same position. He tells himself to take care, not to startle her. She looks up and gets to her feet, picks up her plastic bags, taking a few steps back as she realises that the car is going to pull over. He stops beside her, lowers the window half-way while trying to appear as unthreatening as possible, asks her to get in (as though addressing a foreigner with an incomplete grasp of Portuguese), says he'll give her a lift, perhaps up to the nearest petrol station or the high-way police watch-post. She doesn't answer, looking him straight in the eye. He insists, but she remains fearful. 'It's not going to work, these types of good intentions just do not work . . . ' he mutters quietly before picking up the umbrella and getting out of the car. As soon as she sees him opening the door, she crosses the road. Once on the other side she begins to walk hurriedly south. For a moment he stops where he is, there in front of the Volkswagen, watching her move away (the rain and its weight cover him with deafness and mineral obliteration). He returns to the Beetle, takes the towel and the items of clothing and, cursing uninterruptedly, without any clue what he might lose or gain by doing this, he leaves the car and goes after her.

If, to make matters worse, the National Highway Police were to pull over wanting to know what all this was about, Paulo would say he had no very clear reason. He would confide to them that, these last three years, almost everything he'd done had been done out of a contagious inertia, a blind freedom that needed to be exercised urgently not only for himself, but for all the Brazilians who, having lived through the height of the military regime, now need to promise themselves that they can be just and emancipated and happy, and so much so that they will accept the most obvious determinism by which enemies can be easily recognised and by which the truth is a discovery that is on your side, comfortable, destined to hold out against all things. A line of argument that, if uprooted, placed into the context of a tv comedy show, would be just as useless and pathetic as silence, or as finding that, at such a moment, upon realising that the headlights were still on and the Beetle's engine running, the sensible thing to do might be to walk the hundred, hundred-and-something metres back to the car and turn off the lights, shut off the engine, find a suitable plastic bag in which to wrap the pieces of clothing and the towel, lock the doors, put the key away in his trouser pocket, and only then, with the reassurance of the police authorities (and the applause of the studio audience) resume his chasing after the Indian girl. He stands transfixed in this anguish of speculation and, when he refocuses, he looks south and is surprised at how far she has already got (he'll really have to make an effort if he is to catch up with her). He looks back at the car. Now, holding the umbrella with the same hand that has the clothes, sets off at a faster pace until, once he has come very close to her, he spots how the Indian girl is looking discreetly over her shoulder and slowing down, and a few metres before he reaches her she turns abruptly towards him. He waits a moment, catching his breath, holding out the umbrella and bits of material for her to take. 'I'm just trying to help.' He points his index finger at the things he is holding in his other hand and then points at her. 'It's dry clothes . . . Dry clothes . . . ' She takes them, and the umbrella, too. 'I can take you to some shelter, but if you don't want to, that's fine, I'll leave you here. I'm going back to the car,' he gestures with his thumb. 'If you want a lift, if you want me to take you,' he emphasises this, 'just come with me' – and he uses his fingers to mime a person walking towards the car. The Indian girl looks right at him. In the middle of all that rain, he feels – just glancingly – that they won't come to any solution. And he tries for the last time. 'My name's Paulo . . . What's yours?' She doesn't reply. He imagines that perhaps she can't hear him properly, because there's this distance between the two of them and the noise of the rain on the nylon surface of the umbrella. He realises there is nothing left for him to do, turns back towards the car. He walks twenty metres or so before looking back: she is following him. When he reaches the vehicle he gets in, leaving the passenger door open. She stops beside the car and gets in a muddle trying to close the umbrella. He wonders whether or not he ought to help her and just waits. Then she sits down beside him, her breathing hurried, her eyes fixed ahead of her. A few moments later she closes the door, he starts up the engine and pulls out slowly towards the north. In the eight-kilometre stretch to the restaurant they sit in silence. He keeps his window lowered (because he himself needs to be unthreatening) and the inside of the car gets wet from the rain.

He stops in the space furthest to the left, a few metres from the toilets. The Indian girl gets out of the car. She seems surer of herself; she seems to have understood when he said that it would be better if she put on the dry clothes. She goes off to change. And from the back seat of the car he takes his law-trainee rucksack, pulls out the only t-shirt that's fit to wear, a pair of shorts, a pair of sandals, too, and heads straight for the toilets. He takes longer than he meant to. When he comes out, he looks around in every direction trying to spot the girl. He sees no indication that she's already come out. He goes into the restaurant. To the right there's a snack counter. Savoury snacks from the oven, ham and cheese rolls, slices of cake, all displayed under glass covers. He chooses a seat near the window, far from the other customers, he asks for a cup of coffee with milk. His order is served. He tells the guy behind the counter that he'll be back in a moment, he goes outside. She's standing beside the CRT payphone wearing the clothes he gave her. He gestures for her to come in, she stays just where she is, out of place. He approaches, takes the carrier bags and the umbrella from her left hand and, when he tries to take the stack of newspapers and magazines that she is holding squeezed against her chest, she resists. Then he gently takes hold of her wrist and leads her in with him to where he'd been sitting. 'Do you want a coffee?' She declines with a shake of her head. It doesn't seem unreasonable to insist, 'A Coca-Cola?' 'Yes,' she says (speaking to him for the first time). He orders the soft drink and a serving of buttered toast from the waitress who has taken the man's place, an affected woman who has planted herself in front of them as though she were the manager of the place or even the owner. She doesn't seem up for any friendly chitchat. 'Name' says the Indian girl, 'Maína.' *Christ*, he thinks, *she doesn't even speak Portuguese properly.* When the waitress returns with the order, she dumps the plate with the toast down on the tablecloth. Paulo makes a point of saying thank you. Maína remains immobile, holding on to the stack of papers. After a few moments, in which she takes no initiative, he pours the drink into the glass just recently put there and pushes the plate towards her.

'It's for you. You must be hungry, right?' She puts the newspapers and magazines down on the chair next to her, picks up the half-slice of toast, takes her first bite. 'What's all that for?' Paulo asks, pointing his index finger towards the pile of newspapers and magazines. 'On the road . . . was throw away,' she replies as soon as she has swallowed. 'You like reading?' he asks. 'Got them . . . ' she hesitates as she speaks, 'keep . . . learned at school. Speaking Portuguese . . . little . . . read little. No much practice.' He sees how beautiful the girl is, how graceful her face, even when she is uneasy. 'And how old are you?' he goes on. She replies with a shy smile, says nothing. 'Your age?' he insists. 'I'm twenty-one . . . ' holding all his fingers stretched out, twice, plus his index finger on its own. 'And you?' he points at her. 'How old?' He isn't coming across as threatening. 'Fourteen,' she replies. *What am I doing?* he thinks, aware that the waitress-manager has brought about a small revolt in their surroundings and now the fourteen customers, all of whom look like Italian immigrants, are staring in his direction, judging him, having already made a note of the Beetle's license plate, ready to report him should news break of the misfortune to befall that Indian girl, any Indian girl, in the coming days. *God, talk about naivety, Paulo.* 'Too bad,' he says to himself, as he watches her eat and recalls the seminar on the fortieth anniversary of the Universal Declaration of Human Rights that he took part in last year (he was very interested in the young woman who organised it, a Uruguayan militant from Amnesty International) and the panel on which a tribal chief described the terrible living conditions of the indigenous ethnic groups in the southern part of the country. The chief used the expression 'the Calvary of the indigenous ethnic groups' before talking about the ludicrous number of families living alongside the highways because of conflicts within the villages, because of a shortage of land, because of a lack of space. Paulo hadn't the faintest idea that this was precisely the case of the Indian girl sitting in front of him now.

Living by the side of the BR-116, without her older sister, who vanished from her life more than a year ago, trying to keep her spirits up, weaving baskets out of *cipó* vines, playing as best she could with her two younger sisters, allowing each day to be overtaken by the next, going unnoticed (even since becoming the target of her mother's increased attention, for having twice attempted suicide: the first time, a little over two years ago, the week after a friend who lived in a neighbouring encampment had died for reasons as yet unexplained on a Sunday night when he had apparently gone off for a football match between the local teams; and the second, less than six months ago, when she was sure that she could not bear their difference from the non-Indians, that she would become a melancholy adult just like her mother). Now and again she hears of her forebears and of the indigenous people's resistance in the lands to the south. She even heard this from three non-Indian, Guarani-speaking students who used to show up from time to time at the village (in the days when her family still lived in the village). She looks around her, she sees no resistance at all. Her little sister is playing in the soot, in the dust from the rubber tyres. She goes as far as contemplating how she might kill her before the girl is able to understand her own misfortune. She would have no remorse because she knows – and Maína does everything she can to believe it – that she would be going to a better *life*. Maína believes in the soul, even though she herself cannot imagine what the abstraction that reveals the soul must be like. Every night she dreams of someplace differ-ent, where there are no grown-ups or, at least, no adults like her father who took off when she was nine years old. Without him, things got complicated for her mother and the four children; they had to leave the village. Maína doesn't know quite what to do: she has never been in a restaurant like this restaurant; she has never been in a restaurant at all. A few weeks earlier Maína had started to feel afraid, that's why she ran away. Once Maína dreamed the image of God, he had a fragile body and came out of his hiding place to be with her. For a moment Maína thought this guy might be God or a spirit. What non-Indian would stop on the road and treat her this well? She finishes the snack that he's ordered for her. Now she just needs to use a few words to make him understand that she wishes to get back into the raincloud-coloured car and accompany him wherever he would like to take her, even if it takes hours, the whole day, until she has invented a language that will work for them both, a language from the place of God and the spirits that like to pass themselves off as non-Indians, until she manages to close her eyes tight and (perhaps repeating the choice made by her older sister) disappear.

The road sign read 'START OF ROADSIDE INDIG-ENOUS CAMP (NEXT 28 KM)', and Paulo has already asked her three times where she would like to get out. She limits her replies to the same gesture with her hand to keep on going. So this time, which would be the fourth time, Paulo indicates right, pulling the car over in front of one of the huts. 'Sorry, you're going to have to get out.' He articulates the words carefully and deliberately. She doesn't reply. 'I can't take you any further,' he says. She doesn't budge. 'Come on, Maína. You know it isn't safe to be going around, just . . . ' he can't find the words, 'just around like this, with a stranger. It's dangerous.' He gets out, walks around the car, opens her door. 'You can keep the clothes. I just . . . ' And she interrupts him. 'Give lift to the city. Then I comes back alone. I come back, you let me.' *Well, Paulo, you begged her and now you've got what you asked for.* 'It's just I can't . . . ' Without getting up, she says a choked please. Paulo looks around them, doesn't see anyone, the hut they had stopped alongside gives every indication of being empty, no sign of activity. The girl is at a breaking point, weakened into an absolute conviction that she must run away and that if she fails at this moment she will end up in some other car or headed for some worse destiny. The moments pass; they are part of a test that intoxicates him. This morning when he turned on the hotel radio tuned to a local FM station they were playing a hit by Legião Urbana: *every day when I wake up, I no longer have the time that's gone.* The same line that for much of the journey he'd had in his head and which is now the imaginary soundtrack getting in the way of his making a decision. His clothes dampening, the rain propels him on. *But I have so much time, we have all the time in the world.* There can't be many things worse than her spending the rest of her adolescence and her life stuck on the verge of that filthy road. His house in Porto Alegre is empty, his parents are away, his sister is spending the whole year on an exchange in the United States. He closes the passenger door, resolved to bring her back tomorrow morning at the latest (that's when the imaginary voice of Renato Russo starts belting out the chorus).

In Novo Hamburgo the rain is easing a bit and that should make things easier, but the coordinates Manoela has given him are not exact (the assistant's house isn't where she marked it on the map she drew on a piece of paper with the Pelotas hotel logo on it; nobody knows the alley she marked, swearing it couldn't be easier to find). Beaten-earth roads, the wrong directions taking Paulo down increasingly steep and pot-holed slopes, getting further and further away from the built-up part of town. He has a phone number for Manoela's assistant, but he hasn't seen a payphone to call from in several minutes. Things are only no worse because the little Indian girl smiles peacefully each time he turns to her, as though the whole mess were completely normal, and because they are in a car whose rear wheel traction stops them from skidding on that muddy track. They might already have fallen into one of the ditches if they were in, say, a VW Passat or a Chevy Opala. He gives up and goes back to the convenience store where he asked for directions the first time. He calls the assistant. He wasn't far, as it turned out, his mistake had been taking one turning too early. On the other end of the line the girl makes a point of telling him that the place he'd ended up in wasn't the best place to get lost, it's definitely the most dangerous part of the city, the so-called 'Valmerão Pass'. He goes back to the main road, takes the correct turning. The assistant is waiting for them outside the house with a huge yellow umbrella, she notices that the Indian girl is wearing items of clothing belonging to the group and says only that she can return them any time she wants. Paulo returns the back seat of the car to its normal position. He tells Maína to sit there because the upholstery is dry. She shakes her head to indicate that she isn't going to move.

*

The car is in the parking space in front of the house. Paulo and Maína go in the side door. Paulo takes her straight to the bathroom, turns on the light, shows her where the towels are, says he'll be back in a minute. He walks through the house wondering what he can offer her to wear, he raids his sister's wardrobe (the two of them are nearly the same size), takes a pair of jeans, knickers, socks, the black All-Star trainers with little skulls like the ones you see on pirate flags – his sister said she was going to give them to a charity shop – and an AC/DC t-shirt. He goes back to the bathroom, hands over the clothes, switches on the electric shower, sets it to what he thinks is a pleasant temperature, shows her how to lock the bathroom door from the inside and says he's going to make something for them to eat. In the fridge he finds the pan with the spaghetti he made on Friday. He heats it up on the stove. He opens a can of tuna, he mixes mayonnaise and ketchup and garlic paste in a shallow jar, opens a litre bottle of Coke. He lays out a tablecloth, plates, cutlery and all the rest. He waits for her to come out of the bathroom. They eat in silence. She finishes the food on the plate and then, unprompted, helps herself to more. He goes to his room, collects all the issues of *Trip* magazine he can find, six in total, and leaves them with her. He says to choose whichever ones she wants. He looks at his watch: nine-thirty. There's still time for a quick shower. He goes up to his father's study to check whether anyone has left a message on the answering machine, listens to Adrienne's message inviting him to a party tonight at the flat she shares with Serginho and Carlos. He goes downstairs, has his shower. When he comes back into the pantry, Maína has the magazines open on the table and she is looking at the pictures of the *Trip* girls. Without a word he clears the plates, goes out into the yard, walks over to the garage, gets two sheets of clean plastic like camping groundsheets, covers the car seats, which smell of wet dog, comes back, tells Maína to leave the magazines there, but she prefers to hold on to them all. Paulo picks up a tote bag belonging to his sister, one of the many she has bought and never used, puts the magazines inside, closes up the house, gets into the car and only then begins to hurry so that they will arrive in time for the ten o'clock showing at the Baltimore.

They are going to see the remastered print of *Fantasia*, the Walt Disney animation. First he bought sweet popcorn from old Pestana, whose little cart is right at the door to the cinema; the old man loves telling the unwary that in the sixties he was an employee of the Piratini Steel Company and one of the sixty thousand activists from the so-called Group of Eleven set up in sixty-three by Brizola to bring about the socialist revolution in Brazil. He says he's read every book by Tolstoy translated into Portuguese and, invariably, he ends the conversation with a mild rant on the evils of alcohol (the damage it does to the liver and the pancreas, the disarray it causes to a routine, to social composure) despite the fact that he is quite evidently an alcoholic himself. Naturally, as he has known Paulo for some time (and he can recognise when he's unlikely to find an opening for his tired old digressions), the old man doesn't even start his litany, though as he hands the bag of popcorn to Maína he does say that she is a true jewel of the Brazilian El Dorado.

Paulo tries to describe to her what the experience is going to be like. The images being projected, the moment when the mouse will command all the things and the sounds of the universe. Maína is barely listening. The film has caught her attention, the soundtrack, the colours, the introductions, the stories. He got lucky with the programming: only *The Wizard of Oz* might have topped it (he is sure that 'Somewhere Over the Rainbow', in Judy Garland's devastating interpretation, would change that girl's life); he's lucky she didn't get scared. The film ends. The two of them wait till the light from the projector and the music are switched off. They look at one another. He takes in the girl, all kitted out like a punk-goth with her seed necklace over the fabric of the AC/DC t-shirt and the smell of Phebo Rose soap, sat in the dirty red leather seat of the Baltimore with her canvas bag full of damp pages from newspapers and magazines, fresh from the experience of an invisibility hitherto unknown to her, allowing herself to look, and looking. Perhaps there's some kind of answer there. Paulo knows there is, but he can't do it, it's hard to make out.

He explains that they're going to a party. There will be some odd people there, the kind of people she probably hasn't been around before. Maína nods her head, showing that she's happy, that everything's fine. She says she needs to go to the bathroom, he shows her where it is and waits under the awning in front of the building. And he catches sight of Titi Mafalda with her friends, the three Marias, in tow. 'Hey, senhor Dickhead!' she shouts from a distance in her unmistakable Ceará accent. 'Still hanging out in that *art-house* cinema, then? Standing there with those panty-wetting legs of yours and all these girls going to waste . . . You men are all complete asses, you really are.' Not long ago at all, Paulo had gone out with Maria Rita, the prettiest of the four. Although they'd only hung out a few times, which had been fun to begin with, things hadn't ended well; on the first and only occasion they arranged to go to Fin de Siècle to dance and meet their friends, breaking with the movie-then-dinner-then-her-flat formula, it had been a disaster. It only took half an hour for them to end up standing outside the nightclub, Maria Rita – who without her doctor's permission had stopped taking her antidepressants – completely overcome with hysterics, gnawing at the palm of her right hand till she bled, him trying to stop her, her going back to the self-harming the moment he released her. They carried on this little performance till Paulo let go of her, telling her to go to hell, and went back into the bar. He learned days later that she had spread the word to everyone that he'd given her gonorrhoea, which everyone realised, knowing her as they did, was another one of her lies. 'Hey, it's the Northeastern girls,' says Paulo, needling them already, as the four of them come to a stop in front of him. 'You all right, Rita?' She nods, lets out a restrained smile. 'Come with us to have a few at the Magazine Bar. I'm heading there to see if I run into Passo Fundo; the Gaucho bastard owes me two thousand and it's been an age . . . ' Titi says brashly, with an attitude in marked contrast to the lethargy of the other three. 'Can't do it, Titi, I'm going to a party,' Paulo explains. 'Whose?' she wants to know (she always wants to know). 'Adrienne's . . . ' he replies a little awkwardly, remembering that the two of them never really got on. 'So come here and give me my three kisses.' Just like she asks everyone else, she always asks him for her three kisses (three times, it's the southern excess, she enjoys this). When Titi approaches to kiss him, Maína appears and stands beside Paulo. Titi is quick to react. 'Who's this child, Paulo?' she asks, looking Maína up and down. 'She's come to visit Porto Alegre,' he says naturally. 'And you're her guide?' asks Maria Rita, pointedly. 'It's only for today . . . Maína, these are my friends.' Maína just smiles. Titi knows Paulo well enough to be sure that the best thing to do right then is to take her

Marias and go. 'We're off, Handsome,' and she gives him three kisses. 'Watch how you go, ok? This girl can't even be twelve yet . . . You trying to break the record of the local rock stars? Trying to be like Brando the rapist? Take it easy, Paulão.' Maria Rita doesn't wait, she walks off without saying goodbye. Maria Eduarda and Maria Clara just nod and follow Titi as soon as she heads back off towards the Magazine. 'Give Passo Fundo a hug from me,' Paulo says before the girls are too far off. The two of them step onto the pavement and set off in the opposite direction to Titi. They walk a few metres, and Maína stops when she sees the popcorn seller (who by now has stored away his little cart) sitting on the front step of an office building, drinking straight out of the mouth of a *cachaça* bottle, past the point of recognising her. She places the bag of magazines into Paulo's hand and approaches the old man, puts her hand on his head. Paulo leaves her to it, leaves their moment to pass.

He walks into the apartment telling everyone that there is to be no messing around with Maína: no alcohol, no coke, no weed for her. He doesn't leave her alone for a minute. As soon as the group who were on the balcony vacate the place, he invites her to sit there and look out over the city. 'Pretty,' says Maína, 'light, lot of light'. Paulo doesn't hold back. 'Chaos, Maína.' He doesn't even know if she knows what chaos is. 'It's a pretty place, but not always a good one.' Luana appears with a tray of savoury

pastries, Maína takes two. 'You sure she isn't up for smoking just a little one?' and gives him a wink. Luana, always
Luana. Paulo gives her a get-out-of-here look. Luana turns
around. Adrienne has spread posters of Fernando Collor de
Mello, the National Reconstruction Party's candidate for
president of the Republic, all over the living room and she
refuses to explain this décor; Adrienne and her eccentrici-
ties. The soundtracks of her little parties are limited to
Brian Eno, Roxy Music, Talking Heads, The Doors, Velvet
Underground, King Crimson and Kraftwerk. So long as he
respects the magnificent seven, as she's dubbed them, a
guest is free to put on any music he chooses. Paulo likes
hanging out with this crowd, it's good being a part of the
group without actually being one of the group; it's less
hard work, less stressful. Paulo doesn't find it easy being
involved with groups or people for too long. Everyone
there is teeming with ideas and plans; no doubt at all
that at least half of them, ten or fifteen years from now,
are going to be calling the shots in Rio Grande do Sul and
the rest of the country. In the meantime they're no more
than a gang of stoners who think they're the shit. Paulo is
waiting for the mini-gig by the band Vulgo Valentin that
has been promised for midnight on the dot but that ends
up only happening at half past one. (Adrienne loves to
torment her neighbours, always with the same strategy:
the mini-gigs get going and only finish when the police
turn up asking them to put an end to the *performance*.)

As soon as the boys finish playing – this time it is the woman who manages the building who has switched off the apartment's power mains and is now giving Adrienne the biggest lecture at the door to the apartment – Paulo calls Maína and they leave. The chosen route is: down Independência, onto Riachuelo, past the town hall and then the old Gasômetro factory, back along Duque de Caxias, then taking Borges at Demétrio Ribeiro, on as far as the beginning of Veríssimo Rosa, turn left, turn right, arrive home.

He'll give Maína his room to sleep in, he shows her how to lock the door from the inside (he feels a bit stupid explaining, the girl has trusted him so far, there shouldn't be any further reason to be afraid, but all the same it seems the right thing to do). He goes up to the study, sits in his father's leather armchair, turns on the television. They're showing *The Thing*, the John Carpenter version, which was called *Enigma do outro mundo – Enigma from Another World* – in Brazil. He watches the first half, tells himself he'll stay awake until the bit where Kurt Russell tests his team-members' blood with a piece of hot wire to see which of them is infected. He can't fight off his tiredness. He falls asleep before getting to it. In one of his dreams, he gets up at nine-thirty, opens the bedroom window, walks downstairs, goes straight into the pantry, where he finds Maína sitting at the table, keeping herself entertained leafing through the magazines she was given.

He says hello, she responds with the same word. He pre-pares an omelette with mozzarella, he toasts four pieces of bread in the toaster and pours two glasses of chocolate milk. He says that when they've finished he'll take her back. In the last dream, he is surprised to discover that the previous day he had stopped very close to where her family is. Maína opens the door, he says bye. She gets out of the car in silence but, when she closes the door (through the open window), she says Thank very much. Thank you very much, he corrects her, but she says again Thank very much, and he notices the lightness of her hair in the sun, and she turns her back on him before her mother discovers that her daughter has just been driven home by someone who hasn't even realised he has gone much too far.

a porcelain sky

Originally unpaid, the internship at the law firm had ended up in an informal agreement to share in the profits, and today the payment Paulo receives is higher than a salary at other similar firms. He's been getting along fine for almost two years now (what he needed to feel comfortable as an intern there was that the partners not object to his being a student leader). 'I like genuine people, people with ideas' – that's what the senior partner, a civil lawyer pushing seventy, said when he interviewed him. When he was accepted he was given two 'recommendations': never to disclose the firm's name in his speeches and statements, and never to take part in any kind of activity that could be labelled subversive. In their day-to-day interactions it's common for Paulo to hear the nine lawyers who work there remarking that democracy isn't as solid as people say, commenting on the possibility that the days of military rule could come back, that he should take care – advice that might have made sense in eighty-three or earlier, but not nowadays. At first, Paulo would reply affectionately, call them paranoid, always on his guard so as not to reveal his daily involvement in leftist activism. What would they have said about the time he was in Mariu's, the old-school bar where students drink after classes and student union meetings, when a classmate of his, the son of a high-ranking officer in the military police, revealed to him something his father had mentioned? That his father had handled Paulo's file at a meeting of the so-called PM2, the Military Division's intelligence services that used photographs and daily reports to track and document the political activities of students, unionists, peasant groups, religious groups and anyone else whom the state considered leftist. His mother, strict as she is, would have a coronary, Paulo sometimes thinks, if she knew about anything like this; it wouldn't be all that different with some of the lawyers at the firm.

At this moment, he and the two lawyers to whom he directly reports are in the meeting room, the jewel in the firm's crown, not just for its decorative details (walls clad in English fabrics and all manner of framed items – even manuscripts by renowned jurists), but for the view onto the Praça da Matriz: you can see the tops of the jacaranda trees, the Court of Justice, the São Pedro Theatre, a bit of the Legislative Assembly, the top of the monument to Júlio de Castilhos. They have reached an impasse. Paulo who, as they have already mentioned, is only an intern, doesn't want to agree to halving the percentage he receives from income generated around collection, payments and the termination of rental agreements that he calculates for the Chimendes Machado estate agency. Eleven months earlier, when the younger lawyer, the younger of the two sitting there at the table, had the idea of passing the estate agency account to Paulo in order to free up some of his own time and devote himself to prospecting for new clients, he made it almost impossible to refuse. Paulo didn't like the imposition, the last thing he wanted at that point was to work exclusively for people who make their money exploiting those who don't have a place of their own to live, and, on top of that, to have to put up with the unstable moods of Rafaela, the agency's owner and one of the most difficult people to deal with he had ever met. Certain sacrifices can't be justified in the name of experience. He knew that the new task was no more than a test. He treated it as a matter of honour. He decided to tackle the situation head on. He would get to keep a fifth of what the firm invoiced on the transactions; it wouldn't be a fortune, but it would give him a nice little extra income. This recent idea to change their fee distribution came about when the partners realised that the sums being awarded to the estate agency under favourable judgments (following a change in the legal guidelines) had increased significantly, and it didn't seem reasonable to them that an intern should be pocketing so much money. 'It's not my fault if the procedural criteria changed from one moment to the next, and Chimendes Machado expanded their portfolio of commercial and industrial properties and the value of the cases went up; it isn't fair, you have to stick to what you promised,' says Paulo, who has run out of patience with this conversation. He looks at his watch: one-fifteen. 'I have to go to the Canoas Central Forum to deliver a foreclosure notice . . . As I told you earlier, I won't be coming back into the office today.' The lawyers say that they'll have a think and respond in the coming days. The younger lawyer tells him to call from the Forum to ask whether they need him back in the office for any tasks that might come up. Paulo agrees, but only to be polite. There's no way he's coming back. He's all set to see Maína, for what will be the third time. On their second meeting, they sat in a clearing on the bank of the Guaíba at the end of one of those many faintly sketched lanes that branch off the Estrada do Conde (a subsidiary road with pot-holed tarmac that connects the district of Eldorado do Sul to Guaíba), funnelling out until barely any cars come past; a tiny beach, just a dozen metres long, surrounded by rushes and elephant grass; a lovely, peaceful place, but dangerous in its isolation. This time they'll go out to a plot of land on the Ilha da Pintada, a small, leafy, grassy place on the banks of the Jacuí river, surrounded by a wire mesh, with no constructions save for a little lean-to with a barbecue, a sink and a bathroom, the property of a former Varig pilot who is friends with his father. He just needs to stop at a little shop three hundred metres further up, say he's a friend of the owner, collect the key that opens the padlock and that's it.

Maína is wearing the blue skirt he gave her last time. They sit on the sawn-off tree trunks that serve as stools. Paulo has the exercise book that Angélica gave him. He has written a series of common words and phrases, and scratched out some illustrations and little maps, leaving half of the pages unfilled. He asks Maína not to move, he's trying to draw her. She doesn't do as she's told. She takes off the skirt and shirt, takes the little All-Star skulls off her feet, and steps into the river. He doesn't say anything, just watches her with all the modesty he can manage. She goes in until the water is just above her knees, turns towards him and lies face-down, dips her head under, and re-emerges saying that he should come in, too. (Her spontaneity is shocking.) A thirty-foot wooden launch appears in the distance, towing a fit-looking man of about forty on a single ski; the sound of the racing motor disrupts the silence. Paulo focuses, he simplifies his lines, completes the picture. It hasn't come out well. He considers tearing out the page, ripping it up, and yet he won't do it. Maína comes out of the water, lies on the grass. Paulo gets up, puts the exercise book down beside her, spots the same launch going past at a leisurely pace, without the man in tow. The minutes pass. Maína has dressed and her head is now resting on his right thigh. She thinks it's funny when he surprises her with the battery-powered radio cassette player that he has brought to lend her. He explains how it works and she's killing herself laughing. Now they are sitting on the blanket that he brought to lay on the ground. She knows he's watching her as she leafs through the exercise book. Soon he is going to teach her some new words and they will discuss subjects she'll only partly understand. Maína will take the pencil he used and write 'Paulo' over the drawing of her face, and will hand the exercise book back to him and ask him to write down the story she's just told him, but using the words he would use if he were writing for his university friends (she will get the word 'university' right, both the meaning and the pronunciation), writing on alternate lines so that she can then copy it, letter by letter. In the story she told him there was a colourless girl who very much liked being kissed. One day *the colourless girl was by the side of the road when a squad of bikers passed her and one of them threw an apple at her back. She almost fell over, she was hurt. They stopped a few metres on, took off their helmets, laughed at her. The day, which had been lovely and sunny, clouded over. Hurt, the apple looked sad, sadder even than the girl*, that's how he wrote it down. And she will watch the leaves on the trees and she won't know when his leg has gone to sleep and the time has come for them to go.

*

Many days passed (as in any relationship, theirs created its own idiosyncrasies). There had already been a fifth meeting and a sixth, this is now the seventh, when he picks her up on the road and, in the gap between her opening the door and sitting in the passenger seat, he says, 'Saturday's fucking awesome, isn't it, Maína?' and they look at one another without a couple's complicity but a couple just the same, without his immediately noticing the lipstick on her mouth, the cosmetic pink. Unlike the other times, Maína doesn't have the bag full of papers and magazines to show him what she has read, only the exercise book and the four-colour pen that he brought the last time they met, along with the packs of batteries for the radio cassette player and a pink leotard that he saw in the window of Petipá, the gym-wear shop at the top of Protásio Alves, and bought for her. The exercise book now has Maína's handwriting in green, a colour that makes the letters on the paper look as if they haven't been written, as if they could simply be wafted away. Paulo has brought bags of savoury snacks, cans of Budweiser, mineral water, cans of Coke; Maína's crazy about soft drinks. They have a picnic. She has prepared two stories for him to write down. He says he's all ears. She laughs at the all ears and, without hesitating over the inaccuracies, she starts to tell the tale she has imagined. The first story tells of all the fooling around that happened between Indian men and women in the days when the land had no owner. The other is about an old Indian woman who spent her days on the road gathering up loose pages from newspapers and magazines that had been carried over on the wind, until one day, the day she was bitten by a lizard who wore a blazer (that was the word Paulo chose), she built a bonfire with all the paper she'd collected, and when the flames had grown till they reached the height of a man, a man who could embrace her, she put them on and, hankering after an impossible kinship, disappeared. Maína gathers all her things up from the ground, waits for Paulo to finish writing. Almost twenty minutes later, he hands her the exercise book, she moves closer and contrives a kiss on the mouth, then takes her clothes off. She gets into the Beetle, straight onto the back seat, asks him to get in too. Paulo walks slowly towards the car, sits next to her. Maína tries to kiss him, he evades her. There are consequences, more than he could have foreseen. She says a few words in Guarani; he puts his arms around her. Then he takes off his t-shirt and gives it to her to put on. Silence and the impossibility of a conclusion, although the insistence and the doubts will no longer appear on the pages of the exercise book she has dropped on the grass.

*   *   *

Another day. Maína's sisters cannot guess who the man is who's getting out of the car with those plastic bags in his hands. He tries to talk to the older one, but she doesn't understand what he's saying. Maína recognises his voice, she comes out of the tent and, making no attempt to hide her happiness at seeing him, says she had only been expecting him in two days' time. Paulo hands over the bags with packets of biscuits, cornflower snacks and soft drinks for her. 'I've brought some junk food,' he says. Maína wants to know what junk means. Without waiting for a reply she goes back to the tent. Paulo follows her. He goes into the tent and sees the straw mats covering the floor, the wooden crates with cleaning products, clothes, pans, everything improvised, a table with a stack of six Duralex plates, a can of cooking oil, a few opaque plastic tubs and a pot of cutlery on it. Maína arranges the soft drinks on the table, puts the plastic bags away in one of the wooden crates. She takes Paulo by the hand, leads him to the little wicker bench at the entrance to the tent, asks him to sit down for a moment, then she takes two aluminium mugs, opens one of the soft drinks, pours it, passes him the drink. She purses her lips tight showing her interest in knowing what has brought him here. He takes a sip of the drink. 'I quit my job today. It's a good place, I stayed to help and to learn. The bosses are good to me. They do me good. You understand? It's just I'm not doing what I want to be doing. When I'm there I have to help people, people I don't want to help. The bosses are going to give me some money, money that's mine, and I was thinking of taking some of it and helping you. Except I don't know how to help you. It's not much,' he says. Maína gets up, takes the mug from his hands, puts it down beside the wicker bench, calls her sisters over, tells them to give him a big hug. When it's her turn to hug him, she lets slip, 'We are together, and happy.' (Paulo has had an argument in the office because, after some days, the lawyers told him that they were indeed going to halve the amount he received from the estate agency's legal activities. This decision, which he felt was unfair, made him stand up and say he wasn't going to work with them any longer, and demand that, within the new rules with the decreased percentage, they deposit an amount approximating what he would be receiving from the suits that are filed.) The smallest child sat on his lap without his noticing. He had headed over here out of sheer rage (in order to lessen his rage); gradually he realises what caused it. And – out of context – he replies to Maína: 'Junk is a word for stuff that isn't healthy, that has no value.' Maína puts her arms around him, saying he can come back as often as he likes. 'Things that have no value,' she repeats, talking to herself this time.

In Porto Alegre there's a traffic jam on Lucas de Oliveira. He's nearly fifty minutes late. He goes into the hall, where there must be about a hundred people. A fellow party member from São Paulo who has come especially to contribute to the discussions around public policy in the multi-year plan (the city's main piece of budgetary planning, which is due to be passed through to the Council Chamber shortly) gestures for him to come sit next to her, as she's alone on a cushion for two. 'Did I miss much?' Paulo asks. 'They've been rehashing that crazy argument about which journalist will take over the communications office . . . and' – she whispers even more quietly – 'they talked about the net that's starting to close around the mayor.' He settles as best he can, listens to the introductory remarks and, as soon as the opportunity arises, he asks to speak. The chair of the meeting replies that as soon as comrade Zezinho has finished reading the new framework for assigning senior roles between the different movements and the group of independents, he will have three minutes to do so. It's the independents who are the real headache in this process of forming a government: they are militants who aren't part of any party movement and as a result, when they get together, it takes them longer than any of the other groups to deliberate (on top of this, there's the fact that the candidates they name are not accountable to anyone, since they don't really have anyone above them). Twenty minutes go by, Paulo's turn comes. He gets up, walks over to the table, hands the chair of the meeting a three-page document. He runs his hand over his head. 'Comrades, the document I have just handed to comrade Alfredo is my statement of separation from the movement. Out of respect for some of you, I would like to take two minutes here to present its contents and the reasons for my leaving.' Some were surprised but most already knew that Paulo was there to leave the organisation. 'I am alarmed and . . . ' – he takes on an expression of ecclesiastical seriousness – 'even as an atypical militant, who has always needed the understanding of those who work with me, because I'm vain, I'll admit, and hasty, I'll admit, because I'm not the best example of determination and discipline, I'm truly concerned about the irrational ways in which the factions that dominate the party leadership have shown contempt for democratic debate, replicating the most odious practices of Stalinism. I want to make it absolutely clear to you: I don't intend to repeat today that old lament of someone who has no idea of how difficult it is, the argument with the right, with the social democrats, with the media bosses, bankers, contractors, ruralists . . . I do know, however, that we can take a wrong turn at any moment, just as we've gone wrong before, and I think we need to acknowledge these mistakes . . . If we speak so much about freedom and the internationalisation of socialism and the emancipation of mankind, about the dignity of humanity, we should be guaranteeing the inclusion, the participation of all those who work, who make sacrifices for this, in our own decision-making processes. These decisions, the decisions we make that are the party's decisions, have taken place behind closed doors, they have come about through manipulation, through intimidation, by patrolling the party conventions at voting time. I don't see any sign of democracy, of the democracy that ought to be the foundation of what we do, at the root of everything. I'm troubled, ashamed, by our alliances, by the concessions, by all the turning a blind eye, that we're establishing as standard practices of the Workers' Party. And this is only one of the eight points in my document. Is this the politics of party building that we wanted? I say again: I'm ashamed of what we are becoming. Honestly, I do believe that some of us, some comrades who are in this room, feel like they own this party, they think they're the enlightened masters of the party, behaving like great feudal overlords, like proper gang leaders. Our party wasn't born to be like this. I've seen resentment, vindictiveness. I don't like it, I don't want to be a part of this process of division that is excluding the best in the militant movement, the most critical, those who are technically the most able, just the way Stalin did. Those who are in charge in the movement, and I'm fortunate that you are all here today, you ought to be behaving very differently from São Paulo, where those guys ram whatever they want down people's throats; you ought to be behaving differently from the groups who do nothing but cheapen our arguments.' He looks at his watch, concerned for his two allotted minutes. 'To bring about revolution in the world we need to bring about a revolution in ourselves. It sounds naive, I know.' He takes a deep breath, readying himself for his conclusion (and loses his thread just a little). 'I say again. I look around me and I see people who should never have been part of the Workers' Party, and not only are they in the Party but they've been calling the shots here ever since our win in the municipal elections. We were better off four years ago. I'm sorry, but that's the way I see it. I hesitated about coming today, about being here, standing in front of you. I was afraid of being taken for a coward and even that I myself might judge myself weak, incapable of understanding the big picture, or history, weak for giving up on the struggle, but I want you to know, I'm not giving up, just the opposite . . . I wish you all luck.' One of the two state deputies gets to his feet and suggests that Paulo, 'as a vital partner in the strengthening of the Workers' Party,' might reconsider his position and first have a discussion with the members of his unit. Paulo thanks the chair, tells the deputy he has made his decision and sits back down next to the militant who's come from São Paulo. The interventions continue as though the meeting had never been interrupted by Paulo's speech. He feels relieved, believing he has spoken some truth, something that can move everyone present. After the excitement, they get caught up in a discussion of the agenda, and as the debates and speeches progress he is overtaken by a devastating feeling of not having the stomach to argue with them. Before the final decision is voted upon, without any gesture of goodbye to the woman sitting next to him, he stands up, and with his head lowered, his voice almost silent, he excuses himself again to anyone who might happen to be able to hear him and leaves the room with a strong sensation of having been discarded.

He goes into the club, Enigmas, having promised the bouncer (Gregório 'the Grinder', an old acquaintance from his skateboarding days in the Marinha do Brasil park) that he won't touch the Domecq that he's carrying and which is now suitably stored away in the law-trainee rucksack on his back. He's come here to find Lugosi, the youngest of the place's resident DJs; though there's only three years' difference between them (she is eighteen) and despite his friend's complete alienation from politics, they have cultivated this friendship for the tough times, as they like to say to each other. The nightclub, an LGBT hangout of no great consequence, has in the last year been attracting rent boys (the rent boys who, thanks to an agreement between the club owners, are not allowed into Peter Pan Seven, Polio Garage or Silhouette Cocktail), models of both sexes who are already starting to lose their looks and their jobs and – this is the decisive factor – employees from other clubs on their nights off. Three factors which, in combination with other trends and rumours, meant that Enigmas had quickly gained a reputation as a place that promised a good time, attracting the attention of all kinds of punks and lovers of The Cure and The Smiths. Lugosi could take a lot of the credit for popularising the place, with her goth muse attitude and her ability to choose just the right tracks to play when everyone's fed up having made a big difference. A lot of her friends who are regulars at the Taj Mahal, always up for blowing a load of cash on a night out, even if they don't have all that much cash to blow in the first place, began to show up at Enigmas once she started there.

It's early. There's no one on the dance floor. Lugosi is with her latest old-beautiful-perfect-boyfriend, Castro Two: both of them bored, they've just eaten a portion of chips at the table next to the decks. 'Sweetie, go get us some cigarettes over at the petrol station, tell them I'll settle up tomorrow,' she orders her boyfriend as soon as she sees Paulo approaching, 'and take as long as you like, ok?' Castro Two (yes, there had been a Castro One, even if Castro Two didn't know this) gets up, greets Paulo without a handshake and heads for the door. 'These boys of yours are looking more and more like girls, Lugosi,' he teases her even before saying hello. 'I screw androgyny, you know,' and she moves along so he can sit beside her. 'Well, of all people . . . ' she takes the initiative. 'Yeah well, you're always saying I never come to hear you doing your

DJ thing. So I came. So here I am, girl . . . And, well . . . '
he tries to disguise his haggard expression and his own
drunkenness. 'So what's up?' She knows he isn't here just
in passing. 'I quit the internship and I quit the Party, all on
the same day: today,' and he takes a chip from the cardboard tray. 'But there's more . . . ' Lugosi raises her index
finger like a well-behaved schoolgirl asking permission
to speak. 'And could I guess what this "more" might be?'
she ventures. 'Feel free. I've got all night,' he says, and this
time takes several chips. 'Is it the Indian girl you took to
the Baltimore?' and she gives him an ironic look, her face
a caricature of someone who's just said something she
oughtn't. Paulo shows no sign of surprise, he gestures to
the waiter to come over, calm in his drunkenness. 'How
do you know about the Indian girl?' he asks. Lugosi takes
a cigarette from her pocket. 'I'm right, aren't I?' she says,
and picks up a box of matches from the table and puts it
in his hand. 'It was your friend Titi, she told me. I asked
her what you'd been up to and she said she met you at
the entrance to the cinema with a frightened little Indian
girl.' Paulo strikes the match and brings it toward Lugosi
to light her cigarette. 'She's nearly fifteen, and I'm falling
for her.' He blows out the flame (in that moment he thinks
how it's only with Lugosi that he can speak so candidly).
'Nearly fifteen?' she says. 'It feels like millennia since I
was nearly fifteen.' The waiter arrives. 'Get us a couple
of gin-fizzes, Diego,' Lugosi asks. The waiter gives her an

anything-else-bitch look, and getting no answer he turns his back and walks away. 'You fucked her already?' Lugosi asks. 'It isn't that simple . . . ' he tries to slow Lugosi down. 'She barely speaks Portuguese, she lives in a tent on the side of the highway . . . It's a pretty sorry sight.' Lugosi gets up, goes into the space reserved for the DJ, mixes one track into the next, sits back down with Paulo. 'I get it, she's the Tarzan of the Minuane tribe and you're her Jane-in-breeches . . . Ha ha ha . . . ' She pats him on the head. 'You've outdone yourself, old man,' (she rarely spares him). 'And all that today. Fucking hell. This is a day that's going down in history,' she mocks. 'Nope . . . That's a good one . . . It's your Independence Day . . . Weren't you saying it doesn't make sense any more to do that stuff you do for the Party, that in law the only thing that made sense was the philosophy and stuff, that it's been ages since you've been in love . . . ' He interrupts her. 'I'm not in love . . . ' The waiter arrives with the cocktails. 'Sorry, but you are. You're in love, and you're trying to get over the Christian guilt they shoved up your ass when you were nine and taking your First Communion. You want to have this girl, which is fair enough . . . I lost my virginity when I was twelve to a guy who was eighteen, did you know that?' she says and holds her own tab out to the waiter. 'This first round is on me.' The waiter makes a note of the drinks and goes. 'I have no idea what can have happened to you. I can imagine how weird it must be getting involved with someone who's so different . . . But the passion in your eyes, that's definitely there . . . I know you, sweetheart, I know you very well.' Paulo takes the drinks and passes one to his friend. They clink glasses. He downs the cocktail in one go, he doesn't really appreciate the taste of alcoholic drinks; when he drinks it's with the specific intention of getting a buzz as quickly as he can. He turns towards Lugosi; she looks back at him without blinking, serious, with her light skin and very short black hair, just the way all actresses in horror films ought to be. Wordlessly, Paulo tells her that things are really getting out of hand, which is why he's going to do everything he can to understand Maína, confounding all expectations that might still exist about this middle-class guy, perhaps intelligent, perhaps with a future in some promising profession, the son of civil servants from the upper levels of the Federal Civil Service, both recently retired, a perfect little type from a class with serious ambitions to climb the social ladder. Wordlessly, Lugosi tells him not to expect any great advice from this girl from Higienópolis, the poorly daughter of lecturers at the Federal University, who has been diagnosed with depression and who has already enrolled at three different universities, each time dropping out in the middle of the first semester, and who supports herself, or kids herself that she is supporting herself, playing in clubs. Wordlessly, he will tell her it's good to be there having a drink with her, and, still wordlessly, Lugosi will tell him he's just as complicated as any of these other twenty-something guys who read too much and think too much and believe they know what a girl wants even if in practice they do not. And an hour and a bit from now, when the Enigma's clientele are starting to fill up the dance floor, she'll ask if he wants to split a tab of LSD that the boyfriend of a friend sent over from Los Angeles in a box of flick books (not to go into just how square she and her friend think he is for being so unnecessarily scared when it comes to popping a pill from time to time; he won't even smoke a joint, like a good little doctor, losing out on the chance to understand what's really missing from this world of ours), and, not hearing her, he'll be amused when she puts on 'Relax', that Frankie Goes to Hollywood song full of double entendres, accepting the little slip of paper that she will put in his mouth.

They are in NATO, the bar that Passo Fundo has made his favourite. Paulo wants to go home. In the state he's in, however, it would be a real mistake. His parents are travelling early this morning to Montevideo with friends, that's less than two hours from now. When that happens (they usually go to Montevideo by car) his mother doesn't do her packing till shortly before they go, which means that right now she will be awake with almost every light in the house on, chasing after all the accessories and items of clothing that she cannot possibly leave behind under any circumstances. A conversation between the two of them would be a disaster. Paulo is afraid of what he might say, of acting out the scene that reveals the truth of the universe to someone you love, or of being assailed by an attack of paranoia that will make him want to wish he were dead as soon as it all passes. (Paulo does not like losing control.) No, better to stay here and wait for the dawn. Passo Fundo gets up every fifteen minutes to go to the bathroom to snort some of the coke he got earlier from the Colonel. He and Paulo are at Igor and Luciano's table, two guys who share the same girlfriend, Márcia Boo. She kisses one, then she kisses the other. Cristiane and Magali are there, too, they don't stop talking. Paulo knows he can have either one of them, but whenever he tries to look closely at them in that dark bluish haze he sees Maína's face. The cognac he brought in his ruck-sack is nearly finished, he fills his glass under the table so the manager of the bar doesn't see him, the waiters aren't paying any attention at all: each time he does this, the two girls sitting beside him laugh like hyenas. He contemplated inviting the two of them for a threesome, he even started imagining he was fucking them under the table and then while the two of them were sucking his cock he would be going down on Márcia Boo while she kissed Igor and Luciano, Luciano who's also known as Posh-boy Luciano. This daydream lasted just a few minutes. It passed. He heard someone at the table more than once mention the name David Cooper and the title of the book *The Grammar of Living*, and (as if he were in a tunnel of psychosis in which the possibilities of reaction are delayed) he gets up, theatrically, saying: 'Language was invented in order to destroy communication, which in turn has been used to destroy communion. The final strategy ought to be to use what destroys us to destroy the very thing that is destroying us, in such a way as to allow for areas of hope and the conclusive death of cretins.' He looks around at everyone sitting at the table. 'Many thanks for your attention,' he shouts, as if he were being strangled, and sits. At the other tables there are musicians from the blues band who were on earlier in the evening, a company whose play is on the bill at midnight from Thursdays to Saturdays at the Arena Theatre, two people from the group who will be coordinating Luiz Inácio da Silva's presidential campaign. A few couples in clinches. There is, in short, that kind of harmony in the air (the sharing of a fleeting victory). And at that moment Paulo is a man of steel, he's proud of his bearing, of his courage and his health, he has no doubt that if he had money in his pocket for a taxi he'd go off to find Maína. He'd spend several days there trying to work out the secret of getting used to having so little. And at that moment, Paulo discovers what he is going to do with the money from the office. Tomorrow afternoon he's going to seek out one of those companies that specialise in pre-fab homes, he will get costings, then he will tell Maína. Paulo is at NATO, he has his arms stretched out across the top of the table, his hands with fingers laced together, his eyes lost in an unseemly gladness, and everyone around him knows that he is not his usual self.

on the way

Maína had said it wasn't his problem when Paulo returned
to the subject of building the wooden room, five by four,
so the girls could all sleep more comfortably, saying that
he would use the money from the office to do this. 'It's the
government's problem, not yours,' was her short answer,
which she followed by putting her hand over his mouth
to stop him going on. She looks at the time on her watch
(when Paulo gave it to her, she said it didn't feel right getting so many presents from him), she looks towards the
north, spots the Beetle approaching. By her count, this
is the eleventh time they meet. As soon as he has steered
the car over, she runs to his window, she makes a point of
showing him the calendar she has drawn up on the last
page of the exercise book. He opens the door, she gets
in. He drives to the usual place. When they stop by the
grocery shop to collect the key, he is told that the owner
has replaced it for a different one, that he has changed
the padlock for a bigger one, determining that from that

moment on – and this was the day before yesterday – no one was allowed to get onto the property without written authorisation. Paulo asks Maína whether she wants to go to Porto Alegre. She says yes. Yes, of course.

They are in Paulo's house, in the little room next to the garage at the back of the property, the place his mother used to paint her pictures, do her clothing designs, sew, all this before the slipped disc at the end of last year that made her stop indefinitely (she's talked ever since about boxing up those things and getting the place done up). As soon as they came inside, Maína ran over to the pile of magazines on top of the table, one of those tables that designers use, or architects. She'd never seen magazines like them, they had huge pages inside, pages that unfold, till they end up as big as a road sign. On each page there are a lot of scribbled lines, drawings made up of different coloured dots that almost muddle your vision. Paulo hands her a pair of scissors saying she can cut out anything she likes, do whatever she likes, and that's what she does. She also uses some large sheets of paper and pieces of cardboard that are hanging on the wall. He goes over to one of the bookcases, takes out a plywood box, puts it down on the table, asks Maína to look, opens it. Inside are a dozen little glass jars with classroom gouache, oil paint, different-sized brushes. He shows her how to use the paints, he finds a large roll of sticky tape, says that he'll try and find his sister's old camera, the kind that develops the photos instantly (Maína doesn't really understand what he means by developing the photos instantly). Paulo is some time coming back. When he does return, he enters the room to find Maína finishing the first outfit, the one she's going to wear. 'Preparing some costumes, Maína?' he asks. 'Spirit dress,' she replies, seriously. 'And are they for us?' She approaches him from behind, uses her hands to measure the breadth of his shoulders. 'Yes,' she says, 'for us to know.' He is intrigued. 'To know?' 'Yes, to know,' and she measures the distance from his face to his waist. He shows her the Polaroid, says there's still one photographic sheet left to use. They mustn't get the picture wrong. She doesn't answer. He sets up the camera, sits in the only armchair in the room, watches. Maína gets his outfit ready even more quickly than she's done her own, she opens up the black and brown gouaches, takes one of the finer paintbrushes and passes it to him, inviting him to paint with her. They paint around the edges of the holes that will be the eyes, the one that will be the mouth, they cover the chest and forehead with inscriptions. The paint dries quickly. In those minutes Paulo explains how the polarisation of the photographic sheet works; Maína doesn't take her eyes off her creations for a second. She gets hold of his costume, tells him to take off his t-shirt, puts it straight on to his body; his head is covered, his upper back and trunk down to just below his waist, she takes the purple paint and paints a few more details, she adds the sleeves, asks him not to move. She crouches down, takes his trainers and socks off his feet, then brings her hands to his belt buckle, removes his trousers and underpants. He doesn't react. She takes off her trainers, her t-shirt, her skirt and knickers, puts her one on, she only asks for help attaching the second sleeve. 'Now what?' he asks. 'You can move,' she replies. Moving with some difficulty so as not to tear the paper, he walks over to the armchair where he had left the Polaroid. He positions it on one of the bookshelves, setting the timer to go off in ten seconds. He presses the button. He walks as fast as he can over to her. They get themselves into position. 'Ready.' The flash goes off after winking three times less brightly, it makes Maína laugh under her decoration. 'Shall we go outside?' she suggests. 'Are we going to catch fire like in the story you told me that time, is that it?' She doesn't answer. They leave the room and walk perhaps five metres, which is the mid-point between the two buildings. She embraces him as hard as she can, and his jacket tears over his shoulders. He doesn't move. She bites his chest, tearing off a bit of paper. He takes her whole body in his arms and, without even noticing the paper outfit coming apart, carries her to his room, lies her on the bed, turns off the light, turns on the one in the corridor, strips her naked and strips himself, too. Maína is barely participating, she rolls about in the bed, she slips, forcing him to change the way he's kissing her, the places he's kissing her. With more than half of his body off the bed, he holds on to her hips, his face rough and unshaven slides down her belly, he breathes out, mouth, lips, the slowness of the zig-zagging motion moistens her.

He is staring at the bloodstain on the white sheet. He awoke agitated, like she'd never seen him before, said that he was going out for a run and would be back in an hour at the most. She did not reply, she just stayed there, still, on the single bed. Alone in the house. She needs some thought, she needs some reaction, because the satisfaction she's feeling is huge and reckless and solid (she feels ready, fortunate, she took in the night before, the mingled smells between the two of them, the new texture clinging to her skin). The minutes pass quickly. Paulo comes back (it's very possible that he exercised for less time than he had promised). Maína is in the same position. He lies down in front of her, he says they need to tidy up the house, his parents will be arriving in the evening. Maína gets up, takes him by the hand, they walk to the bathroom. She steps into the shower cubicle, he turns on the taps, regulates the water temperature, takes off his clothes. The warmth is pleasant, it replaces their perspiration. She takes his index finger with one of her hands and his forearm with the other, repositions him (positions herself), and puts Paulo's finger inside, tries not to think about the day when last night's luck will run out on them.

Eleven-thirty in the morning. Silently Maína is tidying herself up (and even when he hands her the Polaroid photo of the two of them wearing the clothes she had created, suggesting that she tape it to one of the pages of her exercise book, she still feels awkward). The house is in order. He says he'll take her to the encampment. They drive away, up the road towards Bento Gonçalves and then out of the city. At the end of the Castelo Branco expressway, not long before the exit to the slope that leads onto the bridge, he pulls the Beetle over, asks if she wants to stay with him for one more day. Looking straight ahead, Maína accepts with a nod. Paulo keeps on going towards the state's northern seaboard. He makes a few amusing comments but, though she looks at him alertly, she does not smile. Almost at the end of the journey they come to the stretch near the Barros lagoon, its expanse made up of water that comes down from the mountains, he pulls into a lay-by, gets out of the car, stands there taking in the north-eastern wind that is blowing hard on his face. She gets out of the Beetle and, finding the smell of the sea curious (not knowing it), she lightly touches Paulo's waist and then puts her arms around him. 'Ok, Maína?' he asks, not turning round. 'It should have passed, but is stronger now,' she says, drily. The lagoon is filled with ghosts, that's what his parents would tell him when the four of them used to drive past in the brown Volkswagen Brasilia towards their old summer house on Capão da

Canoa Beach, his parents always in a hurry, always right on time – close up the house in town, get into the car, don't stop till you're outside the beach house. This haste to do things (and reach places) is supreme in Paulo. This is the first time in his life he's had the patience to stop the car and look out at all that water, standing there wrapped in the arms of this girl who had also spooked him one day. 'For me, too,' he replies, and invites her to sit on the low concrete wall. She runs over to the car, gets a little jacket that used to belong to her older sister, in one of the pockets is the Polaroid picture, then comes back and settles herself beside him. Legs swinging in the air, Paulo's moving less than hers. Maína puts her hand in the jacket pocket, takes out the photo and only then looks at the result, noticing something he already knew: though the composition was good, the picture was out of focus.

In Tramandaí, counting on finding one of his friends who might offer them shelter for a night; at the first attempt Paulo finds Leonardo, who moved to the coast to prepare for the exam to be a public prosecutor. Sitting on the porch of his parents' bungalow, engrossed in a book on criminal procedure, Leonardo is startled when the car comes up his drive. 'Hi, Leo,' Paulo greets him. 'Paulo Guevara and his surprises,' says Leonardo. 'I figured you'd have committed body and soul to the Lula campaign by now,' he teases. 'Some things have changed in the last few months.' Leonardo looks at Maína suspiciously. 'Evening, miss,' he said. 'Good evening,' comes Maína's intimidated reply. He gets straight to the point, 'I need somewhere to stay tonight, Leo. Any chance of staying here in the guest room?' 'Of course, make yourself at home. You know the way, take your things and sort yourselves out up there . . . If you need an extra bed, there's a fold-up there in the . . . ' And Paulo interrupts him. 'No, no need.' Leonardo picks up his book again. 'Right. I've got to finish up a few pages here now. We'll catch up on news at dinner time . . . We can go to a really cool pizza place that opened recently.' Paulo takes Maína's things, leaves the car just where it is. They go in by the back door. In the bedroom there's no sheet on the mattress. Paulo looks in the cupboards and doesn't find anything. Maína looks under the bed; Paulo, laughing, says they're not likely to be there. He'll leave it, they can ask later, he doesn't want to bother Leonardo any more, he knows how much he's been devoting himself to passing these exams since the start of the year. They go down to the kitchen, Paulo pours out two glasses of milk, takes the packet of Tip Top biscuits from the basket on the table. Straight afterwards he washes up what they've dirtied (one of the reasons he's welcomed by Leonardo is that he has never taken advantage of his position as a guest). They go out for a walk along the beach. Though it's nearly five in the afternoon, the sun is still strong, with that punishing north-easterly wind. There are two boys flying kites on the walkway which was damaged by some recent rough seas; there's a big plastic bag, opaque but quite see-through, with seven others inside it and a piece of paper on the outside announcing that the kites are for sale. One is blue and the other is red, they are the same size and design but it's the red that has completely caught Maína's attention, she no longer has eyes for anything else around her. Having expected her to be thrilled by the sight of the sea, Paulo notices this and is annoyed; up till now her only question has been about the fishing platform: she wanted to know what that thing was that was going into the sea. He explained, she said nothing. They walk over to the boys. Maína asks if Paulo can buy the red one that's flying (it's the first time Maína has asked him to buy anything; Paulo thinks, *something has changed*). Paulo fulfils her wishes. Maína reels in the kite and stows it under her arm. They stay till after it gets dark. On the way back, Paulo asks her if she liked the sea. 'The sound of the waves and also the waves,' she says, and they turn right onto Leonardo's street.

Sharing a bottle of beer with Paulo on the porch, Leonardo takes advantage of Maína's being in the bathroom to ask if Paulo knows what he's doing. 'Wake up, Paulo, the girl isn't only a kid, she's also an Indian . . . I don't have to explain to you how much that makes this whole thing a huge bloody chainsaw massacre,' and he looks at his friend, whom he has known since he was ten years old and Paulo eight, feeling as though, in spite of the mutual admiration that still exists, there's no longer the affinity that survived up to their university days. Paulo, who just said again and again that there was no need to worry, seems to be looking out into nothingness. 'All right, Paulo?' Leonardo asks, crossing a line he's sure his friend won't like him crossing. 'Huh? Whatever it is, get it off your chest . . . ' and he puts his hand on Paulo's shoulder. 'Something happened yesterday . . . ' Paulo says, but he doesn't go on. Leonardo won't press him. His old classmate is a grown-up, more mature than most of his age can manage. Even a poor bastard down on his knees begging to be put in jail, even he deserves the benefit of the doubt, he must know what he's doing, there has to be some reason. He picks up the bottle from the tiled floor, refills his glass and then his guest's. 'And the degree, Paulo, how's that going?' he says, trying to resume the thread of the conversation. Paulo takes a gulp of the drink, grimaces slightly. 'I think I'm going to drop out,' he looks at him, seriously. 'I haven't decided yet, but if it happens it'll be now, at the end of this term.' Leonardo can't help himself. 'You never took that course seriously.' Talking about the course is allowed, it's an area that can be freely scrutinised. 'Law's a big lie, Leo, we both know that. You did your entire course reading a Federal Constitution that was shoved down our throats by the military,' he says, and pours out what was left of the beer in his glass. 'This Serramalte of yours is warm.' Leonardo is not discouraged (Leonardo is never discouraged). 'It is. I put it in the fridge when you two went out.' And he teases: 'I'll let you buy me a colder one at the pizza place.' Paulo goes back to looking into nothingness. 'Another reason to devote ourselves to trying to make things better,' argues Leonardo. 'But turning into a well-meaning little prosecutor just to legitimise the power . . . the power of . . . ' and he realises that he has fallen into his friend's trap. 'Just let it go.' Leonardo laughs. 'You know what I find most fascinating, Paulo? It's that the good people, the most credulous and well-intentioned people, they're exactly the ones who give up,' and he gets up to carry the glasses and the bottle off to the kitchen. 'It must be the particularly acute sensibility you people have, that *poetic soul* of yours.' Paulo takes hold of his arm. 'Tell me, Leo,' looking upset, 'what kind of prosecutor do you want to be?' And Maína appears on the veranda, on the side Leonardo was headed. The conversation between the two friends ends there: Leonardo understands Paulo's innate difficulty in taking things less seriously and not getting deeply involved in all of it. He always reacts. It's what makes Leonardo admire him so much, and sympathise, too; he can see his friend's premature frustration, he doesn't like seeing him suffer. 'Let's go in my Uno. I need to get the battery going, but this means the drinks are definitely on you.' Paulo agrees with a smile, a little ashamed. Maína approaches. Leonardo walks over to the kitchen, he's worried about this all-or-nothing situation but, just the same, (believing he can better understand it) glad to see his old friend again.

It was good because they ate and came straight back. It was hard for her to feel at ease under the disapproving gaze of Paulo's friend; he's no different from other people she's come across before, she shouldn't be surprised, but it's so incompatible with everything she has felt since she woke up this morning. She holds the kite that bothers her as much because of its colour as because of its being up in the air, noisy, getting in the way of their visit to the unruly sea, the sea that ought to be blue and luminous, like the ones in the magazines. When she asked to buy it she was determined to break it, to get shot of it the first chance she had, but she waited and understood what she really felt (and what had really changed). Paulo would be coming up soon, he is talking to his friend. Maína would have given ten years of her life to have their language. Fortunately there is the exercise book, she presumes there will be another soon, the assumption comes with the sudden impulse to put away the kite and give its deep red colour a rest. She takes off her clothes, picks up the bucket of Lego Creative Building pieces she'd discovered when she glanced under the bed that afternoon looking for the sheets and, while she waits, she assembles two figurines (she will play with them until Paulo comes into the room, maybe influenced by his friend and unsure of what to say to the girl distracted by the plastic bricks on the bed). In her hands, the figurines live their tiny lives. The girl-figurine can fly, the boy-figurine can't, but he sings to her (in Maína's voice) as they live out their Lego story on the mattress that still has no sheet on it. The minutes pass and the two of them grow calm, the girl-figurine comes down to land, she invites him to sit beside her on the foam, he rests his plastic head on her plastic lap, asks for her hand in marriage, and cries.

Roman drawings

According to Paulo's instructions, when they pass the last of the three bridges that come after the Casa das Cucas, they will be exactly six kilometres from the encampment. Passo Fundo wonders how many times his friend took the same route before he knew for sure that there were six kilometres between the bridge and the Indian girls' tent (that's just one of the questions that goes through his head as the Monza speeds along the BR-116; questions to which there might be no answer). Then they see the two-person blue igloo-style tent belonging to Paulo, half of the Indian girls' tent and, as they get higher than the tops of the trees that block their view of the building work, two men doing the roof. Passo Fundo's cousin slows the Monza, pulls over onto the right-hand side of the road, switches off the engine, unlocks the boot. They get out of the car. Passo Fundo puts another *guaraná* seed in his mouth, looks around at the place. He couldn't say no when asked for help by the one friend who supported him when his father, a retired police chief, kicked him out of the house when he found a bag of more than a hundred grams of cocaine under the mattress slats. (Father and son had reached a kind of truce. In an attempt at reconciliation, they'd even attended half a dozen sessions with the therapist at a clinic near the Moinhos Hospital, one of those specialists in family problems related to substance dependency; as a result the ex-policeman felt betrayed when, even though he knew he was breaking the bond of trust suggested by the therapist, he searched Passo Fundo's room and discovered cocaine in sufficient quantity to be sure that it was for dealing.) Paulo doesn't care what other people say since he's already been branded a cokehead, a loose cannon, messed up and every bit as irresponsible as Passo Fundo (or more), just for being his friend and taking him in on the two occasions he tried to get clean; Passo Fundo tries to reciprocate adequately whenever the chance arises. They unload the eleven tins of paint, the two buckets, the brushes, sponges for the retouching, rags, solvents, a sports bag holding his fleece sweater, a pair of shorts, a sleeping bag, two packets of cream crackers, a bottle of water, a half-full Smirnoff and his clarinet in its wooden case. They carry the things over to the other side of the road. The girl who can only be Maína is the first person to appear. Showing no surprise at seeing them there, she says that Paulo is round the back and then goes into her tent.

Maína knows she hasn't welcomed them as she ought
to, but what could she do? What else could she say? That
the builders had arrived at six in the morning and, that
same moment, had set about unloading the material round
the back of the encampment? That she hadn't come out of
the tent and had made her sisters stay lying there where
they were and asked her mother not to leave either? That
she's been hearing Paulo's voice telling the workers how
careful they were to be, where the room was to be built
and, again and again, that they should be quick and un-
intrusive? The worst kind of invasion, one which could
have been avoided and hadn't been. That (around nine
in the morning, when her younger sister escaped from
the tent and ran over to Paulo, making the others run out
after her) Paulo talked about the men being finished with
the whole thing in two days, assuring them that they'll
be surprised when the job is all done? That she tried as
best she could to be attentive to the four nasty, hulking
carpenters who might under other circumstances have
intimidated her?

Passo Fundo and his cousin don't make it further in.
Following on the heels of the Indian girl, Paulo emerges
from behind the tent and greets them, declaring in a
tone that is solemn and, as such, out of place, that there
is nothing more invigorating than getting involved in
the assembly of a prefabricated house. Not wasting a
second, he tells them just to wait right there. He follows

the girl into the tent. Passo Fundo tells his cousin to leave things with him now, he thanks him for the lift and asks him again not to be late when he comes back to fetch him tomorrow. The lad says goodbye, returns to the car without looking back (Passo Fundo would have given his right arm to know what he was thinking, what he made of all this weirdness), switches on the engine, waves, then gives a quick honk of the horn and pulls out. Paulo comes out of the tent apologising for not having paid him proper attention till now, saying that unfortunately Maína's mother and sisters are not there at the moment, they won't be back till tomorrow afternoon (the girls' excited activity was hindering the progress of the work too much). Passo Fundo asks what needs to be done. Paulo says that the carpenters will be finished in an hour at the most and then it's just the painting left to do. 'We should make the most of what's left of the daylight then, and get the paints ready,' Passo Fundo says before picking out a board nearly two metres long, improvising trestles and positioning seven tins of paint on it. The brightness of the day is almost gone. The one who seems to be the biggest loudmouth of the four workmen announces: job done. Immediately the one acting as an assistant to the others starts collecting up the material into the rented van, which has already been waiting for them for fifteen minutes. Maína comes out of the tent, walks around the works inspecting them. The man approaches Paulo and gives him a series of instructions; Paulo listens to him not finding any of it very important. Night falls completely, there is a crescent moon. Paulo accompanies the four carpenters to the van; Maína and Paulo's friend are left standing opposite one another. 'Do you like it?' Passo Fundo ventures. 'Grey,' she says, directly. 'What?' He is no longer able to see the girl's expression properly. 'I don't like the colour.' And he realises that Paulo never consulted her. 'White is pretty cool,' is all he's able to say. 'She wants grey, because when it rains the room . . . the house . . . won't look . . . it's the shaman side of this girl here,' Paulo says behind him, turning on the torch, shining the beam of light on the building. 'Between you and me . . . ' he says, provocatively, 'Maína doesn't want the house. Isn't that right, Maína?' At that moment Passo Fundo understands why her behaviour was so withdrawn. She leaves. 'Headstrong and proud . . . Could you ever have imagined such a thing if you hadn't seen it with your own eyes?' Passo Fundo bends down to pick up one of the open tins of paint. 'Point the light over here for me, Paulo . . . ' He knows he shouldn't get involved in whatever might be going on between the two of them, 'I don't know whether it'll work out if we put a coat on it without sanding it first.' Paulo is still looking towards where Maína had gone. 'They said it wasn't a problem. Just give it one coat and then the other, four hours later,' says Paulo, positioning the torch on a box to light up the wall of the room that was to be painted first. 'Thank you for coming, Passo Fundo. I don't know if I could have done all this on my own.' Passo Fundo paints a large star on the door. 'It'll be a doddle. We'll paint this whole white elephant of yours in one go. I'll take the ladder; I'll do the top part, you do the bottom. Sound good to you?' Paulo nods. Within less than half an hour, Passo Fundo's arms and legs are beginning to itch (he hasn't told his friend that he is allergic to the smell of oil paint, to the solvents), he tries to get himself upwind. It's dark, his friend won't notice the blotches, the lumps that will start to show up on his skin in a few minutes.

Maína looks at her watch. Nearly ten o'clock at night. She has left the tent open so that they know she will be staying awake for as long as they're painting. That thing that Paulo said earlier (just before his friend arrived) is stuck in her head: about camping out there for a few weeks teaching her sisters to speak and read Portuguese, as well as some other children who might be in nearby encampments. She said it wouldn't work: he doesn't know a word of Guarani, the routine on an encampment is entirely different to anything he can imagine. She can't handle his being available like this, his dedication, with those surprises coming ever more frequently while his gestures and attitude – electric, sure of himself – move him too quickly away from the day and time when she adored him most. Paulo is moving further away because he's unable to be in the present. The present is a burden, it cannot function as a useful tool. 'Hello.' She hears the voice from somewhere out in the darkness. 'Could you get me a glass of water?' She notices the shine of the twisted metal, the buttons and keys of the visitor's wind instrument. 'Yes,' she answers and gets a cup to give him some water. 'Sorry to trouble you. I brought a bottle with me but it's finished.' Maína was afraid that, being a friend of Paulo's, he would be like Leonardo (it took her days to realise just how rude Leonardo had been). 'Don't tell Paulo,' panting again and again as though about to cough, 'but I have trouble breathing in the smell of paint for too long . . . The way he is, always doing everything just right, and the way he's so concerned about other people, he wouldn't have let me come and help . . . You do understand what I'm saying, don't you?' She nods her head. He drinks. 'Do you like music, Maína?' he asks. 'I like it a lot,' she says. He drinks the last gulp, hands back the cup. 'I'll play something for you, then, it'll help me get some new air into my lungs.' He brings his right hand to his forehead; 'Just give me a minute.' She watches him run over towards Paulo's igloo tent and return with a bottle. 'Vodka. To warm my throat up,' and he takes a swig directly from the bottle, then puts it down at his feet. He plays. The music is like nothing else: earthy, weighty the way the sound of a flute can never be, it spreads. He takes his time, barely adding any variations to the melodic arc and the turns it takes. A few cars go by, sporadically, but in no way affecting her hearing. Maína approaches Passo Fundo, picks up the vodka at his feet, pours a little into the cup he has used moments ago. She tastes it. Drinks the lot. Pours herself some more. She walks over to the edge of the road, she feels herself capable of softening it (and when the next headlamps come she wonders – from the old habit she has of just wondering – about covering them over completely even if it's just a momentary collision, blinding them, forging a new being against the wooden room that will be there for ever). She doesn't want to understand how everything ended up like this, she lets him play, thinking this will help to master the bad feelings. It's only when the music stops that she forgets about the road, the hypnotic trance, and turns back towards the tent. Noticing that he is packing the instrument up to go back to his painting, she asks Passo Fundo to tell Paulo to come and speak to her as soon as he can, and thanks him.

The day before yesterday, as they were walking over towards the tiles and wooden slats, Maína asked about the car. Paulo changed the subject, saying to himself that he was not going to tell her about how the money he'd received from the firm hadn't been enough to cover the cost of the building works (the lawyers didn't accept the sum he had calculated; he was only an intern), which was why he'd had to sell the Beetle. He comes down the three steps of the ladder, puts the empty paint tin down beside the other empty ones, the brush in the glass jar of solvent, his back is aching, his right arm is throbbing. He's not sure they are going to finish before it gets light. Putting another *guaraná* seed in his mouth, running the first brushstrokes along the top of the doorframe they had left for last, Passo Fundo says with certainty, yes, they will finish it. The two of them look at each other through the four-paned window whose two frames were lowered, with the opening at the top. It's an hour and a half since Passo Fundo told him that Maína was waiting for him. Here is this somewhat hopeless guy, perhaps the one guy Paulo likes most of all. The two of them look at each other like characters who have grown old, or who are trying to grow old more quickly than anyone else (there's no war, no disaster) and the end of a decade is looming. 'I'm going in, Passo Fundo.' He looks at his watch. 'We can start again in two hours, ok?' The friend waves his paintbrush in a gesture of blessing and then, immediately, with the same hand sweeping the air, gestures to him to go on, to go, get out of here. Maína is awake, she seems to have washed, she's in the dungaree dress he brought her in the very early days (and which she still hadn't worn for him to see). Hair combed and held to one side in her barrette. Paulo tries to make conversation, but Maína immediately invites him to lie with her in the igloo tent, and when she kisses him so enthusiastically he realises that she's been drinking. He asks for a couple of minutes to fill the basin and splash some water on his face, his arms, his hair, takes advantage of the moment to brush his teeth and change his t-shirt (he knows the girl won't care about this, it just seems a good time to do it, now that she's being all friendly, which she has made a point of not being these past seventy-two hours). In the tent he unrolls the extra camping mattress. Maína doesn't wait, she throws herself in clumsily, unbalancing him. She laughs. He laughs. He tries to find her face, with the tips of his fingers he finds one of her breasts. He kisses her. He takes off her clothes. Like a young husband, he assumes the cautiousness she didn't ask for, he brushes his lips over her legs, drawing them out. She is holding handfuls of earth (he guessed at this because of her closed fists, it was confirmed a minute later) and now, in a journey of her own, she scratches granules, clumps, pigments, dried mud, strands, scrapings against his arms, bringing the extra dust to his hair. They have come to a point where nobody can reach them. Nothing matters. It doesn't matter that the Minister of the Army had stated categorically right there in the Chamber of Deputies itself that indigenous culture is not respectable; that Paul McCartney said Madonna and Michael Jackson lack musical depth; that a terrorist bomb brought down the monument to William and Walmir and Carlos, murdered in November last year, in a confrontation with the army in the Volta

Redonda Factory; that the English writer Anthony Burgess, eager to regain the attention lavished on his *A Clockwork Orange*, accused Pope John XXIII of having being the most dangerous man of the century; that a fight is being stirred up between Brazil's General Workers' Union and the Unified Workers Central; that Asteroid 1989FC with its alarming eight hundred and fifteen-metre diameter has come too close to the earth thereby causing justifiable concern the likes of which we hadn't seen for decades; that two hundred and sixty kilometres of electric fencing along the border between Hungary and Austria has been taken down resulting in the first significant break in the so-called Communist Iron Curtain; that cold fusion has been announced to much boasting and then subsequently denied again with much embarrassment; that the ascent of Fernando Collor de Mello's candidacy to the presidency has been so vertiginous; that Colonel Oliver North was condemned for the clandestine sale of arms to the Iran of the Ayatollahs by officials in Ronald Reagan's government in the Iran-Contra scandal; that the Argentines elected the Peronist Carlos Saúl Menem as their president; that Ruy Guerra's feature film *Kuarup* was booed in Cannes; that Brazil was placed by the White House on the list of trading partners disloyal to the United States. Nothing. Nothing matters. And turning her body she moves into a sixty-nine that doesn't work out (it's just over-excitement), her mouth grasping for his skin, his hair, taking his cock

in her mouth, hurting him with her teeth. He holds her
and moves her body into a position in which he can
embrace her but she gets up onto his thighs, gets him
to enter her, moving, shuddering. Passo Fundo had said
to him just minutes earlier: fifteen isn't as young as all
that, you get girls of thirteen starting families in Dublin's
Northside, girls of fourteen who run away from their
homes on the Santa Catarina coast, eloping to marry the
eighteen-year-old boys they've fallen in love with, it's
tradition; twelve-year-old mulatta girls get pregnant by
their first boyfriends in Rio de Janeiro's North Zone, gypsy
girls marry at thirteen. It's tradition. Fifteen years old. It's
not a problem. Passo Fundo is sure of it. Crazy. Nothing
matters. Maína shudders. He comes hard after the weeks
of waiting. Maína wraps herself round him. Paulo feels
her heart beating strongly against his chest. (The world
is turning at just the speed Paulo wants it to turn.) They
have never been so uninhibited with each other before.
She says she feels great. He says it's the drink. She says it
isn't correct to be complicated. It isn't right, he corrects
her. Maína lets go of him, slides off to the side, swears
she'll do whatever he wants: if he is planning to live with
them for a time, she will do everything she can to help
him adapt, she will accept his agitation (that's what he
hears her say) and whatever good he can do them here on
the side of the road. Who knows, what she wants might
really be too complicated for him (he is bigger than her

world, and if he weren't lost in his ideas and feelings he wouldn't be here). She says that if he wants they could improvise a school and show that there can be an escape from living in this ridiculous way. He asks Maína to rub his back a little, the pain has increased all of a sudden, and he says that then she should sleep.

It's day. The work is done. The two of them gather up the materials, pack everything away in plastic refuse sacks. They know that if they don't deal with the tidying up while they are still warm they won't do it. She opens the zip of the igloo tent, walks over to Paulo and then, having said hello to Passo Fundo, says that she's going to change her clothes and will bring her mother and sisters back earlier than they had agreed so that they can meet his friend. You never know, he might even play his clarinet for them. It would be the perfect way to inaugurate the new home. Paulo likes the idea. As soon as Maína has left the encampment, Passo Fundo suggests that they finish the job by dividing up what's left of the vodka. It's a Thursday without a cloud in the sky, there are more cars passing than there were the previous days. Two hours earlier than planned, Passo Fundo's cousin arrives, he's got a crazy expression on his face, like someone who hasn't slept. They position the stepladder the carpenters had left them on top of the Monza's roof rack (Paulo has promised to return it to them by the end of the day). The drink relaxes them, the smell of paint takes on a thermal presence when the sun's rays strike the wooden room, a feature that perhaps only exists in Paulo's exhausted brain. He has already informed Passo Fundo that he is going to have to play his instrument for Maína's sisters, so Passo Fundo is already warming up, going over the first part of the study he will perform (Paulo thinks it's funny remembering that Passo Fundo got interested in the instrument in eighth grade when, as a punishment, he was obliged to attend ten rehearsals of the school orchestra, rehearsals taken by the school principal himself, it was either that or immediate expulsion; he thinks it's funny and comments that he never imagined he'd ever see him warming up for a gig like this). Passo Fundo's cousin asks Paulo if he wants a hand taking down the igloo tent, Paulo says he's going to stay another week, and that's when he notices that the boy is more agitated than usual. Passo Fundo's cousin asks if they don't want to have a bit of a kick-around, Paulo can't stop himself saying maybe, the boy goes to the car, gets a rather worn five-a-side football, laughing to himself, scratching his nose, and with his right hand throws it at Paulo's chest. The lack of sleep and the drink make Paulo give a start, and purely out of reflex he deflects the ball without trying to control it and then runs off after it, wondering what else he could do that would make the situation even odder. Passo Fundo puts away his clarinet, they start up a game of piggy in the middle, in which one of them tries to take the ball off the other two, then some shots at goal and knees and headers. There's no more vodka and it's nearly half past nine. A particularly enthusiastic kick by Passo Fundo's cousin sends the ball spinning quickly with perfect accuracy towards the highway, and the three of them, just kids, run after it, scared it'll get onto the road and cause some kind of accident. That is the exact moment when a highway police patrol van pulls over in front of Passo Fundo's cousin's Monza, and the ball lodges underneath it. Two policemen in Ray-Bans (they couldn't be more of a cliché) get out ostentatiously, wanting to know what's going on, where are the people who live in the tent and what's with that painted house at the back. Passo Fundo's cousin, not realising how much this will expose him, excuses himself and bends over to retrieve the ball. At once the stockier of the policemen draws his gun and tells him to stand up, to put his hands behind his head and step back beside the other two. The other policeman, the skinny one, also pulls his revolver, with an order that nobody move. For a moment Paulo doesn't know what to think. He was getting ready for a verbal confrontation, but not to have two guns pointed at him at the very moment when he stopped paying attention. His almost pathological difficulty in submitting to authority, unfurling itself in the shock of that situation, is such that he cannot pull himself together in the midst of the rage that is poisoning him and, for a moment (which lasts for the duration and the immediate consequences of a slap on the face), the words that ought to be heard are shut away in a paralysis. 'We're not delinquents, officer,' says Passo Fundo's cousin. Paulo still does not react, trying to understand what's going on. The skinny policeman ignores what Passo Fundo's cousin has said and repeats his question about what they are doing there. Passo Fundo and Paulo look at each other. 'Four Indian women, friends of mine, live here,' says Paulo. 'Friends of yours? And where are they?' It's only the skinny policeman who speaks. It isn't hard to tell that his partner, holding the cocked revolver, is a hair's breadth away from losing it. 'In another encampment,' Paulo says, pointing towards the south. 'Lower that arm, kid.' It isn't easy being friendly. Cars begin to stop on both sides of the road: curious passers-by who have spotted something out of the ordinary going on. 'I'm going to ask one last time: what are the three of you doing here?' The people who stopped have begun to get out of their cars. 'I built a house for the four of them.' Paulo looks over behind the Indian women's tent. 'I can show you . . . ' His expression becomes even more serious. 'So they have better living conditions.' The skinny one steps closer. 'And what about the National Indian Foundation, does FUNAI know about this? Do you have a construction license?' he asks, not lowering his gun. 'No,' Paulo looks straight at him, 'it was my idea, the two of them just came over to help me . . . Look, I can show you my papers. I'm a student at the state university, I'm studying law . . . ' he tries to point out. 'Ok, all of you over there,' says the skinny one, now probably playing up to his audience on the roadside. 'Keep an eye on them, Régis.' He goes into Maína's tent; once he's inspected it he moves on to the small igloo tent, takes out the backpacks, opens the refuse sacks, looks at the empty cans and the painting gear inside, only then does he go over to the wooden room. The three of them wait under the gaze of the stockier one. Someone calls out offering to phone for reinforcements if the police want them (Paulo is bewildered by the offer; it's human nature to root for the underdog, he remembers his father always used to say that). The skinny one returns. 'Where are the Indian women? I want to know their precise whereabouts.' Passo Fundo drops his arms, strikes a casual pose. 'You guys have seen we aren't armed. The Indians are going to be back soon. Any chance you can stop pointing those guns at us?' The stocky one takes a step back. 'You stop right there, scum, or . . . ' Passo Fundo moves forward. Paulo steps in between them; the stocky one takes aim at his legs, fires.

nobody reads the unexpected

the fossil and the grip

The VW camper van used by FUNAI and the state government to take Maína to the medical centre at Barra do Ribeiro is running late. White and hollow, the construction behind her has never been occupied. Maína forbade her sisters from going into *that place*. Five months and the ingrained dirt growing in the pre-fab building. Five months since that morning when she arrived and found nobody there but the military policeman (and his 250cc motorcycle with the engine running) scribbling in a notepad, standing in front of their tent. A tall, impatient man with red hair, overburdening them with questions, refusing them the information they needed. It was only afterwards, when he was talking about what had happened, that he took a step back and turned, pointing down at an angle so that they would see the puddles of blood less than two metres away. (Amniotic, consumed in their land.) It's all done now (although the image of all that blood remains confused). Five months to reach this moment when she is wearing the leotard, the dirty one that could have been washed but hadn't been. She likes the way the pink matches the creamy colour of the ice cream that dripped onto the top of her chest and spread down over her stomach. When was that, actually? And when exactly had those things happened that made her think she had the power to say and act as she wanted? Madness. She will never have it. There was an exchange: the change is in her body; the successful natural selection of her yolk (no need even for a doctor), reproduction, birth, Jupiter protecting the earth with its perfect gravity, attracting towards it all the attacks from stray heavenly bodies, in spite of the colonial and foreign massacres, this spectacular immunity, the building of her youth against the clinical prescriptions around the sensation, that recurring sensation that the bladder, the hips, the base of the spine and everything else will collapse (cartilage already becoming bone, the seed already sucks up the liquid around it, swallows, hiccups, the liver and kidneys are already functioning, the seed already has a sex and already urinates). Nobody dares tell her that pregnancy is a good thing. What she finds bewildering are the cramps, unpleasant and tight, at night-time, in her calves. She needs to know. *Go away* when she remembers that she supported him. *Go* she says without being completely aware of it. Sometimes she repeats it – and makes herself ashamed – albeit repeating it to herself, not really even to herself. Her belly is her sisters' plaything, the guest when they play make-believe, sharing out the food that is no more than mud, leaves, twigs, gravel, little crumbled pebbles. The leotard is her belly's favourite piece of clothing. The belly is the life that Maína has to live. And she realises: she has been on her feet there for a long time. She walks over to the other side of the road, sits in the shade of the trees, stretches out her legs, looks up at the Durepox-grey of the sky, runs her hands over her ankles. Her feet are swollen in a way they haven't been before, she feels broad, overloaded. Looking up at the sky, just staying still looking up at the sky, used to be the best way of not needing anything else. She listens to the noise of the camper van's 1800cc engine, the deceleration and the downshift before the brakes kick in. The driver, an old man puffed up and proud, doesn't get out to open the door. 'Hey you, girl, get a move on, we're running late.' Maína looks at her hands, the way the colouring of her skin has changed a bit, she takes hold of the door handle, turns it. 'What the hell are you playing at?' the driver admonishes her. 'What kind of beggar's clothes are those you're in? You look like some circus girl . . . ' he says, making a point of behaving like an unreconstructed gaucho from another decade. 'That doctor, you know she isn't going to like that at all. If we weren't late I'd make you change your clothes right away.' Maína opens the door of the van. There are two small Indians sitting right at the back and an old Indian lady in the middle row, the same row she sits in as the van continues through the other encampments. And during the journey Maína remembers for the first time the moment when, still in a state of shock, she moistened her index finger in one of the pools of blood, then walked over to the white room and, without her feet touching the front steps, wiped her finger against the door, cursing it, damning it once again. The camper van enters the bounds of the city. Maína's attention gets caught up by the roads in the city that she knew when she was six years old, where she watched her first tv and heard her first radio, when she began to register all the objects that the grown-ups handled, when she realised there was a whole world made specially for her not to be able to get into. The driver demands some complicity when he explains the time for their return, when he will be waiting with the camper van parked round the back of the health centre. The building is different, it's been painted. Emerald green, that's the colour. The nine Indians go into the waiting room, there is plenty of space, and there is the enormous poster hanging on the wall opposite the windows with the face of an entreating Christ, exaggeratedly blond, even his beard, his eyes very blue, under which is written 'LOVE YOUR NEIGHBOUR AS YOURSELF.' To love (a verb that's always trying to switch direction). Everybody must love their neighbour. The doctor who will see her, the assistant who speaks Guarani and Portuguese, the permanently nasty driver, the hospital employees, the whole of Barra do Ribeiro, everybody. She is the second person to be seen. They take her blood pressure, measure her height, her weight, ask questions, ask her to go behind the metal screen, take off the leotard, cover herself up in the smock that's almost the same shade of green as they used for the front wall of the health centre, they say to come into the doctor's surgery. She sits in one of the two chairs that are at the only table in the room. The doctor arrives the next minute, she's young, and she doesn't hide her unease at the sight of the adolescent girl she is going to have to examine. Politely (and availing herself of the simultaneous interpretation from the assistant), after introducing herself, she asks whether Maína has been feeling any pain, any discomfort. Maína tells her about the cramps. The doctor jots something down in the notes resting on the blotter on the table, says she'll show her some stretching exercises that will help her with the muscle contractions. As soon as the assistant translates it, Maína shakes her head. There are other questions, some of them identical to those which came before, and they are answered only with nods and shakes of the head until the doctor, changing her tone of voice, asks whether Maína is in touch with the child's father. Maína doesn't wait for the assistant to translate, she replies in Portuguese that she doesn't know who the father is. The doctor puts down her pen, rests her hands on the blotter, looks at the assistant, asks her to leave the room for a few minutes. She gets up out of her chair, walks around the table, sits down beside Maína. Using even simpler words, she wants to know whether everything is all right. Maína remains silent, squeezing the hem of the gown, she can't blame other people, it's her, only her; she is the pivot who struggles with the normality that is so costly to find, and to maintain, for her mother and sisters, doomed to put up with the hormonal see-sawing of her own body for a few months longer. The doctor remains in silence for a few moments and then starts speaking again, about the risk of possible venereal disease, she starts a subtle bit of preaching (though now using friendly words that Maína does not understand) on the many types of sexual coercion and violence. Maína interrupts her saying she just wants the baby to be alive, and healthy. The doctor says that's what she's there to ensure. If there had been a script for this meeting, and if there were also an alternative script, both would have now ceased to make any sense. Maína sits closer to the edge of the chair and asks from what age the child will start having memories that would last for the rest of its life. The doctor says she hasn't quite understood the question. Then, speaking more directly, Maína asks until what age the child can stay with its mother without – once it's big, say about fifteen – being able to remember what she looks like, her voice, her smell. The doctor wants to know why she is asking. Maína says she has a lot of reasons, and also a lot of questions. The doctor says she is allowed to ask them. And then Maína asks about the likelihood of dying during childbirth, asks about what could go wrong and make her die during childbirth: the child living, her dying. The doctor stares, says awkwardly that everything is going to be fine, listing the tests she is going to have to do (she will no longer look at her). Maína can't help but let out a sigh that should only have happened once she had left that place, left that room, finished having that conversation; she will give this doctor she has just met the collaboration she has denied Paulo, to whom, on the first and only chance they got to meet after the imprisonment (however much Paulo tried to explain, it was with this that she associated his disappearance), she told him not to get out of the car, not even to turn off the engine, and deliberately using words as rudimentary as the first time they had met, she asked him to find himself some other distraction and get out of her life.

fractions

London.

The well-articulated intervention from Passo Fundo's father confirming the esteem in which he was still held by his colleagues in the police, added to the condition that Paulo should never mention being hit by the bullet that went into and out of his right thigh without touching the bone (this in order for everyone to arrive at what he, excitedly, called a very excellent agreement), prevented the incident from ending up in administrative and criminal proceedings; the highway policeman who fired the gun, actually the son of a great friend of his from when he was in middle school at Ignácio Montanha at the end of the fifties and long before he ever imagined he'd end up a police chief, as he made a point of confiding to Paulo, had for weeks been using a gun of his own, a nickel-plated Colt thirty-eight in much better condition than those issued by the National Department of Roads and Highways – a twenty-two with a hammer spring and a cylinder breech in a dreadful state. Which was why he would not have to account for the projectile fired, there would be no mention of his outburst on the official record. In the public hospital it was no different: Paulo, the victim who might have been taken for the aggressor, was seen to as a matter of priority and with no record kept. It's alarming how some things get resolved. What could not be remedied, however, was the discord created by his having given in so easily and gone into shock while he sought out the pain that didn't appear even though the seconds were ticking past. As he struggled to stay on his feet, because this would allow him to react (and he was not reacting). And then came the shivering, the fearfulness. And other people talking and shouting instead of him. The dashing around, and the adjustment of tempers. And the pain. Passo Fundo says it was a mistake calling his father and, again and again, how fucked up it all is (his cousin had little paper sachets of cocaine in his trouser pocket). Paulo thought about the Indian girl, and especially about his parents (that his parents should not find out), since he'd left work and college, sold the car, and then there were all those days when he hadn't shown up at home. He would hear his mother, in one of those conversations that were becoming more and more frequent, warning him that she was not prepared to support a son who was a dilettante, a poet, a grown man who didn't work, didn't study. He accepted the ex-police chief's suggestion, feeling a bit turned-inside-out; he also really did want to avoid any mention of the incident (Maína was a subject belonging to him alone), though it is hard to hide a bullet wound, impossible not to limp, impossible not to show his grim mood in front of his parents who are living in the same house and lavishing all their attention on him, just as it was impossible to prevent Leonardo, who was in Porto Alegre taking his exams for a place in the Public Ministry, from showing up to visit and, finding he didn't receive the welcome he had expected from Paulo, talking to his father about that difficult moment that he, the Paulo he so admired, was going through, and about the risk of a brilliant future going down the drain thanks to a delusional compulsion for anarchism, which doesn't sit too well with a move towards maturity. Leonardo's visit had its intended effect. Paulo's mother went so far as to threaten her son with an injunction and called him a 'two-bit little nihil-ist' and said that he had disappointed her. Paulo simply took the opportunity to inform them that he was going to be spending a few months in Europe, washing dishes in restaurant kitchens, delivering food to offices, cleaning, delivering newspapers or whatever he had to do to save money and make his way around the world. On hearing his son's announcement, his father didn't say anything further (Paulo could see that to his father the idea was far from ridiculous, at least it was some kind of direction, a bit of direction for a while), he simply got up and left, his mother did the same. This was a few months ago. He left politics behind, *the fatuousness of politics*, left it to those who like playing at politics. And it almost didn't matter that he was changing cities, going to live in London, to share a two-room flat with five people he didn't know, friends of friends, but who gave him the warmest possible welcome nevertheless, turning over the living-room sofa to him; and it almost didn't matter that he has made good use of this afternoon, the afternoon off from the Italian restaurant where he works preparing desserts, and has done his laundry for the week, and done his exercises in Gladstone Park and the stretching that was prescribed for him by the physiotherapist and, back home, after half an hour soaking in the tub, that he has put on a cool long-sleeved Dudalina shirt, from the time when he used to go around Porto Alegre in a suit, and a pair of jeans he's just bought in Brixton; and it almost didn't matter that he has taken the Tube into town, got out at Charing Cross station right by Trafalgar Square, walked to St Martin's Lane, gone into Café Pelican, run right into Tom Waits at one of the smart tables in one of the most expensive establishments in Covent Garden, almost nothing mattered: the memory of Maína and his feeling of having messed up with her travel with him wherever he goes. There is no place to hide, there are no more fears about what the strips of LSD, the waxy pellets of hashish, the tubes of poppers being passed from hand to hand on Thursday nights at Heaven, the London nightclub, can do to his brain, the *golden* brain that needs to be quicker and more agile than that of any of his acquaintances, his competitors. There's no more Porto Alegre, news from the unforgiveable provincialism of Porto Alegre, and there's no longer the task of getting everything done by yesterday, nor the crappy proletarian revolution in Brazil. All it takes is a public transport pass, a one-month pass on the *metrô*, as the Brazilians call it, with the little wallet where they glue your three-by-four photo in the top right-hand corner to allow you to move around the central parts of town, and a few coins to buy a Twix and a Coke (Maína's taste for Coke got him addicted) and that was that. He allowed everything he had once learned to be transformed into a great ignorance. And there, that's where the urgency was. He sleeps, wakes, takes the Tube, works, fifteen-minute break, works, takes the Tube back, eats the sandwiches he's usually made at the end of the shift, drinks a few shots of the spirits purloined from the bars where the others in the house – almost all of them bartenders – work, chats to whoever is awake (making conversation is the social responsibility of anyone who sleeps in the living room), does the washing up when it's his turn to do the washing up, takes a shower in the adapted cubicle in the kitchen that takes fifty-pence coins and is much cheaper than the shower in the room with the bathtub which, besides being more expensive, is also for the collective use of everyone living on all four floors of the house, reads the newspapers that he picks up for free at the Tube stations, waits till he is absolutely sure that everyone has retired for the night, moves the coffee-table off the rug in the middle of the room, lays out the mattress, sleeps. Fabio, his Brazilian friend who works at Café Pelican, says that Tom Waits was only there to do an interview with a journalist from *Time Out* magazine. Tom Waits, tall and tanned, waving his arms about like an athlete, doesn't look to him anything like the image that appears on the cover of his records that sell in their thousands in Brazil.

Although he is recovering well, his leg still hurts, a lot.

'Ah, *mon cher monsieur*! Per'aps *monsieur* will 'ave anozzer leetle glass of our verrry expensif wine?' Fabio kids around with him, catching Paulo at just the moment when he is watching Tom Waits and the journalist out the corner of his eye. 'What's up, Fabinho? Weren't you heading out?' asks Paulo. 'So the thing is, man, Etienne, that anorexic fag, asked me to stay till it's time to cash up,' and, taking the nearly empty glass from Paulo's hand, Fabio wipes the cloth over the granite surface of the bar. 'You're going to have to stay? Well then, take it easy.' Paulo shifts position on his stool, which is tall and doesn't have footrests. 'Yeah. Another hour and a half. Bastard manager. Well, I suppose it's just tough shit, this is my job. I'll give you some more wine,' Fabio mutters. 'Don't bother. I'll make the most of the fact that I'm at a loose end and you're doing this overtime, I'll go by the anti-apartheid vigil outside the South African embassy. Apparently there are these two big-shot militants who're going to talk about the negotiations to end Nelson Mandela's imprisonment.' He gets down from the stool with no footrests. 'Son-of-a-bitch South African government, this whole segregation thing, I just don't get it,' says Fabio without ever losing his elegant, Italian movie-star pose (an absolute prerequisite for getting a job at the Pelican). 'You get segregation everywhere, Fabinho, theirs is just more brazen than the others,' he muses, 'or rather, it's the first one I'd like to see brought to an end. So look, keep your very expensive wine for some other day. Today our business is with some Mexican beer courtesy of Drake, right?' Picking Fabio up at work was to have been part of the arrangement for going together to the exclusive party for friends of the staff at Bar Sol, the restaurant everyone wants to work at because, besides being a fun place to serve, it's far and away the bar where the customers, most of them American tourists, leave the best tips. Fabio was invited to work there by Drake, who has a Brazilian mother and an English father and has worked at the restaurant ever since it first opened and always manages to get himself back in work there when he decides to come over from Brazil and spend a few months in the city. 'We'll talk at Bar Sol, Paulo . . . And watch out for any trouble, those gatherings outside the South African embassy sometimes end up in confrontations with the police.' Paulo puts on his jacket. 'So I just ask for Drake, right?' and he gives one last glance at Thomas Alan Waits, one of the few idols in his life right now. 'Yeah, he'll be expecting you.' Paulo turns, heads off towards the door. On the street, he turns left down St Martin's Lane, which will take him straight to the South African embassy.

The people who are not on the pavement directly outside the building have positioned themselves across the road on the paved central area of Trafalgar Square. The young black man wearing a white shirt buttoned up to his neck and holding a microphone turns towards the embassy, he says: 'Nelson Mandela is still in prison, but he won't be for long.' The people clap. Paulo is with them now, already feeling the effects of the wine he drank hurriedly at the Pelican. He finds it surreal how explicit they are, these manifestations of belief in the possibility of Mandela being released without bargaining before he dies. It isn't, for him, a question of witnessing what could perhaps be part of a significant historical process; he is there out of curiosity. As it happens, he lied when he was questioned at the immigration counter, saying he was here as a tourist and that he wouldn't stay longer than twenty days in the United Kingdom; he did that out of curiosity. He drinks with people he doesn't know, some of them even younger than him, people from all over the world, he does this out of curiosity. He drinks until things get dangerous, out of curiosity. He hangs out with people who are rich and spoiled, with Turks playing football in Hyde Park on the weekend, people who live it up because they're in London and then become the domesticated little wives of other people who make a point of complaining nastily and telling their friends that their *domesticated little wives* can't cook properly and don't swallow their sperm when they suck their huge cocks, with couples from Madeira with their totally incomprehensible Portuguese, he does all this out of curiosity. He walks alone, in the early hours, from the centre to the north of the city, to Willesden Green, having dropped home the waitresses from Ireland, or Poland, or Jamaica, whom he has been trying to hook up with, even if it's only for a week, spending every night at their place, he does it out of curiosity. He goes into Stanford's, the best map shop in the world, some people say, and looks at the huge maps they have framed on the walls, especially the one that shows the southern hemisphere in the upper part of the *mappa mundi*, out of curiosity. Curiosity, just curiosity, curiosity is what's new now nothing matters man and everyone can go to hell cause now I don't give a fuck and I want to see if this shit catches fire once and for all. Amid *excuse me*s and *sorry*s he makes his way over towards the speaker, undoubtedly more emphatic and positive than the middle-aged gentleman who had come before him. He watches him, comparing. It's as if it were decades ago, as if he had himself never spoken in public, never needed to be charismatic and to convince a group of students, at times in gatherings of more than twenty thousand people, to hate their university vice-chancellors, and members of the Ministry of Education, and foundations run by private universities whose accounts and tax exemptions are never made quite clear enough. He feels odd, not only the dizziness of the wine, it's the dreams and the hope that he can't bear. Such haste, his own haste. So much that it made him stagnate. He hasn't been interested in trying to think. It's the first time he has stopped and paid attention to something important since arriving in London. He doesn't know which struggle is worth it. Where, after all, is this nineteen eighty-nine happening if not in London, New York, Tokyo? Life is moving on. He's in his early twenties and feels like an old man, though not old enough (feeling like an old man isn't usually the same as *nothing matters any more*, though it has been). And the wine having its effect, there isn't a drug that takes you apart in quite the same way. He thinks. She sent him away. Maína's fragility was never weakness. This inability to feel real *passion*, the way some people seem to feel it without making the least effort. Now he realises (as he is overtaken by a feeling of nausea, a nausea that will force him to get out of there) or he assumes: however much he does, he won't be able to get involved again.

'Shall we go to the bathroom?' says the little Portuguese girl who has been clinging to Paulo since he arrived at Sol (she gets all tangled up wanting to talk like the Brazilians, it's embarrassing after a while). 'I'll stick round here,' Paulo replies without any warmth at all, fascinated by the tall black girl with the big glasses who has been watching him for several minutes and who is standing at the entrance to the corridor that leads to the other bar. Perhaps he would have been intimidated by her determination if he were sober, but that isn't the case, he has already drunk all the beer he meant to drink, his superego is suitably caged in, he puts the empty glass down on the window ledge, walks over to the girl. 'Hi,' he says. 'Hi,' she replies, stepping closer, because the noise is really loud in that part of the bar. 'I saw you today' – taking Paulo by surprise – 'I was outside the South African embassy two hours ago,' she explains. 'Are you involved with the South African cause?' he asks (he thinks he hasn't used quite the right term). 'We all are, aren't we?' she replies. And suddenly he feels as though he has seen her before. 'By the way, my name's Paulo . . . What's yours?' She holds out her hand. 'Rener.' They shake. 'Tell me, Rener, where are you from?' he asks. 'I'm from Paris. You know the one? The city that's in Paris, you know?' letting herself smile for the first time. 'The way London's in London?' He tries to go along with it. 'No, in London it's completely different,' and she takes a sip of her soft drink. 'Typical Parisienne,' he said. 'I do like the geography, but I'm not a typical Parisienne, I don't share the

city's mood, I'm not proud of having been born there . . .
I mean, it doesn't make any difference that that's where
I was born.' She pulls him over towards the wall, their
conversation is obstructing other people's passage. 'You're
not a committed neighbourhood-ist, a nationalist. Is that
what you mean?' he says (there's always some room for
error when two people who speak different languages are
using a third language to communicate). 'I don't believe
in nationalities . . . Just like I don't believe in victims . . .
My presence at the pro-Mandela action was just to see
how far the speeches by those two guys would go and if
they'd resort to the old trick of victimising, in the sense of
victimising people and cultures,' she said, firmly. 'That's
the kind of answer I need a whole night to understand,
and another whole night to come up with an adequate
retort' – he is even more convinced that he's seen her
before. 'Ok, so I'm giving you a hard time, aren't I?' she
takes hold of his arm, 'but I can assure you, I'm a pretty
cool person.' She takes the last sip of her soft drink. 'I
like it when people give me a hard time . . . ' says Paulo,
flexing his arms and puffing up his chest in an attempt
to recreate Popeye the sailor's pose without, however,
remembering quite what Popeye the sailor's pose was.
The joke didn't work. 'How about we get out of here,
Paulo?' she suggests, 'Paulo who caught *my* eye out there
and who, as it happened, showed up here at *my* party
and caught *my* eye again.' He looks at her. 'Coincidences,

Rener. Though it's hard for me to admit, life is made up of them.' And someone taps his shoulder. 'You'd better be careful with that black girl, she's extremely dangerous,' Drake says loudly, Fabio is with him. 'Since you're the type of guy who'll even read the instructions on a medicine packet – didn't you read last week's *TNT*? There was a photo of that beauty there that took up nearly half a page of the magazine.' And Paulo realises where he's seen her before. 'That's right, comrade, my ex-colleague from Sol is an important woman, she was named the boldest of the three leaders of this squatting movement robbing the owners of large south London properties of their peace of mind,' he goes on. 'We only occupy properties that are empty,' she says, 'and of course homes belonging to the government.' Drake kisses her on the forehead. 'I love you.' And then speaking in Portuguese, 'I always wanted to fuck her, never managed to do it.' Then switching back to English, 'So Paulo, has she told you she's a huge fan of Nietzsche?' Paulo shakes his head. 'Nietzsche,' Drake continues, 'the Coca-Cola of intellectualism for the under twenties.' Rener leans over towards Paulo and whispers: 'I do like the book *Ecce Homo*, that's all.' Fabio tugs on Drake's arm. 'Hey, genius, use all that philosophical stuff you know and score some more beer for your compatriots.' Drake gestures let's go on, and they leave. 'I love you too, Drake,' she says and, turning to Paulo (and before saying that her problem isn't that she's twenty-six and still likes

Nietzsche), Rener puts her hands on his face and kisses him on the mouth.

Rener asks him to be quiet, the woman who lives in the next-door apartment has a sick daughter. She puts the jug of water and the glass on the small tin tray on the edge of the bedside table, turns on the little lamp, opens the wardrobe, takes out a Marks & Spencer carrier bag, throws it over to his side of the bed, he opens it (it's full of every brand and style of condom), she turns off the ceiling light and immediately tosses a tube of lubricant onto his chest, she says that they are going to do what two uninhibited men should do when they feel there's the chance of a great friendship between them.

Coincidences.

Paulo said he had to be at the restaurant before ten in the morning and it's already eleven thirty-five (straight after the alarm clock had gone off, at nine, Rener had opened the bedroom curtains; she didn't say anything, just made a cup of coffee, left it beside the bed and went back to sleep). From the moment he opened his eyes he was immersed in this stony silence. He must have said what he hadn't told anyone since leaving Brazil. It was a good night in any case. She will introduce him to some guys who will get him to choose an empty building in Elephant and Castle. Arrive when it is getting dark (there's no reason to hide from the building's other residents; greet everyone, be polite, try not to give any impression that you're going to be a bad neighbour), break the sealed padlock put there by the government and remove the metal bar blocking access to the door, break down the door, change the lock as quickly as you can, check that the new keys work, lock the door and only then tell yourself that the place is yours (at least until the squatter eviction proceedings, which can take years to progress, come to an end). It isn't a question of good faith but of sorting out your life, yours and other people's along the way, too. Sorting it out the way she, Rener, has been doing. She remembers having said that any mistakes must not be because of cowardice. Perhaps this was what made him agree like that, but it's hard for her to know, it could have been so many other things. The worst mistake would be to try and guess, now that it's nearly midday and she has to say that in a week's time they will be entering a property valued at more than nine million and she's counting on him, she needs there to be seven people besides herself and she has only managed to get six, there aren't many people who will risk an occupation like this. If things work out, twenty people will get a new home; if they go wrong it's every man for himself. Rener will figure out some way of getting back to Paris and, assuming there are no further coincidences, she and the Brazilian will not see each other again.

palindromes

Rener ties the piece of rubber tight around her arm, runs the alcohol-dampened cotton wool over the bend of her elbow where she is going to make the puncture, takes the syringe, uncovers the needle, examines where the veins are, taps the surface, draws the blood, shows the filled syringe to Paulo. 'Ten millilitres, no more, no less.' Undoes the tourniquet, injects the blood into her own buttock. 'There's nothing like it, I promise you. It's the secret of my vitality . . . It'll reinvigorate you, too, you'll see,' she says, putting the empty syringe to one side and taking another from the packet. She takes the syringe from the sealed packaging. 'Shall we?' she asks, excitedly. Paulo had never heard of auto-haemotherapy, but Rener did not have to say much to convince him and for him to ask her to apply the practice to him. She said that she always plans to draw and re-inject her own blood on the day before an appropriation (that is the convenient word she uses to describe the break-in), because it gives her physical courage. He wasn't sure whether she had meant to say *physical courage* precisely, but that was how he understood it and it seemed more than appropriate. The blood in the muscle acts as though it were a foreign body, activating the immunological system controlled by the bone marrow, that was all she gave as her explanation. 'I haven't needed a doctor since,' she assured him. Paulo doesn't have a problem with the sight of his own blood, getting shot like that stirred something up in him that is not visible, something he is still trying to understand. One second, under exceptional psychological pressure, and a whole life in all its particularities changes forever, accelerates towards something that has not yet happened. He did not even know what day it was when he woke up having spent the early hours tossing and turning in Rener's bed unable to sleep, unwilling to wake her. The needle pierces his skin, it's the second time, the blood warms his body as it enters. Rener has been his guide during these days in which he hasn't left her apartment, even if being guided was not what he needed right now.

> *Maína, I don't know how to send you this letter. I'm going to write it all the same. Here, where I am now, is on the other side of the Atlantic Ocean, a city called London. There's a river that cuts through the middle of the city, I really like sitting on one of the benches they have on the banks of the river. But that wasn't what I wanted*

to tell you. I've been thinking of you a lot, really hoping
that you're doing well. Yesterday I bought a blue dress.
I hope one day I'll see you again and I can give you the
dress I bought. Writing is difficult. I'll try again some
other time. Missing you. Paulo.

Ten-thirty at night, the lamb doner kebab that she brought back from her meeting with the other six who would be going with them tomorrow hasn't gone down too well. Paulo's stomach is hurting more than his leg. He still hasn't been able to understand why she thought it best for him not to come to the preparatory meeting. 'The less involved you become, the better' – it sounded like an excuse. He isn't going to go back to sleep (which has nothing to do with the imminent occupation). Not sleeping, not getting out of bed, just watching the bedroom window panes turning lighter and darker, just listening to the sounds from the endless blocks and towers that make up the council estates of Elephant and Castle and trying to ignore the voices of its children, the crows' cawing, the sounds of the plastic bags brushing against one another as the person carrying them hurries to escape the rain that will be here soon: all this is part of the rules of the boring new game, defying him to ruin everything. And wide awake, watching her sleep, he does.

*

Twenty-two hours later, at the exact moment that Rener sits down at the table with the two glasses of cider saying that this is her favourite brand of the drink, one of the white girls at the next table, one of the three girls who look Swedish, gets up, excitedly gives a few little squeals and shows her perfect breasts to the two young black men who are at the table with her, daring them to touch at least one of them as she sways them from side to side to display their natural opulence, and the two young men just laugh, and she gives another few little shrieks as she looks quickly around to check whether she really is drawing attention to herself and proving that these wonders, that was the word she used, talking loudly, didn't have a single millilitre of silicon in them, and the customers at the other tables applaud, and Paulo and Rener applaud. 'Brixton. I love this place!' Rener exclaims. Paulo downs the cider in one. It's getting dark outside, which makes no difference, the bar is curtained anyway, the curtains are blue velvet, the DJ who is going to be playing from nine-thirty arrives with his case of records, Rener insists on pointing so that Paulo will see him, excited fascination doesn't suit her. Everyone greets him, DJs and bartenders, these guys rule, whether in Brixton or in the City, especially on nights like this, Thursday nights, the hottest nights of the week, the police are focusing on the major demos, the same attention they will give them on Fridays and Saturdays, residential areas are almost totally abandoned. The DJ who has been working the decks brings the track to an end, a moment of silence from the speakers, and 'Last Night a DJ Saved my Life' bursts on. Paulo stands up saying he's going to get a beer, asks if she wants another cider, Rener says she'll stick with just the one she's drinking now, Paulo walks over to the bar, asks for a beer, looks over at the table where Rener is sitting, an indescribable fluttering of dark skin in the darkness, she's even more beautiful than on the night they first met. All pussy's the same, Passo Fundo used to say, older men say that, too, but it's not true. Rener had never surrendered her pussy to him, Paulo had not spoken to Passo Fundo again, Paulo has to go to the flat in Willesden Green to pick up his things. Rener plays with her hair and waves from a distance without any shyness, she's even more beautiful than she was five minutes ago. Rener lives a perfect radicalism, Alice in a state of wonder, enjoying every last drop in the dropper, as she herself says when she's impatient, Paulo must not have understood the subliminal meaning correctly, she's four years and a few months older than him. The bartender puts the large glass of beer down on the counter, one pound thirty. Paulo leaves twenty pence as a tip, he returns to the table, she takes his hand, the hand that is holding the glass. 'You can't get drunk', that is the only thing she says, the kiss between them fits, perhaps it's her mouth, it's fleshy; she says that the best kind of kiss is a kiss between two men,

Where is this going? he thinks, then she takes a mini-torch from her trouser pocket and explains what he is going to have to do: as he's the first-timer in the group he will be in charge of the simplest task. Paulo says nothing, puts down the glass, takes the torch. She goes on: he'll be waiting with the torch on a corner two blocks from the mansion they're going to occupy, it's one of the two places the police might come from if they are called, and she takes a wristwatch from her jacket pocket, Paulo's going to need a watch. The watch is synchronised with the watches of the other six and her own, she tells him to put it on and see if it feels comfortable on his wrist; Paulo obeys. It's tight, he doesn't say anything, he can adjust the strap later, he takes off the watch, holds it in his left hand. They will drop him a three-minute walk from the corner, he will need to arrive there at ten-fifteen, exactly the time when the others will be reaching their positions, and she and the other two who are also going in to break the house's padlocks and door-locks will jump the wall, one will open the front gate and she and the other will deal with the back door to the house, back doors are always easier to get into. It will take them less than five minutes to change the lock; if Paulo spots a car approaching he will turn the torch on and off twice, if it's a police car he will turn the light on and keep it on while he walks off at a right angle to the street, the others will do the rest. Paulo picks up his glass of beer in his right hand, he says he has understood what she has said clearly and that he could be more useful, she says he's already doing a lot and that he shouldn't kid himself, often it's the ones keeping watch who are the first to be taken, mostly when the police arrive with two or more vehicles, but that isn't going to happen, it's all going to work out fine, the house has been empty a long time. And the DJ puts on something by Soul II Soul, Rener asks Paulo to dance, he accepts, a car will come and fetch them, less than forty minutes from now; he holds the watch in his left hand and notices what a good dancer she is.

Contrary to what Paulo had assumed (Rener only oper-ated in south London), they went straight to Hampstead, in the north of the city, the millionaires' part of town. On the way, Rener told him about the building's location and the peculiarities of its owner – one of those modern-day financial gangsters – so that Paulo could understand the real reason for the action. When they meet up with the others they get the bad news. One of them didn't show. 'We're not going to cancel,' said Rener. The look-out plans had to be re-done, the places rearranged, apart from Paulo's, she just asked him to be as alert as possible and gave him a bigger torch than the previous one, one that could be seen from far away (the guy who didn't show up was to have been the in-between person in Paulo's group; now there would no longer be anybody positioned between him and the person at the front gate ready to go in, to warn the others or assist them in their escape, should anything go wrong). She warned him that having a larger torch could get him into trouble more easily. He answered that's fine. This happened a few minutes ago; now Paulo is walking towards the corner where he will have to wait. He wasn't able to loosen the watch strap any further because it was already at its widest. Rener asked him not to take the watch off his wrist. 'People who keep taking a watch out of their pocket and putting it back again attract suspicion and we don't want that, do we?' Paulo keeps the watch in his pocket anyway. He reaches the corner, looks towards the house that Rener and the others will be going into, he takes the watch from his pocket, looks at it. 'Excuse me, young man, have you got the time?' He hears the voice and turns. It's a lady with a caramel and white cocker spaniel sitting without a lead, his muzzle in the air beside her. Where did she spring from? How could he not have seen her coming? 'Sure . . . ' He looks again at the watch, getting over the surprise and already trying to find the words for the numbers in English in order to give her the information. 'Ten-sixteen,' without looking her in the eye. 'Thank you very much,' she says. 'Welcome,' he says. 'Buster can't abide using his lead any more, but he's devastated if I don't carry it with me when we go for our walk,' and she indicates the lead in her hand. Paulo looks at the dog, trying to be attentive. 'He's a very beautiful dog.' Evasively, 'Have a good night.' 'Where are you from?' she asks. He looks back towards the house. 'I'm from Portugal,' he says, making something up because he feels that in such situations being thought European might be beneficial. 'I don't know anything about Portugal, but I do like the Portuguese people,' she says, and adds, 'if I were from Portugal I'd never end up in England.' The dog stares at Paulo. 'It's very sunny there, isn't it?' Paulo says nothing. The dog runs off in the opposite direction to the house. The woman is impassive. 'Don't worry, Buster knows how to take care of himself.' Paulo puts the watch back in his pocket. 'Is the strap broken?' she asks. Still he says nothing. 'Talk to me.' There's a certain cadence to her speech that hypnotises him and makes him unable to imagine how he might free himself of her. 'Addie, that's my name. You don't need to tell me yours.' Now where the hell has that dog gone? 'You're with the gang who are going to go into that mansion down there aren't you? The one owned by that Egyptian with the bogus company? Large torches always give squatters away,' she goes on. 'Don't worry, I'm not going to start screaming for help, asking someone to call the police. Other people have tried to get in there before and haven't managed it, you know. There were hired security guards, that was less than a month ago . . . I think the owner slacked on the security, he must have thought: lightning doesn't strike the same place twice. But I know it does, and not only twice. Do you agree?' Paulo has no choice but to listen to her, he takes the watch out of his pocket, looks at it again: ten twenty-two. They must have gone in by now. 'Promise me you'll be good neighbours,' she says. 'I promise,' Paulo says despite himself. 'Can I give you a piece of advice?' she asks. 'I don't mean to be presumptuous, but I feel I have to tell you this.' Paulo nods, his eyes never leaving the house as he waits for some kind of signal. 'London isn't the place for you. It might seem as though it is, young people from all over the world come here thinking it is, the coolest place in the world, but I can see it isn't. You're torn, and being torn is not good. What I mean is: go back to Portugal and sort out whatever needs sorting out there, before it's too late.' Paulo sees the signal from the torch, responds with his. 'Thanks for the chat, young man. I must go and see what Buster has been up to. I hope to see you round here again,' and she walks away. Paulo doesn't know what to say. Rener is coming towards him. Paulo walks over to her and, when he is closer, he sees the concern in her expression. 'What happened, Paulo? We've been waiting for you for nearly half an hour.' Paulo takes the watch out of his pocket: ten forty-four. He can't understand what has happened. 'I met a lady, she had a dog with her . . . ' Rener doesn't wait for him to finish. 'A lady with a dog? That's so unlikely.' Paulo hands back the torch and the watch. 'You don't want to keep the watch?' she asks. 'No, thank you. I'm going to Willesden Green, to sort out my things.' She takes his hand. 'Stay

at my place . . . ' He looks annoyed. 'Or stay here, there's
going to be plenty of space.' He looks in the direction the
lady and her dog went in. 'I'm going to need your tools,
Rener.' Paulo lets go of her hand. 'Whenever you need
them, *brésilien*.' He considers asking if it's ok with her,
his leaving now, but Rener who has been serious gives a
broad smile and calls him 'one lucky son of a bitch'. He
returns her smile and doesn't tell her that his stomach
and his leg have stopped hurting.

the master's student

Luisa was absolutely certain that the members of the selection panel had been impressed by her, the twenty-three-year-old lately graduated in history from the Federal University of Rio de Janeiro, with unusual determination, who had come down to Porto Alegre in order to secure a sought-after place as a postgraduate at the Federal University of Rio Grande do Sul. 'From one Rio down to the other,' said the chair of the panel before letting slip in so many words that she would be most welcome on the master's programme. Then she took a bus to the centre of town, went straight to the hotel on Praça Otávio Rocha. She decided to stay in the city until the results were released. Seven days to take in what would be awaiting her in that Distant South if she were to be accepted, seven days far away from the dullness of Urca, from the brand-new Chevette her father had given her, from her childhood friends, from the groups that hang out at Lifeguard Post Nine on Ipanema Beach. 'Make yourself at home, Miss Luisa,' said the man behind the hotel reception desk as he handed her the key to her room. Luisa Vasconcelos Lange, only daughter of Colonel Ambrósio, that placid man, exemplary husband, conscious of his realm of influence, capable (through his

kindnesses, his sophistication, his affected reserve) of establishing
a network of absolute control over every move made by his subor-
dinates, his close friends, his wife and now, since her graduation
more than ever before, by his daughter. Luisa, however, has always
managed to escape. She knew that she would never be able to realise
certain desires if she remained under that control. She went into
the room, turned on the air conditioning, took off the suit that she
had chosen specially for her interview with the panel, showered,
put on a dress like the ones southern girls wear. She went out to
explore the centre a little more. She walked to the São Pedro Theatre,
went up to the mezzanine, struck by the five o'clock evening light,
sat at one of the outside tables of the theatre café, looked at the
menu (everything looked promising), ordered a chamomile tea, a
slice of apple cake. She took in the Praça da Matriz, the cathedral,
the historic buildings, the residential buildings and the ones filled
with offices, she told herself that this would be a better place than
her Rio, distant, self-sufficient, where she might perhaps discover
what to do with everything that brought her closer to the freedom
of a life without regrets.

names in vain

The seventeenth of December. Two recent polls have confirmed the low popularity and almost total lack of approval of Margaret Thatcher among the British people. Steven Soderbergh, aged twenty-six, has shot the film *Sex, Lies and Videotape* in five weeks spending little more than a million dollars. The Berlin Wall no longer exists, and the front page of every newspaper is quite certain: the western world will never be the same again. The mausoleum housing Lenin's body in Moscow is closed for renovation. The French are still going through their endless programme of commemorations for the two hundredth anniversary of the Revolution. A few hours from now, according to today's issue of the *Observer* magazine, a cartoon called *The Simpsons* will air for the first time on American tv. Paulo has already lost track of how long he has been in London: the tally of days does not reflect what he has already experienced here. He has lost the habit of speaking Portuguese (common though it is to meet people from Brazil, Portugal, Mozambique, Angola, even some from East Timor and Macao); he has become a squatter, not the altruistic kind but one of those who break into buildings they find empty on council estates and *transfer* possession for prices that vary between eight hundred and two thousand pounds. He negotiates with people who don't dare to take a risk themselves, who are in London to work, to save and send money back to their family in some godforsaken place in Asia, Africa, the Middle East, the western part of South America. He works alone; eventually he hires two look-outs, guys from Camberwell. He never breaks into places for Brazilians, he doesn't want to get a reputation among Brazilians (whatever it might be), there's nothing to be gained by that. Brazilians talk too much. He won't do break-ins for Italians or Argentines, either. Since the end of October he has been buying Brazilian weeklies from a little shop in Bayswater. News from Brazil doesn't help him to live better (those months when he kept himself distant were the good ones), yet he needs it. How else would he know that, at the start of November, a *favela* in São Paulo rechristened Nova República had collapsed under the weight of more than forty metres of rubble from the landfill being built next to it? (Nova República's former name was Núcleo Getsêmani; the change of name was due to the euphoria experienced in the wake of Tancredo Neves' victory in the electoral college, bringing to a close, according to

the political scientists, the country's military dictator-
ship.) Whole families were buried forty metres under.
Nova República is in Morumbi, one of São Paulo's richest
neighbourhoods, home of the tv presenter Silvio Santos,
who did everything he could to run as a candidate in the
presidential race and who did end up being a candidate
for a few days but was unable to remain in the contest
following a decision by the Electoral Court. The residents
knew that such a disaster was imminent. Those who
survived said they'd had nowhere else to go. Paulo can't
forget the news, this particular piece of news, and still
asks himself how it's possible that some people should
be so fixed in one place. Paulo can't sleep. It is election
day. Paulo is standing outside the Brazilian consulate in
London, he is drunk enough to have gone there in search
of news. People are waving Workers' Party flags on the
pavement outside the building, the liveliest are shouting slogans, they say the Workers' Party doesn't need to
pay for its militants because the party's militancy works
from the heart, the time has come for a change, the time
has come for a decent minimum wage, for honesty and
transparency, time for the workers to choose the country's
direction. Paulo could have arranged things so that he
would be eligible to vote, like those people are doing, but
the deadline lapsed, he let it lapse. He can't get involved,
nothing new about that, and he cannot tear himself away
from the consulate. All that joy, all that hope: love, love

locked up in manly breasts, like it says in the anthem. Paulo was always impressed at the number of people who became militants motivated by love. There is barely any traffic on that street, the only activity being that of the Brazilians, the sound of the conversations in Brazilian Portuguese that fill up the gaps between the buildings. Paulo stays until voting closes (arms crossed, unnoticed, contrite), he stays till people have dispersed, he stays till not many others have stayed, in conversation with one another as though what they said really could affect what was going to happen from now on.

Rener had invited him round to hers for this pasta with tomato sauce over two weeks earlier, she was sure today would be a difficult day for him, and because she said she could no longer bear to keep meeting him in bars, and because he's got to stop living off Twix and Coke. Paulo knows exactly what she thinks. He walks up the stairs in the building in Elephant and Castle, stops outside the flat. Rener is the closest he has managed to get to family these past months; it's been hard to be with her. He knocks three times. She says to wait a moment. She opens the door, her right eye is bruised and there's a cut on the left side of her forehead. 'Hi, *brésilien*,' she greets him without any awkwardness. 'What happened, Rener?' He's surprised. 'Looking pretty cute, aren't I?' she says ironically. 'Brand new Halloween makeup, I've had it on since Friday. Three mammoth sons of a Lebanese businessman, the owner of a house we went into on Wednesday, appeared out of nowhere and threw some punches.' She pulls him inside and closes the door. 'There were three of us there, me and a couple, still messing around with the electrics so that the rest of their family could move in as soon as possible. They caught me unawares. Three against three, it wasn't hard for them to get us out of there. I ended up leaving my tools behind, my Walkman was left behind, they lost their things, too. I misjudged it. I wasn't careful enough. I learned my lesson. I've already drawn a line under it . . . Want some wine?' And suddenly Paulo feels as though he's in a patch of quicksand from which he will never be able to escape. 'What they did isn't right, Rener. Let me have the address of the house, I'll go there tomorrow and fetch the stuff that belongs to you and the couple.' He walks straight over to the bottle of gin by the herbs next to the oven. 'If you think I'm going to let you go there, you're crazy. What's done is done.' She takes a glass from the cupboard and passes it to him. 'Ok, we'll discuss this later.' He knows now isn't the time to insist. 'Any news of the elections back home?' she asks, changing the subject. 'I ended up going to the Brazilian consulate . . . ' he replies. 'And?' He pours the gin. 'I wasn't in the mood to talk to any of the people who were there cheering the parties on . . . To be honest, I found the whole thing a bit embarrassing . . . ' He puts the bottle back in its place. Silence falls between them. 'The sauce is ready, I made it myself . . . ' She takes the initiative: 'I'll prepare the pasta then you get to eat the best spaghetti with tomato sauce in Elephant and Castle.' Without bothering to raise the glass in a toast, Paulo drinks the gin. He knows she doesn't approve of what he's been doing, he knows that in this kitchen he is the official representative of *the Dark Side*. 'Let's get drunk, *francesa*. Save the pasta for another day. I'm not hungry.' She puts the pan back in the cupboard. 'You can't quite stomach it. That's what you mean.' She takes his hand and leads him over to the sofa in the living room. 'You drink your gin, I'll smoke my hashish, I'll have a few sips of the expensive wine that you ignored, and let's go to bed,' she says. 'So be it,' he retorts. 'Do you think your candidate stands a chance?' she asks. 'I don't think so. Oh, I don't know . . . ' He takes off his boots, puts his feet up on the pouffe. 'What do you know about Trotskyism, Rener?' he asks. 'The same as everyone else. It's the name given to the doctrine invented by an embarrassed communist who tried playing at revolution and didn't have the balls to confront Uncle Stalin. In short: a wimp,' is her reply. 'I was a Trotskyite in Brazil, and the more time goes on the less I know what that meant. I've been thinking . . . ' She interrupts him. 'You think too much, Paulo,' she says. It's strange hearing this. 'I think I'm just as competitive as the guys I used to attack back in the days when I was a militant. Sometimes it's like I only started being a militant because I wanted to be different,

I needed to be on show, I needed attention. I'm empty, Rener, hollow.' She laughs. 'Hollow men,' and she pays him a compliment, 'I don't think you're one of them, Paulo.' He gets up to fill his glass. 'I'm rich, did you know that?' This time he will get a few ice cubes. 'I don't want to talk about that. You will always be welcome here so long as we don't talk about that,' she warns him. He comes back into the living room, turns on the ceiling light, he can see better: her face is all smashed up. What little physical attraction had remained (when, last time, he had to make an effort to deal with her issues with sex) was no longer there. There's no doubt they are friends, in so far as each has a lot of tolerance for the other. There is a strange and uncommon trust between them. They talked about what happened on Friday. Rener smokes her joint, while she tells him the details. He fills her glass with more wine, asks all he needs to know to find out where the house is. She lets down her guard, tells him what she really felt about the violence she suffered. He doesn't put his arms around her. First she says the name of the street and then the house number. The conversation continues, she says that he could have been her great ally. It is different to how he imagined it, they end up fucking, and Rener offers no resistance when he puts his cock in her vagina.

Then he makes her some tea to have with the aspirins and runs his fingers through her hair until she sleeps. Now it's two in the morning and he isn't sleepy. The chronic discomfort that begins, and focuses, in his back, above his lumbar region, gradually spreads. He gets out of bed and leaves the room carrying his clothes with him, very careful not to wake her. He pulls the bedroom door to, trying to do it fast enough for the hinges not to creak. He puts on his trousers, his shirt, his socks. He does the washing up that had been left in the kitchen sink. He puts on his trainers, his jacket, sits on the sofa, waits. He can't remember what he did at the beginning of the week, the only thing he can remember without any difficulty is walking for hours through the city's suburbs, boarding buses at random and getting off in the most unlikely places, trying to get to know it, to learn it by heart. He doesn't always manage to learn it. Identical streets, identical houses, only the full mailboxes to tell them apart, the curtainless windows showing the empty rooms, curtains that are never opened, lights that are left on day and night, lights that are never turned on, lawns and flowers, bushes in gardens and unpruned trees. Hours he spends lying down listening to the same track on a CD. The time that never stops. The growing inattention, the growing impulse towards explosion and robbery. He cries and he can barely breathe for the guilt. Rener is patient enough to let him pretend. The words he has said to Rener, the conversations, were what remained of his dream. The future of Brazil never troubled him as much as it did this afternoon. He feels old (and Passo Fundo is

no longer nearby to feel old with him). He wants the life
that the Indian girl on the side of the road re-awoke. He
couldn't quite stomach it, and he still can't.

Half past five in the morning. The dawn cold sharpens.
Paulo gets up from the sofa, opens the apartment door,
leaves. He walks to the Elephant and Castle Shopping
Centre, waits for the bus that will take him to Camberwell. Before six he arrives at the house of the two people
who usually help him with the occupations; he knocks
on the door till they wake up. He offers each of them two
hundred pounds, saying he needs back-up on a collection
visit that he needs to pay before ten o'clock. They accept
his proposition, Paulo says he will be back at eight, they
go back to sleep. Paulo stops in at a 7-Eleven, picks up a
Twix and a Mars drink. He takes the bus out to the squat
in Chelsea that he broke into two months ago to be his
permanent residence, his private place, his perfect place;
quality carpet, central heating, excellent paintwork on the
walls, the type of luxury few people have. *Life doesn't get
any better* is what goes through his head, it's in the nature
of this strategy to feel as though he's playing the game,
to be crazier than his *opponents*. (Deep down he's just the
same and he doesn't notice.) He goes into his flat. He puts
the Public Enemy cassette into the tape deck, presses
play. He turns the volume up to four (never annoy your
neighbours). He changes. He gets his workmen's boots
with the steel toe-caps, the knuckleduster he received

as a recent part-payment, a cap and his shades. He puts *guaraná* powder in what's left of his chocolate drink. He covers it, shakes it, drinks. He consults the cheap watch that he bought in Brixton, similar to the one he gave Maína. He puts the watch in his pocket. He gets two oversized plastic laundry bags. He goes out. He walks along the Thames as far as the Tate Gallery, takes the bus back to Camberwell. He arrives half an hour before the agreed time. He buys a Twix in the little shop opposite the bus stop. He looks at the newspaper headlines as he eats it. Nothing about Brazil. He goes back out onto the pavement, walks to the nearest public payphone. He calls his parents' house. The telephone rings until the answering machine kicks in. 'Hi . . . It's Paulo. You ok? I was calling to find out about the elections . . . And to say my *holiday* here is going great . . . ' He doesn't say anything for a few seconds. 'Just to say I'm fine, I don't need anything . . . ' and remains silent until the recording comes to an end and, a moment later, the line goes dead.

The three young men enter the patio, the back door is open. Paulo puts on the knuckleduster, the other two are carrying iron bars, a fifty-centimetre bar each. Paulo goes in first, the only person he meets is an Indian man who introduces himself as the electrician. Paulo asks where the owners of the house are. Understanding the nature of the situation when the other two come in holding their iron bars, the Indian man says that the guy who owns

the house and who hired him will be back soon with the
bit of wiring that needs to be changed. Paulo says that's
fine and asks him to take a seat on a bench. He gathers
up Rener's tools and the clothes belonging to the couple,
trampled on and heaped up in a corner of the living room.
He doesn't find the Walkman. He puts everything into the
bags he has brought with him, hands them to the two
guys who have come with him. He doesn't know what
he'll do with the electrician, this guy who, Paulo now sees,
has an annoying face. Now isn't the time to hesitate, he
has got this far. He asks how much he's earning, the man
says he charges eighty a day. Paulo takes two fifties out
of his wallet and asks to see the other man's wallet. The
electrician hands it over without hesitating, Paulo opens
it, removes his travel pass ID. He checks the photo to be
sure that it really is the same man, puts it in his pocket,
tells him to get another one made at Arsenal Tube station,
puts the notes in the part of the wallet where the travel
pass was, says that's for his day plus twenty for the disrup-
tion. He holds out his hand in greeting, the Indian man
shakes it, and Paulo says he can go. One of his companions
asks Paulo if he knows what he's doing, it's stupid to let
the man go like that, he'll call the police. Paulo just says
that they can go, too. The electrician excuses himself and
gathers up his things, he leaves. Paulo explains that he is
going to stay, he has a Walkman to claim from the owner
of the house, and then he will stop by their place to pick

up the big bags. He asks them to leave one of the iron bars. One of them says staying there is madness. Paulo's ego swells when he hears him say this. The two of them leave. Alone in the house. (What a grotesque stage he has set up.) He puts on his hood and his glasses. He positions himself by the door, he tests the weight of the iron bar, its inertia, its movement. He doesn't stop to think, doesn't look for any logic. He hears the noise of the gate and the steps coming down by the side of the house. The shadow, oblivious, moving at the windows, close by, exciting. The sound of the door, the sound of the handle, they're one and the same, the door opening, the movement already seeking a response. His own movement, the movement of attack, the knot that seems to grip all the knots that hold those two strangers together. The second blow to the back, the same height as the first, he doesn't think about the cowardice of taking the other man by surprise; the cry, and the single kick that knocks his opponent down to the floor, a kick from the leg with the good knee, a kick to the head, stamping on the right side of his face and a blow straight to the hip. The doubt. The spit. Conquest and then withdrawal. The air that is never fresh for someone who can't sleep. On the pavement he dares not look back. The bar is hidden inside his jacket, the knuckleduster unused in his pocket; he starts to think again. What make of Walkman was it? He takes off the hood and glasses. He walks on for a few metres. Birthdays.

He waves at the passing taxi, the driver stops, asks where he's headed. Chelsea (where everything seems always to be in order). The driver says he can get in. Paulo gets in and settles himself on the seat, his stomach has already stopped hurting, and when he looks out he spots the cocker spaniel and then the lady.

mosaic

She chooses the name, and two days later he is born.

It's much more difficult than Maína had imagined, she will need clinical monitoring, other consultations like this one, this fifth consultation since Donato was born. She can barely control her impatience. Her difficulty communicating with the doctor, the same woman with whom Maína had been so cooperative at first, the doctor who, after asking Maína to turn off the radio cassette player, writes PUERPERAL CONDITION in large block letters on a little consultation slip and leaves it on the table for her. And this, like all the gestures that came before it, takes no account of the dread that Maína felt for the first few hours of the child's life: the revulsion she felt as she held him in her arms. There has to be some other reason besides the expulsion of the placenta and the reaction this provokes in the nervous system, in the pituitary-hypothalamus axis, because of the sudden drop in hormone levels. This, too, was noted down, but not on the same bit of paper, not in today's consultation. Nothing can explain Maína's desire to harm the baby. Every single day: probationary days. Months waiting for the recontraction of the uterus. In search of moderation. Paying no attention to the doctor, she presses her son to her chest and tells him in Guarani that it's time to find a way out. She says goodbye, knowing how hard the doctor is struggling to get over her ineptitude for attending to indigenous girls. If she could, she would never see her again. In the car park the driver *grants her permission* when Maína says she's going to the ice cream place. 'Fifteen minutes' (in this space before meeting up with the FUNAI official in order to register the birth). She crosses the street, walks up to the entrance of the shop, climbs the steps. She goes straight over to the counter, shows the money she has brought (she is not a beggar), points to the tub of vanilla ice cream: one scoop, in a cone. She sits at the table by the little wall that separates the table area from the pavement; she has chosen the spot that any other customer would have chosen. She rearranges the baby in her lap. She smears his lips with the icy-cold mass. At this moment three schoolgirls make a noisy entrance. One of them stops, makes a face and approaches. Maína behaves *as if to her equals* and, as soon as they have introduced themselves, asks if the girl would like to hold Donato. The schoolgirl thanks her, says she isn't really that good with children. Maína laughs and says, lying, that nothing could be easier than holding a child.

three

The fifth of March, nineteen ninety-two, the sky is the best shade of blue, the Minuane wind that usually sweeps across the Southwest at this time of year still hasn't made its aggressive appearance, the leaves are holding onto a green that as yet shows no signs of tiring. The number of cars starts to dwindle until there are just a few on the road (and only heading towards Porto Alegre). Now there isn't a single car passing the encampment, and the BR-116 is a landscape taken from a magazine, and for the first time since Donato was born Maína is able to hear the tranquillity without the interruption of engines and wheels putting tonnes and tonnes of pressure on the tarmac. She puts some trainers on her son (he needs to get used to them). They head towards the middle of the road to look out at the horizon. They play. If any vehicle were to approach they would hear the sound from kilometres away. The little boy moves away from her hand and from one moment to the next, without any help, and as he has never done before, he runs off towards the south, runs until he feels he's too far from his mother. They will stay there several minutes. Perhaps no one will tell them that a lorry carrying dangerous chemicals has overturned at the exit to one of the bridges further up and the highway police have had to stop the traffic in both directions. And she softens as she watches him: he cannot help but contrast with that damn horizon.

honour words

From the outset, it didn't take him long to learn that when you're dealing with squats you mustn't draw attention to yourself – exactly the opposite of what Rener did. Interviews, photos here and there, the old Robin Hood weakness. It wasn't hard to find her, it wasn't hard to work out who she was; even in a city where nobody is interested in finding out who you are. Another valuable squatter rule that Paulo learned was to choose buildings that don't create problems: a two-room council flat was his favourite kind of lead. Rener, however, wanted confrontation. She really wanted it till she found it. The Lebanese men had no trouble tracking her down, *inviting* her to take a walk and putting her in a private cell (and this time it was no longer just the brothers who had kicked her out of the occupied house but an older cousin, well-connected in the circles that the London police call the city's Really Fucked Bits). They didn't go so far as to torture her, they kept her in a perfectly soundproofed room just to be safe, until they got to Paulo under forty-eight hours later. There was no beating, they did little more than push him around and handcuff him. He had to hand over his passport, his papers, all his documents from Brazil. They set terms for bail, that was what they said. Bail, reasonable and feasible, so as not to have to end his life and the life of his black friend, who came this close to being raped, she could have been, and still could be, since she was an angel fallen from heaven, that was what they said. Paulo only got to talk to her for twenty minutes before they were separated, he paid what they asked for, he used up all his savings and was left still owing them a thousand five hundred pounds. There would be no problem setting up an instalment plan, that was what they said, give him the chance to pay it off in instalments, with two per cent interest accruing per month until he had met the total cost of the life insurance, that was another phrase they used. The lives of a Brazilian guy and a French girl who looks like a model are worth a lot more than that, that's what they said. At Paulo's insistence, Rener returned to Paris; she never knew about the agreement he had made with the Lebanese men. He lied that he'd had to give them two thousand pounds, that was all, and that they would kill them if they didn't leave London, which they had never said. They took his luxury squat in Chelsea and forbade him ever to occupy another property again. Paying rent to live somewhere would be good for him, it would give him a new sense of the market, that was that they said. This meant that Paulo had to get a job, that was when he started working at Whispers, a yuppie bar in Covent Garden, where the basic cocktail list included no fewer than a hundred and twenty alcoholic drinks, he came top in the selection process to fill two vacancies to work on the first-floor bar, he rented a room in some guy's house in Kilburn. The guy works as a first mate with two other friends, taking sailing boats to and from the Greek islands, boats belonging to people who like to sail to a certain place and then don't have the patience or the time to sail back. The house is always empty, it's modern, and it has a private patio that is completely grassed over. The money he takes home from Whispers is great and his customers include the most beautiful girls in Covent Garden, much better than the ones at Sol. Paradise for any Brazilian, or rather for anyone at all in his early twenties who wants to work in London, were it not for the constant pressure from the Lebanese men who would show up at the bar once a week asking for free drinks and constantly announcing new additions to the total amount owed. In the movies, in books, in comics, the hero always finds some way of getting the most brilliant revenge and escaping, leaving behind him the crushing defeat of his enemies, and yet, however many nights he spends wide awake thinking, he has never been able to come up with a way out. Getting hold of a new passport at the Brazilian consulate, asking his parents for money, or one of his acquaintances, and taking off completely on the quiet; that wasn't for him. He is more paranoid than ever, he has hated himself.

It is the second time Paulo is trying to change gears in the Ford Fiesta they have just hired; he bangs the door with his fist and realises that same second that he needs to use his left hand and to stay on the left-hand side, particularly on the minor roads like this one that he has taken to reach the house of his Portuguese workmate, the guy who is going to join him and the two Moroccans who also work at the bar, one as a busboy and the other as a bartender (in whose name the car was rented, since Paulo has no passport or papers); none of them wanted to drive the car in that busy traffic because, despite having licenses, they haven't had much practice. The drizzle will complicate matters a bit, but it's part of the fun of getting out of the city and curing a hangover on the road to New-quay, a surfer beach in the south-west of England. Driving is just another reason to stop thinking about everything that has happened in the last few months. The Portuguese guy gets into the car, says he's going to surf every wave and fuck all the girls they find and that as soon as they're out of London he will take over the driving and show them how you drive on a European motorway, something he's sure doesn't exist in Brazil. Paulo isn't good at handling the Portuguese guy's agitation, he'd imagined that his colleague would be calmer outside work but apparently not, just the opposite. He says he needn't wait till they have left the city if he really wants to drive, he can take the wheel right now. He gets out of the car and from outside gestures for him to do the same. They swap seats. Paulo feels the weight of his hangover. Up till this moment he has managed not to think about what the Lebanese men had said to him the night before. After pouring them two glasses of Moosehead beer and telling them that with this month's interest and everything else he now owed them the final two hundred and sixty pounds, after which he will have settled his debt, that he would be giving them the money in forty minutes when he went on his break, he heard the older one saying they had decided to charge him a two thousand pound fine for Rener having left London without their permission. Paulo said nothing, went back to serving the group of yuppies who were waiting for him at the other end of the bar. On his break he went down to the staff room, opened his locker, took out the money and outside he handed the two hundred and sixty pounds to the Lebanese men, asking when they were going to give him back his passport and the rest of his documents. He knew the answer already, but he wanted to hear it all the same: only when he paid up the fine. He looked up, trying to see the London sky which in the centre of town always hides the stars, he turned his back on them and – even though there were still fifteen minutes left to the end of his break – returned to work, took a bottle of bourbon without checking whether the manager was watching him or not, poured himself a glass with some ice and Coke, the official drink of any self-respecting bartender, and started to drink. The Portuguese guy won't shut up shouting Alright like a madman, imitating a Texan accent, overtaking cars on the motorway, gesturing at their passengers, especially when they are women. The soundtrack is The Cult played at maximum volume. Paulo is really annoyed now, he turns off the music and, speaking in Portuguese, mostly so that the Moroccans don't get involved, he tells the Portuguese guy that he's the biggest idiot on the face of the earth and to pull the car over immediately. He thought he would get the chance to rest on this trip to the coast, but running away from your problems, even those that have just appeared at the last minute, is an inexcusable fault. The Portuguese guy pulls towards the hard shoulder and stops the car. Paulo gets out, saying he is going to take over the driving, the other guy doesn't argue with him. Paulo apologises to the Moroccans and says that from here on in only he will drive. They get back on the road. Paulo drives at more than a hundred and forty (the car has a good engine, the road is excellent; Jaguars, Mercedes-Benzes, Porsches pass them at more than a hundred and sixty), one thought is supplanted by the next, he tries to predict what he will do when they get to Newquay, what it'll be like in the B&B, since they haven't made reservations, what it will be like dealing with the Portuguese guy who has gone into a sulk and hasn't spoken another word, how he's going to be able to wrench his passport from the Lebanese men, what he will do if the car is stopped for some reason and they ask for his license, what he'll do to go back to having a life in Brazil, when he will go back to Brazil, when he will see Rener again, what it'll be like when he tries to find Maína, when he will go back to being proud of his country, when he'll have more news of what's happening in Brazil, how he's going to manage to get to sleep like a normal person, when he will stop giving himself a hard time, when he will reach the top of the world, and he hears the phrases *I won't make it* and *It doesn't matter what I do, God doesn't exist.* He sees the caramel and white cocker spaniel at the side of the road (he isn't sure if he really does see it, he isn't sure of anything), and panic sets in. Scared to breathe, scared of not being able to breathe any more, scared to talk, of not being able to talk, not being able to swallow, scared to think, of not being able to stop thinking. He pulls over, opens the car door, gets out, his steps shaky, holding his head as though it might come unstuck from his neck, walks off the road and kneels down looking at the ground, the ground which at this moment looks like nothing, his eyelids almost shut. The others get out of the car, ask what's going on. He says quietly that he is going to die, he says it in Portuguese, he says it in English. He can't stop thinking. He says he's about to have a heart attack. The world is never going to change. There is no meaning to life. And nothing can be more futureless (and hopeless), more awful and terrifying.

Luisa and her reason

Nineteen ninety-three (Luisa never returned to Rio de Janeiro).

The doctor they interviewed weeks earlier at the meeting with representatives of the National Association for Indigenist Action in Porto Alegre spoke emphatically about that Indian girl, aged seventeen or eighteen, called Maína, about how they really needed to meet her in order to understand properly what it is that modern life is doing to the current generation of Indians in Rio Grande do Sul, to people who have never before had to live with all this technology and so little space and such poor conditions. They no longer have the recipes for medicines and traditions for healing from decades past, they don't have places where they can find leaves, roots, herbs, there is no jungle and there is no countryside, there is only this relationship of always failed rapprochements, and the distrust they feel about accepting the medicines offered to them by non-Indians. 'You people have a translator, don't you?' the doctor asks. 'You should start in the villages, but do also speak to the ones who live on the roadside, do speak to the younger women, they have a lot more to say, specially the one I mentioned. Don't forget, write it down.' And Luisa wrote it down. Luisa has been telling Henrique that they need to hire an Indian secretary. Henrique, who is actually Henrique Magalhães Becker, eleven years older than her and a trained geographer with two master's degrees, in Human Geography and Statistics, and two doctorates, in Management and Geography, her professor in one of the extra modules she made herself attend during the master's since she wasn't getting as involved in the Porto Alegre social scene as she had planned and as a result had plenty of time left to devote to her studies; Henrique, the man of multiple allegiances, confident and practical, who, in that first semester of nineteen ninety-one (and already three seminars into the module by the time she came to give her presentation) became the love of her life. And she, Luisa Vasconcelos Lange, did not rest until she had managed to take him to bed, until she had made him fall in love with her and hold her hand in front of the other master's students and professors on the postgraduate course and invite her, as soon as she had defended her dissertation with honours, to live with him in his house, which, as the only grandchild, Henrique had inherited from his maternal grandfather, a narrow building on a long strip of land with a great patio, a barbecue, two plum trees and a vegetable garden round the back; number eight hundred and thirty-nine Cristovão Colombo, near the corner with Ramiro Barcelos. The problem isn't with the Indians they are going to interview. The translator is excellent, a white boy currently doing a master's in Language and Literature at the Santa Catarina Federal University, but, hardworking as he might be, he won't be able to help them map out the Indians' profile in the minute detail – using audiovisual media to make a documentary record – that they have been hired by the Getúlio Vargas Foundation to provide, mapping the broadest picture they can of the status of the Kaingang and Guarani Indians in Rio Grande do Sul, an undertaking that will require three months of intensive fieldwork and a further two tackling data, recent bibliographies, press cuttings, surveys in partnership with public institutions, and the preparation of documents and reports. Luisa still has not understood why Henrique agreed to take this project on, the money is not much compared to what he is used to earning, she imagines he took the opportunity to give himself a break from the work he has been doing for big corporations; he won't earn what he hoped to, but he will be able to travel around the state, understand the lives of a people about whom nobody ever talks (he once said to Luisa that despite his Germanic biotype he has Indian blood; his great-grandfather, a Chilean Indian, was abandoned at the entrance to a farm in the south of Chile, brought up by a family of Spaniards as though he were their biological son, and ended up on the border of Uruguay and Rio Grande do Sul, where he married an Italian widow who owned an inn and with whom he had four children, among them a daughter with very light skin, Henrique's grandmother, who came to study in Porto Alegre, married a businessman from the Lageado neighbourhood and had just one child: his father); this was the closest he came to what could be called a break from the consultant's routine he has devised for himself.

Henrique sent the other team, which Luisa christened the B-team, to the western part of the state, a total of five people in a diesel camper van just like this one in which they're travelling as a foursome right now. Luisa insisted on operating the camera herself so that there would be free seats in the van: one of the interns would handle the sound and the Indian they would find and invite to join them would help the second intern with the data collection. After a while, they would meet up with the B-team in Iraí, almost on the Santa Catarina border. That's what was agreed.

The camper van leaves Morro Santana (one of the hills that make up the so-called Porto Alegre Crest, the chain of hills comprising Morro Santana, Morro da Companhia, Morro da Polícia, Morro Pelado, Morro da Pedra Redonda, Morro Teresópolis and Morro do Osso), where the Kaingang gather *guiambê* vines for their handicraft work, a region that has been threatened by growing property speculation. They take Avenida Protásio Alves until they are beyond

Porto Alegre and then drive on to the roadside encampment where the Indian girl lives about whom the doctor talked so much. There are Indians who have become civilised, accepting the rules and organisational structures of the non-Indians, but there are also those who claim to be wild, the ones who, living near the cities or even within them, consider themselves at war with the invaders. Luisa understands that there is no other way to face the facts, that there is no point marking out territories or getting help from well-meaning NGOs and government officials; the disputes over land never end. She was disgusted when she heard about the case of the chief who tried to lease out indigenous lands for his own private gain. She is besotted by this subject; Henrique has already told her that the audiovisual survey might not yield all that much if she isn't able to separate her particular enthusiasms from the work they've set out to do, it's vital to remain alert to everything and not to become attached to one particular problem or other. All the same, he has agreed to amend one day of their itinerary, since it's easy enough to get to the encampment where this Indian girl lives.

With her hair cropped short (Luisa had never seen this on an Indian woman before), she does not seem too friendly when, after they have looked at the baskets and fans of local bamboo hanging from the improvised beams, dry sticks stuck at an angle into the earth and tied with vines close to the hard shoulder, they ask her whether

her name is Maína. There is no one else to be seen in the encampment. Maína asks them what they want. Henrique introduces himself and explains the survey work they are doing, Luisa then takes over and asks whether they might film an interview with her, she explains that they heard about her from the doctor who looked after her during her pregnancy. Maína, her expression still serious, tells them to leave the camper van just where it is and come inside. As though they had been waiting for just the right moment, three children emerge from the tent, come to meet the visitors. The oldest, quite a lively girl, appears with a smile and asks whether they have brought them any gifts. Luisa tries to stroke her head, but she dodges her and runs off towards the van, the younger girl follows her, and the boy, who doesn't look like he can be more than three years old, stays behind. Maína takes the boy in her arms and, still looking quite unfriendly, asks whether they would like a lemongrass tea. Luisa accepts and notices that round the back there are foundations supporting a wooden floor that looks as though it used to be part of a house, and now resembles a giant table. 'What used to be there?' she asks. Maína replies that it's a stage for performing Russian ballet. Luisa doesn't know how to handle that response, she walks ahead without saying any more and climbs onto the structure, gesturing to Henrique to come join her. The two girls are entertaining themselves with the interns, escorting them as they unload the tripods, the cases with the two Sony Betamax cameras, the microphones and audio recorder. Maína says to make themselves comfortable, she goes into the tent. Henrique climbs the steps and stands beside Luisa looking out towards the west. 'What do you reckon this was? What do you think of her?' Luisa asks. 'Take it easy, Luisa.' Henrique taps the floor with his foot, testing to see how firm it is. 'Shall we record up here?' Luisa suggests. 'I don't know, it does seem a bit unusual here,' he replies. Luisa comes down, walks over to the tent, asks permission to enter, and goes in. Inside she finds Maína's mother, who greets her saying that the tea will be ready in a few minutes, and an unclothed Maína arranging strings of beads and seeds around her neck and her waist. Luisa tells her there's no need to do herself up, that it's only going to be a quick chat about what she thinks about her situation, about being there on the roadside, and about what she thinks of the situation for Indians who live like them. 'I'm an Indian girl, miss, Indians go naked . . . I don't have any problem being filmed like this,' she says, looking straight at Luisa. 'If you could make one request that I would be able to grant you,' Luisa says, 'what would you ask for?' 'Financial support, a study scholarship with a place in a student house where I'd live as a student studying in a state university.' Luisa is impressed at the Indian girl's fluency. 'Very good. It's a nice choice, it's a dream worth having,' she says in a sisterly tone. 'I don't know how to deal with dreams, miss . . . Indian dreams are different from you people's . . . It's not right to play at dreaming, like it's not right to play with promises. A few days from now I'm going to be eighteen and, however much I read and however hard I try, I still haven't been able to understand the world you live in, I still haven't found the door to get in . . . A scholarship to study would solve my problems and those of my family . . . I'm not going into the city to work as a maid, I'm not going to be a whore . . . I'd rather stay here selling my craft things, taking care of my son, of my mother, of my sisters, waiting for handouts from the government and people like you, coming here to play nice with us . . . ' Luisa raises her hand in a gesture to stop. 'Put on your clothes, there isn't going to be an interview.' Maína's mother, who has had her back to the two women, turns towards them. 'I'll make you a proposition. Why don't you join us for a month? We need another assistant. I think it would be quite an opportunity. We'll give you food and lodging and we'll even pay twice the minimum wage. We've got to go to a place called Fazenda da Borboleta up near the source of the Jacuí, we need to get some notes that only the researchers up there have got, that'll take us a day, and on the way back we can come by here again to find out what you think and what you've decided,' says Luisa. 'I don't need to think. I accept,' is Maína's reply. At that moment her mother asks Luisa to go outside. Seeing what this means, Luisa (barely thinking about it, and as has increasingly been her way of doing things lately) jumps in. 'We can find someone to stay here with you and the children while Maína is with us.' Maína's mother thanks her with a shake of the head and, looking sidelong at the visitor, once again asks Luisa to go outside. Now Luisa does. Maína's mother walks over, tells her to listen in silence to what she has to say. There is no room for any more adventures and if Maína wants an adventure with these people who have appeared out of nowhere she can go, but she's taking her son with her. To each her own burden (she used an expression very like this). She would manage with her two sisters, she will always be able to rely on help from the people who live in the neighbouring encampments. Maína has never been apart from Donato, the way her mother has understood things this is going to happen for the first time; although it was not clear from the answer she gave the visitor a few minutes earlier, parting from Donato is not what Maína has in mind. She takes off her necklaces and the strings around her waist and gets dressed. Anyone who says that a person controls the things her head devises is lying; it is possible to choose what you want, but not the time nor the way in which things around you will happen. Maína has learned to be patient, but she has become bitter, too, for her this is that thing they call growing up. She thinks, and she worries: she doesn't know what they will say when she asks for her son to go with her. She will assure them that he's well behaved and placid (she must remember to use that word) and that he never cries or gets in the way, which is true. It's the chance she's been waiting for. If there are benefits, she will not be the one to get them. Children behave in a peculiar way. Children don't remember too much. Maína does not yet know what her son needs. Maína needs to give him the chance to choose, even if this takes a while. Donato will come with her, he's a good child (she must remember to say that he is placid). They must accept, they have to accept.

Luisa knows that Henrique doesn't like that she decided about the Indian girl and the child on her own, which is why since yesterday he hasn't addressed a word to her beyond the essential. It isn't just a tantrum, that's not what he's like, she knows that; he's like this because he feels his authority was undermined in front of the rest of the team. The equipment had already been all set up when she appeared saying that there wouldn't be any interviews. Perhaps he'd been wrong when he said it would be a project for them to undertake together, a test of how much 'professional affinity' there is between them. She wants to be with him, basically, that's the only thing she is sure of. She runs her hand through his hair while he is driving. It is the truce that he must agree to. She puts her hand on his knee, strokes it, she kisses his cheek. They are leaving the Botucaraí mountains, they will go through the Centro de Soledade, because Henrique needs to copy on a photocopier all the documents and maps he got hold of from a Kaingang leader, they're from the end of the nineteenth century, things that were obtained in some fight or were left over from some usurpation (not forgetting that there were Indians who settled there in the eighteenth century, fleeing the attacks on the Jesuit Missions). They entered the city. Without warning, Henrique stops outside a chemist, asks Maína to come in with him. He buys jars of baby food and disposable nappies for the child. They return to the camper van, they drive on as far as a stationer's offering 'Copying Service'. Luisa gets ready to make the copies, she asks Maína to come in with her and learn something that she might have to do herself one of these days, takes the child from her lap, hands him to Henrique, who holds him with the vulnerability of someone who is infertile. Luisa will not have his children, the children they always talked about until they discovered that there was nothing to be done about his condition. Luisa looks at him before going into the stationer's and is glad to see that the man she so loves might have in his arms an even better reason for spending the next few days driving around for kilometres and kilometres on the highways of Rio Grande do Sul.

all the colours of what is
the least important

End of the third week. São Francisco de Paulo is one of the chilliest places in the state, particularly at night. Maína had quickly become friends with the interns. They went out to eat at the snack bar that the locals have told them is the most popular in town, to try the burger dubbed by the owner the 'Aro Fenemê' (after the brand of lorry wheels), a pressed sandwich (as is the custom in the region) with three kinds of sausage and five kinds of cheese served without lettuce or onion, just with one large slice of southern tomato and a lot of mayonnaise. Luisa and Henrique have stayed at the hotel with Donato. Henrique is completely attached to the boy. Luisa gets up from the bed, takes a sparkling water from the minibar. Donato is playing on the single bed that is beside the double. Henrique is watching the news. The national news is showing footage of bundles and more bundles of *cruzeiro* banknotes being packed up on conveyor belts on their way to the incinerator in the

Central Bank, while an analyst is remarking that Brazil is the country with the third highest inflation in the world, after Zaire and Russia. Luisa asks him to turn the television off, she can't bear it any more with this headache she's got. In the last few days nothing has been able to lessen her migraine. Henrique says she needs to find a specialist and stop self-medicating. She changes the subject, saying how surprised she is at the Indian girl's liveliness and that she's thinking of a way to help her, perhaps taking her to Rio for the first term of her doctoral studies next year. Luisa knows Henrique is planning to stay in São Paulo for a bit, but vehemently rejects the idea of living in the Paulista capital herself. This has been the cause of the slight friction between the two of them. Henrique barely hears her, just lowers the volume of the set slightly so he can still catch a young, smiling economist announcing that a leading firm in the calculator sector has over the last year been investing in the production of fourteen-digit calculators where the normal would be ten, that they have been doing this purely as a response to Brazil's current reality. Luisa sits on the bed where Donato is playing, she says that tomorrow she will do a filming session with Maína alone and, gently squeezing the boy's toes, she tells Henrique, without making him take his eyes off the television for a single second, that the Indian girl had suggested being filmed naked when they first met.

*

Nine in the morning. Maína is reluctant to be filmed, says that things have changed too much these past weeks, she is no longer keen on the idea of exposing herself. Luisa suggests recording just a few minutes with Donato on her lap. Maína says that if it's going to be with her son then she absolutely definitely won't. Luisa says she doesn't understand her and, laughing, turns off the camera. At noon as Maína is tidying papers and folders, Luisa films her from a distance. When she realises what is going on, Maína folds her arms, yells in Guarani, but seeing that Luisa is not going to give up, says in Portuguese (her Portuguese that is getting better and better) that it's ok; she sets aside what she is doing and gets up and moves, half-inclined to run, to imagine something from the cinema (or what she remembers from the cinema), or possibly even to dance.

nobody reads the unexpected
(second part)

The morning shower is the most dangerous moment in his day, the water beating down on his head, the relaxation in those bright surrounds of the cubicle, the waterproof white paint, the acrylic of the sliding door, positive thoughts gathering, what the doctors call a flight of ideas. Paulo is not on any medication, nor will he take any. Psychiatric treatment requires a link to the city's health system and to the city itself that he has never wanted to establish, there is no one to take responsibility for him, a more pessimistic diagnosis might see him caught in a trap from which he might never escape. The cocker spaniel follows him around the rooms in the house. Sometimes the lady shows up and makes a comment on what he might do in order to better fulfil his role as head employee in that cheap seven-room hotel on Fitzroy Street, a two-star establishment less than a hundred and fifty metres from Euston Road and three hundred from Tottenham Court Road. He only leaves the hotel to deposit his salary in the bank, to buy toiletries; if it were up to him he would absolutely never set foot on the pavement. His job is to receive the guests who have been sent by the booking service that goes directly through the owner, an Italian who turns up there once a week; to set the tables for breakfast, served between seven-thirty and ten; and to supervise the cleaning service. Three floors and a basement, where the office and the pantry are to be found. He still cannot look directly at the sky, he can't imagine getting into a car, going into Warren Street station, the feelings of vertigo are unbearable. In the hotel, he spends most of his time in his bedroom listening to the cassettes that the other employee, a Welsh guy, copies from the CDs he buys and passes on to him, he translates the lyrics to the songs, he gradually becomes able to read some comic books (English comics are very violent) that his colleague lends him. Sometimes Fabio, who is now manager at Café Pelican, shows up for a visit, and the effort that Paulo makes to demonstrate that he is leading a normal life is enormous. He has told no one what is going on. Sometimes his discomfort is visible, especially when Fabio, trying to cheer him up, tells him his jokes and stories of his escapades with women, where laughter is the compulsory response. The debt to the Lebanese men has been settled, Paulo never cried in front of them, never showed weakness. (Paulo does not take any medication.) One novelty is this compulsion he has to write whatever comes into his head. He thought it could be the disturbance known as hypergraphia, but he has asked the medical student who has taken up residence for a fortnight in room eleven about it, and it's unlikely, people with that particular kind of mania can't stop writing, he can. Writing is merely comforting. It's not like drafting pamphlets inspired by the increase in monthly wages, student demands, the end of censorship or in favour of some trade union demand. No. It is a way of putting the day into some kind of order, of having something to do when his jobs are all done, when he cannot imagine what to do without getting anxious. He lines up his duties as though they were a chain, a row of boxes on which he places his hand on each number in sequence, he thinks about what to do, carries that out, then thinks about the next task, carries that out, in this way assuring the tranquillity of his days and saving money to return, defeated, to Brazil.

atomic and subatomic

Henrique turns up at the encampment. He is alone. As soon as Donato sees him he runs over towards him. Maína finds it funny, this little three-year-old doll who is so receptive to the presence of a guy who just four months ago was a stranger. Henrique is downcast, he says he stopped by because he was missing the boy so much he couldn't bear it. He has brought some little books, the kind you give children under four, he brought a box of tabletop games for Maína's sisters. He asks if he can stay for lunch and hands her a bag with a roast chicken and polenta. Maína hugs him and says thank you. It is a while before she asks about Luisa, and he replies that they have decided to separate. Luisa has gone back to Rio, she will do her doctorate there, because from one moment to the next she had decided that she had been far away from her parents for too long and, yes, just because she is wilful and impulsive. Maína leaves him playing with Donato and prepares a pot of rice; her sisters entertain themselves with the Chinese chess, whose rules he tries to explain while Donato uses him as a human climbing frame. Maína's mother says she is going to prepare a sweetcorn porridge for Henrique to have for dessert and to take away in a jar for later, it will help to perk you up, she assures him. While the rice is cooking, Maína hands Henrique a package, says that there are two envelopes inside, one with his name on and the other with Luisa's, they're a couple of things she would like them to have as gifts. She only asks that his not be opened until after they have eaten the porridge and that hers is only delivered to her when the two of them have made their peace. Henrique takes the package, saying he isn't sure he will be talking to Luisa again all that soon. Maína says she's sure they will get back together before long, she says Luisa loves him too much, that she has never seen anyone love somebody so much. Henrique leaves the package next to the bench where he is sitting, goes back to playing with Donato. It's a lovely day, with a breeze that couldn't be more pleasant. Maína asks her mother to help her take the table from inside the tent to under the tree on the northern side of the encampment. She tells Henrique (who tries to get up when he sees the women carrying the table) not to move, today he's the guest of honour. They fix the legs of the table so that they aren't wonky and cover it with a flannel tablecloth with a Christmas pattern that her mother has kept for years, something they use only on special occasions. The lunch has taken on a festive atmosphere. Henrique has left the van radio on loud, the girls asked him to, they are as noisy as ever. Maína proposes a toast, saying she never learned so much in so little time from anyone and that she will miss them. They clink glasses. Her sisters don't really understand why they do it. Henrique jokes that Maína really did learn: she learned the dramatic touch that Luisa used to bring to even the simplest occasion. They laugh. Maína says she is going out to fetch some leaves and herbs and make some tea while they wait for her mother's porridge. Henrique says he has plenty of time. Maína takes the basket (which is a bit large for someone who is going to gather leaves and herbs but nobody notices). It's a lovely day. She goes into that small bit of forest that grows on the north side of the tent, walks maybe thirty metres, climbs the tree, reaches the branch she selected years earlier, ties four good, strong knots, waits for a series of lorries that always scream past to add to the loud sounds from Henrique's van. (She thinks of the time she talked to Luisa about God, and perhaps because of all that studying, Luisa said proudly that she would rather not believe in the possibility of there being a God. She asks Him for Paulo's disappearance, his total disappearance, for many years.) She puts the rope around her neck and jumps.

spring

Donato

A child aged five barefoot in the sand, standing in front of the sea for the first time and directly under the noonday sun of a baking summer day like this one, needs a good while to understand what his eyes, unable to see clearly at distance, can make out. Which is why as Henrique bodysurfs the waves of Siriú beach, Donato remains petrified at the vastness of the turquoise horizon which outweighs any other image or object that gets in front of it, subtracting any image or figure to enter its enormity, just as he subtracts Henrique, on this their first trip outside São Paulo. The nanny has come along, too, sitting next to him on the back seat of the five-door Ipanema, making up stories while Henrique drives cautiously alone up front. Donato does whatever he can to be adorable during their playtime, and again when they colour in pieces of paper with a felt-tip pen, constructing Brazilian Air Force jets out of them, which right now are crammed into the wicker bag beside the blue bucket and the green rake on the strange solidity of the sand. Playing along with her games was, he found, a way of not being in the way; it was how he cooperated with Henrique, being cooperative, accepting the possibility of freeing himself from the blurred memories – indiscriminately shot through with lapses – that will soon cease to exist, of finding happiness in their cohabitation and accepting it as the counterpoint to something that is the palpable part of solitude (of a solitude that has also been his), yes, a thousand times yes, cooperating, being cooperative, inventing a kind of succinct order in this, a recreation that will be useful in every future, near or far, feeding the desire that one day, in one such future, he would be able to ignore it, since, like any other child, what Donato really wants is sheer normality and the normality of fear that comes with the destruction – the unrealisable destruction – of the televisual images in his head (the insignificant thing in the midst of which he recognises a foolproof code to bring him happiness, every day), pocket-sized monsters that become bigger monsters, spheres with the entire future of humankind and the universe depending on them, blows, fleeting in indescribable clothes, stimuli oscillating between the initial yellow and the most tragic red, and, then, all of a sudden, someone, someone he can't make out, takes hold of him under his armpits and lifts him more than a metre in the air, and now he's no longer looking at the sea (there is only the impenetrability of the sky) and he feels a reverse electricity running through him absurdly slowly as though gravity were propagating itself within another person, planted, uprooted and replanted in another person, and it isn't a good match, it doesn't fit, with the vertiginously fast and strange situation that is really a weight filling his chest, a cartoon at that precise moment when the guy's plane has run out of fuel and is falling, under the potent emphasis of a Japanese soundscape; now, the culmination of the sky gives him the impression of being frozen in blue before his eyes, it's distressing, a lack of completeness carrying the shock that he was not able to conceive and that (with another, a worse electricity) happens again when, as part of the same action, his feet sweep up to the height of his head, and he tries to scream, but his voice does not come out (and if it did come out, it would surely be someone else's, the person he needs to be and whose speech is decisive, it's the command from the pocket-sized monsters turning into bigger monsters), it is trapped in his stomach and surrounded by ways of giving up, and there's no way to go any higher which is why now his body moves in a different way, and in the trajectory between all these moments, and still with difficulty, he, Donato, understands what it is to fall. 'But Nato, you weigh a ton . . . ' he hears a woman's voice and, before thinking that his feet are about to touch the ground, he realises that he's going up again, going up as though he were attached to springs, and he keeps moving, launching up in an acrobatic take off, like characters on tv, free, asking himself whether this is what life is like, whether these will be his powers and this his heroic initiation, twisting a hundred and eighty degrees before returning to the firm hands that catch him before he tumbles and keep him at the height of the woman's face, the kind of woman from the television, but whom he cannot identify, just as he could not identify her voice. 'Heavy and huge, my little Indian . . . ' The woman looks right at him. 'You don't recognise Luisa,' she says and finally brings him back to the ground. 'I've brought you a present,' and takes from the bag she has across her chest a carved wooden owl, some fifteen centimetres high. Donato says nothing, but he recognises the object that was once his toy. He holds out his little arms, almost jumps onto her, holding her tight with an aggression that is not his own (as though everything around him were diminishing in significance), and turns back towards the dunes and stays like that, immobile, intoxicated by the scent of wood, of vine-extract paint, of the earth and the fat that are still encrusted in it, and an anxiety comes to him that is mixed in with a televisual certainty of inhabiting the solid shape of the owl, flying within it just like the flying animations that he watches every morning on the tv in the living room of his father's house, he wants to fly, to wind his way along the fibres of carved white cedar. The woman runs one of her hands over his head, with the other she waves to Henrique, who has already seen her, and asks: 'Is Henrique giving you a lot of trouble, Juruna boy?' The child is still dazed, trying in his own way to remember what the voice of the owl was like, the feminine voice that was inside the owl (or surrounding it), but the owl is mute and every moment more diminished in familiarity. 'You don't remember Luisa any more, do you? . . . Shame. Fourteen months is an eternity, I know . . . But you haven't forgotten the owl. That's good . . . ' The woman looks back towards Henrique, he's walking out of the sea now. 'A new life . . . ' She touches the tip of Donato's nose and, without another word, walks over towards the edge of the water. Donato looks at the owl, then at the people who are nearby (there aren't many, most of them sitting under their parasols), his gaze stops on the nanny, she's about five metres away and wearing sunglasses, it's impossible to know which direction she's looking in, whether she has seen him or not. And he freezes, he can't manipulate the details or draw them out, he cannot even retain them. Somewhere not too far from that seaside, very probably in Garopaba, there are tv sets turned on (Donato doesn't know this) and on them a paediatrician is being interviewed on the midday news. Obligingly, she is explaining that a child's motor functions, whether through movement or through touch, are what he uses to reinforce his visual attention, allowing him to explore and provoke his surroundings. Donato does not manipulate his surroundings, he doesn't provoke his surroundings. Donato merely reflects upon being at the wonderful height of those dunes further off to his right, just like drawings, sandy giants, monsters offering up their breastplates, which might be where the bulk of the memories are to be found that he is not finding in the wooden owl. Henrique and the woman are keeping themselves occupied twenty-something metres from where Donato is standing. They are talking about him, even if he doesn't realise it, because he has his back to them (and also because he's no more than a child), articulating his thought as he has never before articulated it, spending the minutes as he has never spent them, before walking towards the vulnerability of that quite new landscape, before keeping his eyes fixed on the dunes, trying out a few steps, looking at the oblivious nanny, dropping the owl in the sand, and running, really running.

Months have passed since that time on the beach, the woman has a name, but the name is not spoken by him very often (it's a name that still does not fit in the apartment where he lives with Henrique and the new nanny, a name he still does not want). She, the woman, can't decide whether to come and live with them in São Paulo, she's asked for a bit of time to think about it, whether she is really going to leave Rio de Janeiro, the kind of life it is possible to have only there. Donato knows how to listen to her, he learns a lot from listening to her talk, she is quick and unpredictable, Henrique is not as unpredictable. Which is why it is Cássia, the personal assistant Henrique employed when they rented the Sumaré apartment, who takes him in today for his first day at pre-school. Sending him to a bilingual institution is perhaps the better and cheaper option, but by enrolling him in this one, where English is the main language and seventy per cent of the places are given to the children of foreigners living in Brazil, Henrique believes he is making sure the child will suffer less. Donato will learn English and improve his Portuguese at the same time, he will have to cope alongside other children who are also having to adapt. Henrique, his father, is not sure about this decision, but he wants the best opportunities for the son he has chosen. It wasn't easy getting the letter of enrolment, Donato will know that one day. If Henrique had not been advising a group of north American industries with an interest in the improvement of Brazil's patent law, a group whose spokesperson is the vice-president of the school's parent-teacher association, it is unlikely that the headmistress would have made an exception. Of course, there are requirements, a number of requirements that are far from simple. As the admissions coordinator emphasised, the school management's greatest fear is that Donato should end up holding back his fellow students' progress. So they agreed that he should receive intensive coaching outside classes to compensate for his linguistic deficiencies, and at the end of May he would undergo an assessment. The word *change* is one of the words Donato understands best. Hardly taking into account his young age (as an Olympic gymnastics trainer would, for example, with his kids, or the teacher of a prodigy just out of nappies in search of possible musical genius), Henrique told him that a full life demands big changes, he said that everything is ready, but that the change will require commitment from them both. Donato feels his love and really tries hard to follow him. And when the taxi stops outside the school, Cássia asks the driver to wait for her, she will pay afterwards, she knows they're late, she walks with Donato to the reception desk where there is a young woman who speaks to them in English, the welcome greeting makes Cássia uncomfortable (she is quite clever, able, but her English isn't that good) and makes her say merely, unsure whether her Portuguese is being understood, that Donato is a new pupil. The young woman immediately starts speaking Portuguese with quite a heavy, strange foreign accent, excusing herself saying that the children there, on the whole, have a good grasp of English and it was only force of habit that stopped her from welcoming them in Portuguese. Cássia cups Donato's cheeks with her two hands and wishes him good luck. Donato briefly smiles back at her. The girl from the school takes him by the shoulder and leads him towards the classroom. They walk along corridors. They stop outside the room where his lesson is taking place, his chaperone knocks on the door. It's not long before there is an opening, and he sees his future classmates sitting in groups around hexagonal tables. The teacher looks at him and smiles. The young woman from reception goes in with him, the teacher has already been briefed about the particularities of this new student and, at least this time, she addresses him in Portuguese. After announcing his name to the rest of the pupils, she shows him where he is going to sit. The table she is pointing to has three children at it (it is the only table in the room that isn't full), he doesn't look at their faces, the one who is next to him, a girl with black skin, touches his arm and says in a French accent that her name Rener, but her nickname is Brown Sugar, he looks at her with a smile and, in Guarani, says it is good to be there, the girl also smiles and says his hair is a lovely colour. The teacher walks round handing out blank paper and crayons, the one he gets is dark grey. It is his first assignment, and he completes it easily because all he has to do is do the same as the other three at the table. The minutes fly by. Half the morning had passed and it was break time and all the children went to an enclosed playground, where there were toys that needed to be played with in twos or threes, team against team. Most of them behaved as though this was all theirs, it was their property, as though they had practised the night before or were using some kind of telepathy, because they were so exact and integrated as they coordinated their activities on the seesaws, on the slide, on the monkey bars, on the rocking beam, on the swings, on the jungle gym, and on the wireframe rockets, the same pieces of equipment that appear in the background of the photo of the whole class taken at the end of that same morning after the teacher handed them small jigsaws to assemble and stick onto a piece of card as homework (in the photo, Rener is looking straight at him, she's beautiful, slender, completely unembarrassed; she insists that it was that day she gave him the nickname Curumim, from the Tupi-Guarani word meaning a boy, but that is not true). That morning was the closest it was possible to get to the phrase 'group bonding' in the whole of that year of nineteen ninety-five. It was only the following day, when the teacher handed out more complex activities to do, that he understood that it wouldn't work simply to watch what was happening and copy it. As the weeks passed, language quickly stopped being a rarely used tool. And on the day of the assessment, overloaded with unknown words, with gaps that had no tactile equivalents, Donato understood that he needed to be exactly as his father wanted.

The end of the year. Lada Niva is the make and model he most likes to say, followed by the Fiat Uno, the Saab

Scania, Toyota Bandeirantes and a long and varied list of other names almost all of which are compound nouns connected to the inexhaustible world of the automobile. Besides these, he likes words like fireman, pilot, lifeguard – this latter, as it happens, printed in yellow on the back of the red t-shirt he is currently wearing as he and Henrique are on their way to Guarulhos airport to meet the woman. They are on the Tietê riverfront road, one of the few places that make him less impressed by the things shown on television, it's almost his favourite place in São Paulo. Countless vehicles with endless differences that make him demand from Henrique the proper names and the proper updates to the models (about five minutes ago it was the Maserati, seen for the first time), all taken in as fast as the quick-fire answers given to the questions that he himself takes on the task of asking. This is the greatest proof that he has integrated perfectly into his new life. Comfortable being Version BOY: UPPER-MIDDLE CLASS, SÃO PAULO devoted body and soul to his collection of Matchbox and Hot Wheels miniatures. Today is the first day of his summer holidays. He feels proud because Henrique, as though speaking to an adult, told him at breakfast that all his expectations as regarded his school performance had been achieved and so, next year, he would be staying on in the same school. This is good, because that girl is there, Rener, who of all his classmates inspires him with the greatest confidence about what to say, how to speak.

Because he has merited it by his own efforts (this was the expression Henrique used), they would spend the rest of the morning at that bookshop, Paulista, for him to choose two books. Henrique was not explicit as to the language, but Donato knew what his father expected of him. He chose one in Portuguese, one in English. Donato understands the enormous dedication shown by Henrique, his father Henrique, to making the two of them a family. At school the older teachers talk quite a lot about family and about God (the word God troubles him less than the word family). In the drawings he does, it is only him and Henrique. Donato likes to draw someone holding his left hand. Starting from today he knows that he can draw the woman, she will be the one holding his left hand. Donato hopes he will be able to draw her a lot, to draw her forever, he hopes that she makes an effort (as much as the two of them) to get a *very good* or an *excellent*, just as he has managed to get in almost all his assignments at school. Donato understands the enormous dedication shown by Henrique. Donato understands Henrique and, most of the time, he tries to pre-empt his actions so as not to disappoint him. The first and only time he responded with aggression to a classmate, he was taken to the office of the headmistress, who told him, 'You are lucky to have been taken in by someone as good as senhor Henrique'; she told him that undisciplined attitudes like Donato's would only disappoint him. Disappointment is a word

Donato does not like, but it helps him to understand the
world all the same, even more than other words that
are better to say. Disappointment justifies words like
careful, a word he relates to Guarulhos (the name of the
airport, which comes from the Guyanese tribes, that is
what Henrique explained to him before they set off in
the car today after the bookshop). Guarulhos is a word
Donato likes, but he finds it a bit strange, a bit heavy in
his mouth, like another word he found strange the other
day, though not as heavy, the word *anaphylactic*, which
he tried to say but could not. Henrique then insisted that
he try again. He tried and couldn't do it, and Henrique
articulated the word with measured care. He tried again
and couldn't. This was not the first time he pressed him
to get it right, to correct himself and say a word that was
interrupted or not even begun. In situations like these
Donato feels like he is playing pick-up sticks on his own,
and in this game he is not allowed to be defeated, and yet
he will never be allowed to win. Over the summer, when
they are spending more time together (and because this
time the woman will be there as a spectator, a spectator
you can count on to be a spectator), Henrique will require
of him, and with some rigour, the correct pronunciation of words in Portuguese and in English and, later,
when March comes around, speaking with fluency and
precision will be an absolute duty for Donato, *enough
of this childishness*, he will say to himself in that way he

has, and years later it will be like juggling. In Guarulhos they find a space in the car park easily. When they reach the arrivals area they learn that the flight is expected to land half an hour late. Donato takes his father's hand, Henrique is his father, and squeezes it. And when he gets his attention, albeit only briefly, he says – as though they were exploding in his mouth – he says the words he had not been able to pronounce on the way, he pronounces them in sequence, one, two, three times, defeating an opponent who will never be in his imaginary game of pick-up sticks, offering his response to Henrique's dedication that they should be a family, like the family the older teachers teach at school.

The woman and his father are not getting along. Donato can't help them. Henrique won't leave São Paulo, and it would appear that she has got a job at a university in Rio de Janeiro. Donato thinks it will be good when they swap around the visiting arrangements and he and his father go to spend a bit of time with her in Rio. Donato leaves the owl on his desk and from time to time when he stages a battle between it and another toy the owl always wins. The photo of him with Rener (which he only takes out of the drawer on these occasions) is the referee.

*

Years later, Luisa and Henrique finally work it out. She moves to São Paulo.

The Rainha trainers are the most basic black indoor-football type. To a lot of his classmates Donato is stuck-up, to others he's the victim of total brainwashing by a step-father who's a Nazi (when they apply this adjective to him, they obviously don't consider the fact that a Nazi, a Nazi white man, would never adopt an Indian boy). At the age of ten he is probably the only child in his year immune to the consumer temptations typically experienced by his age group. Henrique took every precaution to clarify the meaning of the word capitalism for him, the way it works and is organised, even the psychology behind this term, and the reason why wealth is scarce and human needs unlimited, and how this is the most important rule of all, even if there are fraudsters who promise that it isn't. His teachers talk a lot about liberty and fraternity; whenever they can they illustrate the economic repercussions of these two choices, Mr Lavirmes is one of the ones who makes a point of not hiding the fact that the school's pupils are candidates for future leaders of their countries, stress-ing that it's no use studying if you don't know the social implications of what you're studying. On the whole, this kind of lesson does not mean much to most of the pupils. To Donato, these concepts and explanations make more sense when they coincide with his father's: when there isn't enough for everyone it's necessary to have realistic criteria for dividing up what there is, what you have, what you can get. Price. Donato likes this word – short, direct and reliable – because it is practical and has been a part of his vocabulary forever, he understands what it represents, whether in the supermarket, at the stationer's, picnicking in the park, on the football pitch, in clothes, on the trips he takes with Henrique around Brazil, in the cars that used to so fascinate him and no longer do, in the shopping he does with Luisa; for weeks the only thing Luisa has done has been to shop. Donato knows many things, but he does not really know what the future is. The future is still Henrique's choice. Donato knows he needs to learn to think, he knows he needs to study and he needs discipline, he knows intelligence is worthless if you don't have discipline. Donato doesn't feel bad and he doesn't compete and he doesn't secure alliances with his classmates; he steers clear of the traditional games of hierarchy, of the worldly magnetism of the three or four students who are more confident than he is, the inevitable captains, the rangers who one moment bring the group to a place of perfect harmony, to a companionship that has a muscular concision to it, to an almost martial brusque-ness, and the next moment to the worst of discords, to arguments, to progressive stages, to absolute distancing, to acts of revenge and – not to ignore what is merely a statistical likelihood – to real conflict, a fight, a haymaker punch, trip, kick, hook, headbutt, blood. Donato is a zero.

Neutral territory. Switzerland. He has become used to being an object of mild curiosity to other people both within and outside school. At his classmates' birthday parties he would suffer a little when there were other children who didn't know him and who weren't quite sure what to do when they came across an Indian. Sometimes it was good and hilarious, at other times less so. Little Rener learned to profit from this socially. Black French girls are at an advantage over Brazilian Indian boys. Donato is the main attraction at her birthday parties, every year she reinvents her friend's story, about how they met, about him being a kind of shaman who will avenge his people, who is only among the white people to learn how to master them, practically a Buddha (her mother is a Buddhist and she knows everything about the religion), an Avenging Buddha. Donato is horribly embarrassed but, playing along as best he can with Rener's pathological need to embellish, he appears each time in the most exotic outfit he can manage. This time, they agreed, he would wear a dark suit, white shirt, red tie and a badge saying 'ASK ME HOW'. Rener is in a pink dress. Someone commented that the only thing missing was a garland of flowers in her hair and another said that it wasn't a birthday, it was a wedding. Neither Henrique nor Rener's parents suspected the little performance that their children put on every year, but Luisa noticed their arrangement and kept their secret. It was she, in fact, who hired the suit when Donato asked her to. She knows he is a boy of few words, she knows that when he speaks them he pronounces each one as correctly and emphatically as he can, an impostor playing the role of child (prevaricating in between lapses to hide his reptilian failure to take off). He is condemned to a process of rigorous selection, down to the very commas; condemned to calibrating the air in his lungs, to their tightening, so precociously familiar with the pressures of an extensive vocabulary, because rarities are to hand much more readily than the copious babble of the day-to-day. And this is nature playing one of her dirty tricks. When he started to stutter (almost at the same time as he decided not to) he realised that the everyday was his worst enemy. His whole body seemed to resist what should have been elementary, a simple occurrence; in order to tame it he needed to take it by surprise, use routes that caused shock, surprise, and hope that this surprise might be quicker and more dynamic than the bluntness of his tongue and his brain, his diaphragm and his hands. His hands. He heard it on a tv programme once: only people who are insecure or those who are not very persuasive need their hands to express themselves, to get where they want. Donato needs his hands, but he won't allow himself any shortcuts, he's sure Henrique wouldn't allow them either. Donato devotes himself to difficult words and generally to whatever is difficult, that is where his levers are; he almost never found them when he was a child. At

Rener's parties, he hardly talks to people (his stammering is not revealed), he lets his friend talk for both of them. Those who already know him, already familiar with the dynamics of the games, just help out here and there, supplying the attention necessary to make the story invented by the famous Brown Sugar a bit more credible. At the end of the party, dressed as bride and groom, as the others said, the two of them laugh at themselves, she hugs him and promises that one day they will own a circus troupe, and he just promises that he'll fix something even more striking for next year. Everything is yet to come.

Resignation. Separation. The three of them at the table in the flat in São Paulo. Luisa and Henrique are arguing more than ever. Donato thinks Luisa is always trying to compete with Henrique (and he thinks this is fair), but he doesn't really understand too well what is happening between the two of them. And the argument is all set to become a row. Luisa is trying to persuade Henrique not to invest everything they've got in this project he has invented and which has been dragging its heels, in terms of financial return, since ninety-six, when the internet was still feeling its way into the world and even more so in Brazil, when the global network of computers was a curiosity orbited by shots in the dark (it was not long since access had become available on a commercial scale, it was not long since the green-and-black screens had been abandoned and the graphic possibilities for interaction via monitor had expanded). His idea was to create a *'hub for distributing specialised information, on a subscription basis, to corporations, social groups, new investors, political agents,'* information based on research and surveys aimed at those who are seeking *'new, alternative strategies for economic development and social interaction'* – that was what Donato read in one of the prospectuses that are always scattered around Henrique's study. It was vital to make the most of this new tool to democratise discourse and analysis and to make money. His father imagined that, if there were a sufficient number of subscribers in Brazil and abroad, he could make the company self-sustaining in two years. This did not happen. His ambitions, however, continued to grow and to push him towards ever-greater injections of money. As he had stopped doing consultancy work there was no other source of income. In the second year of the enterprise, Luisa joined as a partner, half-half, with the money from the *settlement in advance* of her parents' inheritance. An ultimately traumatic outlay when her parents discovered her intentions for the money, and later, with the appalling performance of the project, almost a reason for breaking off family relations. Henrique talked about returning the money, but Luisa was furious at her parents' interference; that, however, was almost a year ago – today it's Henrique she is furious with, for not recognising that it is time to stop. He says he will continue with his trips to try and sign up new subscribers and new partners, he will travel the whole of Brazil if need be, he'll try new contacts in Europe, some foundations, the universities, some visionary out there, some philanthropist. A visionary like you, says Luisa, provoking him, like the thousands of others set to lose a lot of money trying to guess at the future of the internet. This is the moment when Donato excuses himself, gets up and goes to his room. On the wall beside his bed is the drawing he did years ago, it came out well, in it you can see the three of them, well dressed, smiling, but not holding hands.

Thirteen years old. Usually he sits all the way over to the right, at the fourth desk from the front. He spends the twenty-five minutes of his break almost always in the same way. The final destination is the library. The itinerary is simple: the bell rings, he waits a minute till most of the class have left, he takes the CD player Henrique gave him out of his rucksack, he always brings a pearl from his collection of more than a thousand discs that are kept in his living room (today he has brought *Surfer Rosa* by some guys called Pixies, a pretty old band who inspired Nirvana, the supreme rulers of the universe). Then he takes his regular walk around the playground under the covered walkways. He will spend a minute or two with the groups of boys, always small groups, with whom he gets along; one of these groups is made up of Américo, Ramon and Julián, this latter a Bolivian, pale and feeble, with grey-blue eyes, a potential candidate for his best friend. He doesn't waste more than five minutes on this circuit, for the time being he moves on to his *small daily dose of obsession* moment: tracking down Rener wherever she is, even if it's just for a glance and a wave from afar. Since last year they've been in different classes, it's one of the school's strategies, to mix up the classes in order to increase the students' *sociability*. This time he didn't need to look for her. She runs over with a CD to give him, it's Serge Gainsbourg's *Love on the Beat*, she says this is who he should be spending his time on and not with the Nine Inch Nails of this world (he doesn't even like Nine Inch Nails). Donato looks at her gratefully, puts the CD in his jacket pocket, asks whether she might want to go with him to the library, she laughs and says that if she ever chooses to trade her break on a sunny day for the library he should have her locked up in a madhouse, she gives him a kiss on the cheek and returns to her circle of girlfriends. Donato walks, then, to the start of the corridor that leads out of the school, turns left and walks on to the library. This is his refuge. Saying hello to the two women working at the counter and the head librarian is his refuge, mixing up the names on the spines of the books is his refuge, thinking that he understands the poems by

Brazilian writers is his refuge, that he understands Walt Whitman and Camões, who are not well served in the classroom, is his refuge. Refuge. Here he has the sensation that he is not wasting time and (squeezed together in the corridors with the other students, the interested ones and the ones who most probably have just adopted a strategy of invisibility like his) he also has the sensation of possessing some kind of autobiographical authority. Here he doesn't need to submit himself to trials of strength, charisma, leadership, shrewdness, humour, popularity, here he doesn't need to discover how much he resembles his classmates, the future leaders of their countries, here in the impersonality of the iron shelves and the silence that has seeped into the rest of the furniture, he spends the only minutes in which he allows himself to feel afraid.

Luisa said it would be a complete waste of time going up the Pão de Açucar on a cloudy day like this one in Rio de Janeiro. Donato knows she's taking unfair advantage of her right to reorganise the outing agreed by the three of them. Her threadbare excuse is her perpetual migraine, she says she woke up at five and didn't go back to sleep. The reason, looking at the situation objectively, is solely and exclusively the fact of Henrique having been called in as a last-minute replacement for a Mexican analyst at a think tank in Teresópolis, a private meeting to come

up with public policy suggestions organised by a group
of young businessmen from Minas and Rio (the money's
good, in the financial crisis he is going through there
was no way he could say no) and, because of this, he is
prevented from returning before Thursday, that is, three
days from now. Now the itinerary is up to her. Donato
doesn't want to think about this too much, he has a map,
he knows which buses he needs to take. He never puts
himself on a collision course with Luisa, he just ducks,
weaves, leaves little notes. In spite of the occasional embar-
rassments caused by his stutter, he considers himself
at a great advantage to the rest of the social universe:
he is better informed than most of the adults around
him and entirely confident as regards his inability to
make mistakes caused by absent-mindedness, an excess
of pride, resentment or vanity. He leaves a note at the hotel
reception, takes the circular-route bus at Leblon towards
Gávea, Jardim Botânico, Humaitá, Botafogo. He gets off at
Voluntários da Pátria, the main street in Botafogo, walks
to Rua das Palmeiras, to the big house numbered fifty-
five. He goes in. He walks around the courtyard, there's
a stylised thatched hut that has been set up right near
the entrance on the left of the main building, he spots
the class of children aged around nine who are probably
starting one of those guided tours and joins the group.
The teacher, a really young redhead, looks at Donato,
says nothing. They go into a hall with an exhibition of

ceramic objects, pieces representing Asurani art made by the people of that name who live in Médio Xingu, about a hundred kilometres from the city of Altamira in the state of Pará. The guide's little jokes make up for his weak presentation, rather unconvincing and lacking relevant information even for a gang of students from any old municipal public school. All is going well until the teacher emphatically states that the greatest mistake made by the white man was to remove the Indian from his habitat and because of this 'we all have to fight for Indians to return to their natural state, living in harmony with nature . . . ' Before she has finished, Donato raises his hand. This throws her, there's a moment of doubt (you can see it in her eyes) and she gestures to him that he may speak. He says that she is wrong, it would be best to take every last savage they can find in the forest and civilise him, give him a real chance to 'ensure his dignity in today's world without needing favours from anyone, before the process of decimation has been completed.' He concludes by saying that the past will never come back. The teacher is stunned; two students immediately ask 'miss, what's decimation?', and, fortunately, the guide launches into one of his comedy routines and Donato goes off to explore other parts of the Museum of the Indian less propitious to his enthusiasm.

*

Another school year has passed. They are both fourteen (Rener is just three months his elder) and this meeting on the staircase that goes to the teachers' car park has not been prearranged. Donato's face is turned towards the alcove framed with very light quartz stones with a statue of Our Lady of Lourdes in one of the far corners and is still stunned at the news that Rener will be leaving Brazil in eighteen days' time and, along with her parents, will be going back to live in France. Stop being such a hick, Curumim. You'll learn to get by on your own, she says. He turns his face towards her. I know how to get by, Rener. It's just, I . . . I kind of . . . I'm going to miss you, I'm really going to miss you a lot. She responds with a melancholy smile. This whole time we've balanced each other out, haven't we? He nods. You've helped me not to become the school's walking freak show. She looks grateful. And you've given me grief to keep me from becoming the local Naomi Campbell, she says, her lips quivering. Exactly, he says. Rener's eyes fill with water. Don't worry, I'll be all right . . . There's only two more years. They both know two years is too long. But pay attention, Donato, drying the tears that are flowing down her cheeks, it's time for you to learn how to play the game better. He frowns. Better than I play now, Brown Sugar? I'm a complete goody-goody, I always do everything just right. She gives his shoulder a gentle shove. That's not what I'm talking about. Being like that is only going to open doors for you in the future, she says. So what are you talking about, then? She looks down. About how blind you are to things that are going on around you . . . your naivety, your passivity, your . . . leaning her elbow on her knees and clasping her hands together in front of her. Leaving this school, getting far away from you, it's going to be a relief. I'm sorry to be telling you . . . almost in a whisper. But what . . . he tries to interrupt her. She doesn't let him. I'm sorry to be telling you like this. Really, I'm just sad and I'm taking it out on you . . . still in a low voice. Rener, Rener, Rener . . . She lifts her head and looks at him. Look, Curumim . . . Since the first day of pre-school I've liked you . . . And that feeling of affection has taken so many different shapes, in so many ways, that sometimes I've doubted whether it really exists. Even my girlfriends . . . I swear on my life, I never told anybody a thing . . . even they know I've always liked you . . . and they know I've always protected you . . . Or do you think you escaped from being one of the school punchbags because you've got nice eyes? Hmph! Anyone messing with you would have to mess with me . . . You even called me Mônica for a bit, like in the comics, remember? she says. I used to get furious, didn't I? He agrees. And she gives him another gentle shove. How many times did I make English Douglas ask you to play football with them at break time . . . I'd even insist that you had to play up front, never in goal. Donato considers telling her about the poems he wrote for her, but instead says: the older guys always did like you. *There are at least twenty poems.* See what comes from being the school skating champion . . . *He memorised one in which he calls her Dino.* I always suspected as much, Rener. I mean, you pulling the strings. Hiding in the shadows. *Poems don't belong in the world of Rener.* Women know how to do that kind of thing. I confess it was really fun, the cretins in our year respected me not only because I was, let's put it this way, irresistible, but also because the guys in the years above did whatever I told them, including intimidating, with all the subtlety of a builder's mallet, any younger ones who stepped out of line. Ah, my Parisian blood . . . It's not my fault that's what I'm like. And what do you feel now? About the cretins? *A dinosaur within a poem.* Please, Sugar, don't start . . . Hardly anything has changed . . . Everything has changed . . . You know . . . I've gone out with Mark, and Gabriel, I've fooled around with two other guys . . . I've never kissed anyone, he admits. Really? . . . Why am I not surprised? And he moves forward (three spaces at once). I like you, Rener, really like you. This year was hard, loads of things I hadn't had to deal with before became important and I discovered I had no idea how to handle them. You live to study, she says. Isn't that what we're here for? I still don't know for sure . . . Now I'm going back to France and I'm going to have to start from scratch . . . I know I won't adapt . . . And he surprises her: I love you, Brown Sugar . . . Since when? Donato doesn't reply, he can't be as frank as she is. Three or four minutes pass without either of them saying a single word. A group of their classmates is walking towards them, approaching casually; after all Rener and Donato are like two sides of the same coin. Rener notices and gets up to meet them. Donato stays where he is, he knows Rener will take the group far away, because that is her way of protecting him and, right now, of torturing him for what he's done, too. He knows that he will need to find some new reasons for being in this school. He should have kissed her. He should have stopped her getting up.

With the story he drafted at the desks in the library, Donato wins the school's playwriting competition. His prize is the money to stage his play, *Crucial Two One*, at the end-of-year party. He has little more than three months to choose his actors, rehearse, sort out a set. He never imagined he would do it, it was the first time he had entered. If Rener had been in Brazil he'd have got her to play the lead in the story, which takes place in an indeterminate future and an indeterminate place, where a government, an indeterminate government, has developed a way of resuscitating people which will guarantee them twenty-one more hours of life. The service is offered through a monopoly and proves to be one of the most effective ways of securing money for the public coffers: as the price is high, only the rich can afford the procedure, and the first condition imposed by the government on whoever buys it is that in the first seven hours of their extra life, they will fulfil their obligations to the Internal Revenue Service, to the public exchequer, undergoing a cross-examination under the effects of a drug which, for those seven hours, will make them unable to lie, and also that they will resolve any lawsuits under way with any private firms that have an agreement with the programme. Any buyer who, on his own account, is not in a position to shoulder the total cost of the service can be sponsored by other people, thereby being at the service of these sponsors for half of the fourteen remaining hours – this method tends to be bought by large firms to obtain information and secrets from their executives who would otherwise die without revealing them.

He gets a lift from Julián's mother as far as Avenida Paulista. He said he'd get the metro but decides to walk; he likes strolling down Doutor Arnaldo when he is feeling calm. Luisa will be thrilled at the news; it was she who took him to see his first children's play. He gestures to the guard to open the main gate of the complex. He takes the key out of his rucksack, opens the door. It's cleaning day today, so the silence is strange (Friday is the day Luisa makes a point of staying home to organise her work). He opens the kitchen windows, the late afternoon light invades the room, the kind of light that makes the city better, showing up the crockery in the sink, the cereal box and the dirty ceramic bowl, just as he had left them that morning. He finds his phone, calls Luisa. 'Hi, can you talk?' he asks. 'Yes,' she replies, drily. 'Dona Leila hasn't been,' he tells her. 'I know . . . ' She is shaken (but he still hasn't noticed). 'I've got good news. I won the playwriting competition . . . ' he says. 'Huh?' She doesn't seem to be hearing him properly. 'The one at school . . . You and Henrique said . . . ' – he is euphoric. 'Great . . . ' she interrupts him. 'You're at home, right?' says Luisa. 'Yes,' no longer euphoric. 'I'll see you there, then.' She hangs up without even saying bye. He knows he'll have to clear up the kitchen so he doesn't waste any time: he takes the rubbish from the bin, puts it outside. When he comes back in, he turns on the radio and the television (a recent habit); it's not ten minutes before he hears the radio bulletin with an update on the turboprop plane carrying a number of businessmen that disappeared from air-control radar around eleven in the morning on a flight from Teresina to Brasília. It's enough to make him squeeze the dishcloth in his fists without drying them properly and, trying to control his breathing, pick up his phone to talk to Luisa.

The body was one of the last to be found by the recovery team. After the many bureaucratic procedures had been seen to, it was sent to São Paulo. The coffin remained closed for the two hours of the wake. Luisa said she was not going to tell anyone, let alone pay for a death notice in the newspaper. 'It's not Henrique's style.' It was not her style. Donato did not ask to see what was left of his stepfather, nor did he go along when they buried him, he just sat outside the Gethsêmani snack bar imagining the mayhem if they'd had to bury him in Porto Alegre. An impressive number of friends showed up. He wondered what would make someone drop all their obligations and go to a wake at three in the afternoon, if he himself, the son, the adopted son of the only child of a couple, already deceased, is able to feel nothing but the enormous desire not to be there.

Luisa has been on medication for more than a week and it would probably be wise to refrain from any activities that require good reflexes, such as driving Henrique's Honda Civic, in which the two of them are now sitting, travelling at more than a hundred and twenty kilometres per hour down Anhanguera. She holds the steering wheel and drives as if it were her own car. He watches her: her movements and the expression in her voice make her seem a stranger, a stranger he wouldn't know how to deal with. She says she is not going to accept a settlement, she says they have to trust the Brazilian legal system. 'If someone made a mistake, no doubt about it, they're going to pay.' Donato looks out at the landscape racing past the hard shoulder, tries to avoid the complicity of his presence with Luisa's, just as he has always intuitively avoided his informal kinship to her all these years; he tries to avoid it before, as well as becoming a stranger, she becomes disdainful (because of their having reconciled in such an abrupt and Siamese way). 'Your father's Porto Alegre friends are going to want to kill me,' she says. Donato doesn't reply, but turns back to look at her (letting his silence seem an ill-at-ease way of keeping the peace). So she goes on: 'They don't all read the papers, they don't all pay attention to disasters, they aren't all working on the assumption that I might think they will be out of our lives for good now . . . ' She rolls her window all the way down, sticks her head out. This lasts just a few seconds. When she returns to her proper sitting position, she sighs, a sigh of satisfaction. 'I need to get some petrol.' She drives on for a few kilometres, indicates right, leaves the road, enters a Texaco service station. 'I'm not sure I'm going to be able to stay in this city . . . ' She stops beside one of the fuel pumps. There's an attendant gesturing to her to move the car up to the pump in front. 'I'll have to get out,' Donato tells her. 'Wait. I have a proposition to make . . . ' she says, before putting the car into gear and starting up slowly. 'You graduate from high school,' and she brakes again, stopping the car just before the pump, 'and in January we'll . . . ' Donato unlocks the car door. 'What's it to be, miss?' the pump attendant asks her. 'I need to go to the toilet,' Donato says and opens the door. 'Just a moment . . . ' she gets confused. 'Excuse me a moment, Luisa, sorry . . . ' Donato says and gets out of the car. 'I'll wait here for you,' she says. He walks over towards the convenience store and disappears from view. 'Petrol – the Super . . . Fill it up,' she tells the attendant. He fills the tank, checks the oil. The boy is taking his time. Luisa pays with a credit card and, when she is thinking about heading over to the shop, to check that he's all right, she is surprised by the sight of the girl in the Texaco uniform. 'Miss, sorry to bother you, but the young man who arrived with you asked me to tell you that he's got a taxi home and he'll meet you there.' The girl is looking over towards the convenience store. 'Could you tell me whether he . . . never mind.' The pump attendant asks whether she wants her windscreen cleaned, but she barely hears him. She's going to drive to Avenida Lorena, call up a girlfriend (but which?), get a coffee at Suplicy, then a drink, two, three and find some hotel to stay at, so Donato is left alone to understand just as quickly as possible what it means to look after yourself; but she is playing this scenario out in her head in order to lessen the pain not of having lost the man she has lived with for more than fifteen years and loved unconditionally, but of having been abandoned by the only person who could have been there with her, supporting her with a bit of decency through the distress of not being able to imagine how to wake up tomorrow morning and from where to wrench the strength to admit that from here on in there would be absence, a new absence, a solid block which refused to fit into reality.

Donato chose to wait seventy-two hours before resorting to the police for help or seeking out whatever acquaintances he could think of. He lost track of how many times he called her phone. He clung on to this remorse and, inside himself, to a resentful interpretation of everything that had happened so far. He doesn't know what to do, he doesn't have the strength, he doesn't even have any spontaneity. He has already waited more than a minute. The voice on the other end said it was from the São Patrício Clinic, informing him that one Dr Nelson would speak to him shortly. On the holding message, a voice saying that the institution offers a welcoming hospital environment, and the techniques and staff suited to the treatment of people who find themselves suffering from emotional troubles, guaranteeing the best clinical conditions for their most rapid recovery. The doctor picks up, explains that Luisa sought them out for voluntary admittance, she has been medicated and she's doing well, sorry not to have called earlier but when she checked herself in she only supplied contact details for her mother in Rio de Janeiro, and had just asked that they notify Donato a few minutes ago. Donato asks if he can speak to her, the doctor says that a nurse will call him within twenty minutes and will connect him to the patient. He notes that they will only be able to talk for five minutes, to stop her getting too tired. Finally the doctor says he can visit her tomorrow afternoon, just for forty minutes, and if 'everything goes according to plan' she will be out in a fortnight. The minutes pass and the time he's spent waiting reaches a bit over an hour. The phone rings, the voice says hi and asks how are things. He says he's ready to leave the city, that he can finish his third year somewhere else and they'll never need to set foot in São Paulo again. She sighs and says he's crazy to think about transferring from such a good school, he's got to graduate. As he listens to her, he thinks he's going to have to get empty cardboard boxes from the supermarket to pack up the books, clothes, pictures, films, CDs belonging to Henrique; to make the ghost of his father dissipate before she gets back. Then he focuses back on what she's saying and excuses himself, he says hurriedly that he will definitely visit her tomorrow (and he's cruelly taken up by the idea that he has the lucidity the other person needs, and this is something new, a new power, unearned, unjustifiably grown-up).

Luisa's decision to adopt renewed the feeling of complicity between the two of them. The series of appearances before the judge, the Public Ministry, the Children's and

Youth Supervisory Council, meant that they behaved perfectly to show off the solid structure of their new family. Assessments are awkward, they encourage those being assessed not to take them seriously. They are standing, now, outside the civil registry office. They have come to the city centre specially to get the certificate on which, from here on in, will appear the names Luisa Vasconcelos Lange and Donato Henrique Lange Becker (his name has four names now). It takes just a few minutes, as it is the end of the working day and there are no longer queues at the windows. Minutes from now he will sit down with her at the table of a popular restaurant in Higienópolis and they will order a bottle of Pol Roger Brut Reserve. The real extravagance will begin, however, when she orders a second bottle of the same champagne and challenges him to join her; he is after all just about to graduate with honours, very possibly with the highest average in his year, to première a play, as both playwright and director, and to move away with her far from São Paulo. He doesn't hesitate, he allows the waiter to fill his glass. The head waiter is going from table to table holding out a bag of round, numbered chips in imitation mother-of-pearl, one for each customer, referring to the establishment's week-long twenty-sixth birthday celebrations by way of justifying the interruption. There are two draws per evening for the chance to win one night in a luxury suite at the Paulista Plaza on Alameda Santos. Once he is sure everybody has

been given one, the waiter randomly draws exactly the
number that is in Luisa's hand. She asks Donato to make
himself known, to shout something: he is the man of the
house, after all. The head waiter approaches and hands
them an envelope which explains that the night at the
hotel can be used at any time and includes consumption of
up to a hundred *reais* of food and drink. She asks whether
it would be valid for that very night. He straightens himself
up and immediately assures her that it would. She asks
him to fill their glasses and she proposes a toast, another
one. They finished eating the lobster in *pitanga* sauce and
she ordered a tiramisu for dessert accompanied by two
glasses of Kir Royale, and then he suggested that the two
of them go straight from there to the Paulista Plaza. She
smiled with tense lips and let out a why not? As they
drove down Avenida Paulista, looking at the buildings
from the back seat of the taxi, she said that the two of
them would never be coming back here, that a few weeks
from now there would be no more São Paulo ever again.
In the hotel they were given a suite on the penultimate
floor. They had no luggage, which didn't stop the bellboy
from accompanying them to their room with the twin
single beds they had requested, and showing them how
all the gadgets worked. The hotel employee withdraws.
The two of them are sat on the sofa, the lights turned out,
sharing their exhaustion. The brightness of the buildings
thickens in the polluted air and is enough to light them

up, leaving room for doubt about where their boundaries are. Then the accident. Coming closer. Donato moves his first kiss against Luisa's mouth. She witnesses his awkwardness, his determination to discover, and is left wordless, confused, distressed.

It's terrible when you discover yourself to be meticulous and methodical in the extreme and you discover, too, belatedly, that the person at the top of your list of the school's greatest stage talents suffers from terrible insecurity about his actual capacity to get up on stage, make it count, face the terror, just put it all out there and perform as he has done so well in rehearsals. First it was the cold that rendered him voiceless, then he discovered it was flu, then it developed into mild sinusitis and then severe sinusitis, then acid reflux, then those palpitations in the left side of his chest, which are clearly baseless given that he, Vicente Fino, is evidently thin, healthy and has no history of heart attacks or anything of the sort in the family. You go all in, you take a risk, because after all he, the play's male lead, Little Vicente Fino, again, is an anxious little Jewish fag, and charismatic, with a big fucking face like a startled donkey able to rearrange itself into any expression, just as representative of a minority as you are, Adopted Trapped Donato, you who are an Indian, just like the most Indian of Indians, with that unmissable Indian face, like you find in the documentaries by those brothers, the Vilas-Boas, and who had the wretched fortune of being brought up by a white man, a pale little deceased white man, full of ideas that ultimately, tragically, ended up unrealised, like this play which has created so many expectations and that at this moment looks set not to happen. You haven't stuttered this much in months, because everything happened without your being the centre of attention, and now you've spent the last fortnight in the midst of a tempest, the true Prospero with a tempest shoved up his ass, and you're stuttering like a lunatic. Now it's five-twenty in the afternoon, the auditorium doors open at seven and, apparently, the play is to start at seven-thirty tonight on the dot, because after the performance come the party and the drinking. The problem is that the Great Vicente Fino is at the ear, nose and throat doctor, he has no voice and, according to his mother (who at the moment, as one would expect, is with him), has a thirty-nine degree fever. The prognosis (you've just hung up): Vicente will not go on. And there's not a blessed soul alive who knows all the lines, only you know all the lines, no one will be such a sucker as to expose himself and become the scapegoat if everything goes wrong. The worst thing is knowing that most of the audience will be there because of Vicente. They are his friends, including some from outside school, who actually appreciate theatrical lunacies. You, take his place? No, you'll stammer, you won't manage any fluency at all, you'll slow down the pace of the dialogue, which is the play's trump card. And Kika comes into the room without knocking. 'Sorry to barge in like this, but I have to say something . . . Can I?' Kika's face is very close to yours. The breath that comes out of her mouth is the best that anyone could ever produce. Fuck, Kika really knows how to come on to you. 'Go ahead.' Kika has lovely eyes. 'I know you're the director.' Kika has quite some breasts. 'And you,' he replies, 'do the lighting and the sound.' Kika has a fringe like Regina Duarte from when Regina Duarte was young and hot and was called Brazil's sweetheart. 'The thing is, you're going to have to take Vicentinho's part,' Kika says. Focus, Donato, this is not the time. 'I'm not an actor,' he argues. 'But it's the only way . . . Wear a mask . . . It won't make any difference. What matters are the lines.' Kika is so very good at moving those lips. 'You're forgetting how they're done,' he ventures. Kika might put out for him one day. 'How they're done?' says Kika raising her sexy arms. 'How the lines are said . . . I'll ruin everything' (and ladies and gentleman, the person who has just spoken is the Director, Adopted Donato, who still has the nerve to fantasise about Kika sucking his cock at a time like this). 'Forget about how they're said,' says Kika. 'Why did I have to invent this damn play?' says the director. 'We can do a dramatic reading,' says Kika. 'Kika, give me two minutes to think, here, alone.' Kika opens the door. Would you believe it, this pert ass of Kika's? 'The whole cast is outside . . . ' Turn round further, Kika. 'What an utter cock-up . . . ' Just turn around now, Kika. 'You haven't got two minutes, you have to perform . . . Wear a mask, it'll work, I'll ask Alessandra to track down one that covers everything from your top lip upwards.' Like, so that it, that lip, can help me go down on you, Kika? 'What difference would that make?' the director asks. 'Oh, no idea, it's just something you use . . . You adopt a persona . . . ' Kika, Kika, Kika. 'Don't talk to me about personas.' The director gets annoyed. 'But Jung . . . ' Kika provokes him. 'Oh, Kika, please . . . now is not the time for Jung.' 'Well, then?' and she gives a smile, the deadliest of Kika's weapons. 'Tell them to find the mask.' Donato gives in. Donato wasn't even smitten with Kika like this, but today Kika is too much. Kika leaves, Donato sits down at the table on which the pages of dialogue are scattered, the scenes, the acts, with technical cues, the play's key moments, he opens the elastics round his folder, puts all that paper inside, puts it in his bag. He goes out to talk to the group of actors, he stutters almost the whole time, but his words link together into a strong lecture about the text he wrote and about the critical contribution of everyone there towards making the result so much better than he had imagined. Bit by bit he realises that he is managing to calm everyone down, to ensure at least a minimal degree of unity. Alessandra appears with two masks made by a friend of hers called Guilherme Pilla, they are plastic masks that leave the lips and jaw completely exposed, likewise the eyes. Donato tries on the first and feels so comfortable that he doesn't even bother with the second.

And now, on the stage and in the mask, in the important role of male lead, Donato imagines being Henrique, and this doesn't frighten him as much as it should.

At the Rolling Stones' concert on Copacabana Beach, Luisa hugged Donato and said, her mouth right up to his ear: 'Have you got any idea what it'll be like in Recife?' He turned his face towards her, taking advantage of the deafening noise, and, under the effects of the five cans of Itaipava beer he'd drunk, he laughed cockily, in the way he thinks he would have laughed at Rener – had Rener been there, obviously, and had he not persuaded her he was never again going to write letters to her or send messages and that he was going to try and forget her forever. His feet in the sand (and more distant than he has ever before felt from the French girl; he used to think he existed only for the French girl) he pulls Luisa towards him and, surrounded by a mass of one million three hundred thousand euphoric people, brings his mouth to hers and bites her lips, his hands slide round her waist and stop firmly on her ass, she puts her own hands on his and encourages him to squeeze her as hard as would be expected of a man who knew women. Donato could never have imagined what it would be like, this detachment from every other gaze. As soon as Keith Richards finished singing 'This Place Is Empty' Luisa invited him to leave and they walked to the apartment on Joaquim Nabuco where they were staying. He wanted to wait at least till 'You Can't Always Get What You Want', but the Stones and all the cultural memorabilia he had been able to accumulate in thirteen years can't compare to what he's feeling now; any information right now is useless. Luisa and her muscular body and her sharp sense of humour that many twenty-year-old women would envy, confidently leading him by the hand through the maze of crazy people that Avenida Atlântica has become, leave no room for doubt: she is the final thing of his stepfather's that remains for him to take.

**what's to be done
with the usual?**

metals protecting metals

After Recife. (Recife as a place of transit.)

The first thing that upset Luisa was the trip to Goiânia in eight days' time being brought forward. The news arrived mid-morning, carried by the electronic sound vibration in her phone reproducing, at thousandths of a second's difference, the serious voice of the Deputy Vice Chancellor for Research at the University of Goiás; and what really knocks her off her feet once and for all is this call made to her landline, notifying her that the removal van which left Recife fourteen days ago with her things (and other people's, too, in keeping with the common practice of transporting two or three removals at once to reduce the freight costs to the client) had overturned less than four hours ago in Santa Catarina, on one of the widened stretches of the 101, fifteen kilometres from the entrance to Tubarão, and had, unfortunately, caught fire and

destroyed all the furniture, carpets, mirrors, dishes, por-
celain, silverware, household appliances, 'all of it, madam,
regrettably, all of it . . . ' says the employee of the Pernam-
buco company, impassive, distressing her so much that
she loses her balance, stumbles, knocks over the luxury
hundred-litre silver-model Samsonite she has just rolled
in from the bedroom to the living room. The weight of
the clothes set aside for several days and the nearly two
dozen essential books she needed to take mean that the
plastic structure crashes hard onto the laminated wooden
floor with a noise that can, no doubt, be heard even outside
the house, even considering that the house is on Avenida
Cristovão Colombo, one of the busiest roads in Porto
Alegre. At that moment, as is to be expected, Donato
comes running down the stairs. Barely moving her lips
Luisa says that she's ok, starkly belied by the hate radiat-
ing from her eyes. He nods, folds his arms, waits. And
what could have been a brief conversation lasted more
than half an hour; she had to speak to the employee, the
manager and the owner of the removal firm, and it only
didn't take even longer still because, in her argument
with the owner of the firm, Luisa yells all the insults she
possibly can and hangs up on him. 'Bad news?' Donato
asks. 'The removal van . . . There was nothing left. Can
you believe it? . . . The dressing table that belonged to my
grandmother . . . ' she says sadly, 'God, there's no way
that can be replaced.' He is silent. A few minutes pass

before she says, 'And what about your things? They've gone, too.' Without looking at her, he says: 'We've lost so many things already, Luisa . . . ' and looks over towards the kitchen, probably considering that this would be a good time to fetch a glass of water with sugar, a kindness that Luisa would refuse. 'You did insure everything, didn't you?' She doesn't answer. 'We will be able to buy more furniture, won't we?' he asks. 'It isn't going to be that simple,' she says. 'Then you're going to have to postpone your trip to Goiânia.' He used just the argument she was most afraid of hearing. 'Don't even think about suggesting that again, understand? They want me there tomorrow afternoon, and tomorrow afternoon is when I'll be there. Our money's run out. There's no way I can ask my parents for more.' She is firm. 'I can't afford the luxury of chucking away another research grant.' She hadn't noticed how low the living room ceiling was. 'And the insurance payment for the removals they didn't deliver?' he says. 'I'll sort it out from there,' she replies, determined. 'What about the idea of my going out there to visit you?' And here, in this thought process of his, begins what she might call the second phase of the game of death. 'That's the millionth time you've asked me that today,' and she walks away. 'And it might not be the last.' He follows her and touches her shoulder. She turns to face him. 'You know that we've fallen into a hole, and I'm not referring to our little financial disaster. You know we need a break from each other.' He sinks down, his hand slides down her arm, he sits on the floor; he remains silent (which is his answer). *Luisa, Luisa*, and a series of things run through her head that she will have to sort out with the greatest possible amount of emotional stress, negotiations that will lead to legal wrangling and years of waiting for a final result. Some of her emotions are rushing out of control, their boundaries are no longer clear, they are the normal behaviour of someone in a dangerous gear, because not long ago she was young and adaptable. *Damn.* She watches him, she doesn't know what exactly the plan is, all she decided was that she needed to nudge her life forward, which is why she forced herself to move to Porto Alegre, to this house that isn't even hers, the only possession remaining from Henrique's inheritance (he was able, fortunately, to make a legal arrangement, keeping the house in Donato's name and far from the reach of the creditors who seem to have increased following his death; she was his business partner, she is answerable for a part of the debts). The house is the monument to the ruins of a dream, with its two storeys and its southern precariousness. And Porto Alegre, even after everything she's lived through in the city, is scarcely better than the end of the world, where, now that Donato is so surprisingly capable, she can abandon him and forget about him for a time. And then, by chance, he looks up and his gaze meets hers, making her stop thinking, making her go up to the bathroom where she forgot her washbag, fetch it, bring it down with the intention of going into the kitchen to get some filtered water, but the moment she walks through the living room, finding him there prostrate, she decides not to take the medication in secret; on the contrary, she will pour herself a glass, come back to the living room and crouch down beside him. And at that moment there they are, the two of them, side by side, in the living room of the house where their removals are no longer going to arrive, it is a sub-phase within the second phase of the game of death. Luisa puts the washbag and the full glass down on the floorboards, lies on her back. 'Let's make a deal,' she says, her green eyes looking up at the ceiling, aggressive. 'Let's spend those forty days . . . ' she's cautious. 'And forty nights,' he interrupts her. 'Right . . . ' Interrupting the conflict that is already emerging. 'Let's spend that time a long way from each other and then we'll do that therapy we agreed on . . . ' The living room ceiling seems even lower now. 'And then we'll decide together.' *Don't do it, Luisa.* 'Together . . . ' he ventures. *Don't.* 'Of course. Together . . . ' she interrupts him (her rejoinder) and, not getting up, she takes the washbag, unzips it, pulls out the strips of Valium and Rivotril, pops out two pills of the former and one of the latter, then she pauses (leaving him ample time to react), then puts the pills in her mouth, and after feeling around next to her as though she were blind, takes the cup, lifts her head, drinks. She raises her back off the floor, sits up. *Do it Luisa.* 'All I know is I'm going to bed, my flight leaves at eight,' she says, and settles her hands between her outstretched legs with the strips held between her fingertips. And before Luisa realises what's happening, he takes the strips from her hands, puts down the Rivotril, pops out a pill from the strip of Valium, puts it in his mouth, swallows. 'What are you doing, Donato?' she asks, grabbing the packaging out of his hand. 'Me? Nothing. It's going to be no problem . . . No problem . . . Isn't that right? All of it no problem at all and rent a DVD. A no-problem DVD, no problem at all in this no-problem life,' he retorts. 'We don't have a DVD player.' She won't allow him to make a scene. 'Oh, that's right, Luisa . . . and we don't have a table and we don't have chairs . . . Or an oven, or a fridge, or beds . . . all we have are the mattresses . . . the mattresses you bought no problem with your no-problem money, the money that's going to come from the research grant from your new university and, of course, my computer, oh, and my clothes, and my owl, and . . . let me see what else . . . yes, nothing.' She knows this is not the moment to lose it. 'I'll transfer money for you to buy a fridge and a microwave . . . And you also have that new credit card . . . I'm sure this handsome boy won't get himself into any trouble.' *Do it Luisa.* 'I'll use it to book a few days in the most expensive hotel in Goiânia . . . ' he gets up with a threat, 'you just wait.' Already on his way to the staircase, he starts singing: '*I'm not saying it was your fault . . . Although you could have done more . . .* ' 'You wouldn't dare,' she says. *'Oh you're so naive, yet so . . .* ' 'Come back here,' Luisa shouts. 'You're such a smiling sweetheart.' It's no use. 'You're just pretending you can't hear me.' It's really no use. *'That every time I look inside I know she knows I'm not fond of asking . . . True or false it may be . . .* ' and he stops on one of the last steps, turns to her and says: 'I'm going to the club to swim.' Luisa brings a hand up to her mouth. 'You can't. The Valium you just took . . . ' And this is only the beginning. *'True or false it may be . . .* ' he goes on, *'she's still out to get me . . .* ' She hears the bedroom door closing upstairs, tells herself that she has done what she was supposed to do. Soon she will write a note, a note containing a set of instructions, that she imagines leaving in the middle of the living room when she goes to get into the orange taxi, flaming orange typical of Porto Alegre, that will take her to Salgado Filho airport, where she will check in her huge suitcase and go up to the cafés (yes, that's what she has planned) and ask for a green tea or a fennel tea and drink it with half of one of her tranquillisers, she'll take a couple of deep breaths, look at the other people, oblivious at their tables, and only then will she feel relief.

Donato walks through the turnstile of the Nautical Union Guild, ignores the surprised expression on the face of the employee working on the door, walks towards the Olympic-sized swimming pool. He changes in the changing room. He does his warm-ups and stretches under the awning over the staircase you take to get to the swimming pool from the changing rooms. There are other members swimming in lanes one, four and six. He greets the employee who looks after the pools, acting as lifeguard to the members. It's his first time here. He puts on the silver silicone swimming cap, goggles, dives into the end of lane three, he forces himself into a front crawl for the first two hundred metres and then onto his back kicking his legs, he forces himself to swim until he stops in the middle of the pool, attaches himself to one of the buoys, coughing, he's swallowed some water. The employee who looks after the swimming pools gets up (it must be four metres deep where he is – not a place to let someone play at being ill), takes off his flip-flops, his t-shirt with the Nautical Union Guild logo on it and dives into the pool, straight into lane two. Donato is still clinging to the buoy. 'Everything ok, kid?' asks the club employee. 'I'm fine . . . I just felt dizzy' (he is no longer coughing, just breathing anxiously). 'Have you been drinking, by any chance?' he asks. 'No. I got a bit dizzy . . . It was strange . . . I lost concentration, I felt a kind of vertigo . . . I started sinking as if . . . ' he coughs and stops, 'as if suddenly I didn't know how to swim any more.' It had been a long time since he'd gone swimming and since he had taken any risks (Donato took a risk). 'Come on, get those goggles and that cap off so the blood can flow more easily in your head. I'll come with you to the side,' says the club employee. And, hanging on to the floats separating the lanes, they make their way to the side of the pool. 'Better?' he asks. 'I'm a bit drowsy.' He was stupid. 'Can we get you over to First Aid?' he suggests. 'No, I just want to get out, get my clothes on and go back home.' They go down to the changing room. The employee who looks after the swimming pool asks the employee on the door to call a taxi. They don't have to wait long. The boy gets himself ready. The two of them walk to the entrance of the club, the employee who looks after the swimming pool asks if he has money and if he really is ok. Donato gets into the taxi, the club employee gives him a goodbye wave. Donato feels a sense of calm, a peacefulness he has never experienced before. There's no doubt about it, he's high on medication. The car pulls away, and he thinks that being high makes it easier to accept and understand what it's like to be alone.

Luisa comes into the bedroom without turning on the light, she walks over to him, lies down in what little space is free on the mattress and puts her arms around him from behind. He doesn't wake up. She notices the strong smell of chlorine in his hair. She squeezes him tighter without getting any reaction. She partially uncovers him and kisses his sweaty back (sweaty because he's covered himself in an eiderdown on this baking hot night). She shouldn't have come to the bedroom, being there goes against everything she had planned, but nothing matters now, she slides the palm of her hand over his body, letting the minutes pass. She wants his temperature to stick to her hands and she wants there to be no past between them; that is when she lets go of him and moves away, but at the moment she rests her hand on the floor in order to get up he pulls her back and kisses her on the mouth. She turns her back on him, but doesn't leave the bed, her clothes and the cover are preventing their two bodies from touching. He hugs her, she doesn't move, tears roll down her face, smear her makeup, she feels his hard-on pressing against the top of her left thigh and she lets it be. 'I'm going with you to the airport,' he says. 'Please, this madness has already gone too far.' Luisa has never been so sad. 'But . . . ' he tries to argue with her. 'Shhh . . . ' she cuts him off. 'Mum . . . ' And she insists: 'Shhh . . . '

Two in the afternoon. Donato wakes up, goes down to the kitchen, fills a glass with water, drinks it and immediately spots the brown envelope in the middle of the living room. He walks over to it, picks it up off the floor. On the side that had been face down were the words: 'TIME TO GROW UP.' He opens it: inside there's a two-page letter. There is an apology first. Then a set of instructions. He is to go up to her bedroom, get the suitcase that is still closed with the airline company tag attached, open it. She says in one of the lines that follow that perhaps he should start with the exercise book and then move on to the DVD, since there's no television or Betamax video-player on which to watch the tapes that are there, nor a tape-deck to play the cassettes. There are also the two letters, one of which had been addressed to her and the other to Henrique. Everything about his biological mother and about the three-year-old him.

He opens the exercise book, reads as far as he can. He goes back to the Polaroid photograph, looks at the two of them: Maína and Paulo. Her face hidden behind the mask, the face that appeared in the edited footage on the DVD (Luisa explained in the letter that she had transferred them from the Betamax tape to a DVD in Recife (Recife as a place of transit) and then edited them to leave only the minutes in which Maína appears. If he wants to see the rest he will have to get hold of a machine for copying the tapes, which are now museum pieces) and a few drawings that are in the exercise book. His face is also in a drawing in the exercise book, but it's any old face, there's no way of knowing. Donato gets the computer, inserts the DVD into the drive. In her letter Luisa says the footage was recorded when Maína was a little younger than he is today. He sees her moving, smiling anxiously: he can barely keep his eyes on the monitor. She is beautiful, the most beautiful woman he has ever seen. Biological mother. *Mãe*. The voice he tried so hard to hear in the wooden owl. He opens his Gmail and writes to Luisa. *'You have no idea how much I hate you for this.'*

He had to go to a place called Galeria do Rosário to get hold of a Sony machine (which according to the shop assistant was made in nineteen eighty-eight) and also a ten-inch colour television. He was doing the right thing because transferring the tapes to DVD would have been more expensive. He watches; he finds nothing worthwhile, except for the minutes showing the three women, his grandmother and his two aunts, the place by the roadside, where they might still be today, although he suspects not.

It wouldn't be hard to find Paulo. In the exercise book there are the contact details for this woman called Angélica in Pelotas. One thing might lead on to another, they might meet, but Donato thinks not.

He buys a cheap tape-recorder. Paulo's voice appears in just a few places on the cassette; it's a considerate sort of voice. Paulo's voice will become a kind of nightmare within his nightmares. Waking up alone at home in the middle of the night will be a sort of training for dealing with his own cowardice (while it is transforming into something else, into a duty he will have to fulfil), everything is only a question of learning. That's something he's good at. Paulo's voice is outside the owl.

He walks the city. He reads the exercise book over and over again. He reads the letters that Maína left for Henrique and Luisa. It was Maína who asked Luisa not to give him the material till he was older, she was the one who asked Henrique to adopt him and never to reveal to him the way she had decided to die (he already knows, Luisa has told him in the penultimate paragraph of the letter). He studies whatever he can find in the way of books, dissertations, theses, newspaper and magazine articles about the Guarani people in the state. It takes him nearly a month. In that time, during which he doesn't answer Luisa's phone calls or respond to her emails, he starts feeling a nostalgic longing that, having no object, he never imagined anyone could possibly feel.

extract of a nightmare between two grown-up people

It was a very big house. The light coming in through the open windows made the walls even whiter, emptier. The forty-four-year-old man who introduced himself as Spectre was carrying a tray of sweets he said he'd bought in the German patisserie on the street where he lives. He was there to talk. There was this growing hatred, this antagonism between the two of them. There was no point having prolonged arguments, no point in acts of chivalry, in diatribes, in rebellion. Spectre was finally beginning to understand that there was no way of predicting what was going on in the head of this guy: the Guy. The Guy, who was either some kind of lunatic or in possession of the most colossal naivety. Spectre was determined to defeat him through exhaustion. The card he had hidden up his sleeve was the city, the city that inspired revenge: revenge was perhaps the only way to make it listen to them. There were clothes scattered around the room and wooden masks on the mattress. In a white t-shirt and jeans, Spectre was unable to contain his excitement. The Guy explained that he did not have a plan, that it was merely a personal, painful process and that he still didn't know how long he would keep it up. Spectre listened. The brightness of the day abated and then the temperature dropped, too; Spectre opened the parcel of sweets and asked the Guy to fetch them something to drink. It could be anything. The Guy got up, went to the kitchen, brought a bottle of whisky and another of mineral water. He put the glasses down on the wrapping paper from the patisserie. Spectre smiled awkwardly, forcing an innocence that did not come naturally to him. They drank, they ate. Spectre waited (even while waiting he could make progress). It got completely dark and then the Guy turned on the light, Spectre poured out another two whiskies, almost twice the size of the two previous rounds, and ventured that this escapade needed some record kept and that they could start right away. We will only exist if we accept each other, said Spectre, drunk now, having downed what remained in his glass. 'It's time for you to go,' the Guy informed him. Spectre stood up suddenly, took off his trainers, took off his jacket (the two of them are in identical outfits) leapt onto The Guy and tore off his face. 'I knew it was a beautiful face,' said Spectre with a twisted tongue, 'very, very, very beautiful,' already moving away from the Guy with his face in his hand. 'Give that back,' said the Guy, quite without aggression. 'No, I shan't give it back . . . Here it is, yoo-hoo . . . come and get it . . . ' The two of them were the same height; Spectre was not all that strong but he was sure that wouldn't make any difference. The Guy did not attack him (he would have been well within his rights to do so by the rules of chivalry). 'You're a spoilsport,' Spectre grumbled. Then the Guy, who was the owner of the house, the very big house, walked over to the door and opened it. 'Bye,' he said. 'I'll behave,' Spectre promised, and gave him back the face. The Guy closed the door and there the two of them were, two ghosts in a house with white walls, neither of them knowing what was going through the other's head.

Donato took the bus to the city centre, and from there to the outskirts of Partenon.

Docinho arranges the mess of papers on her desk, opens up the Severiano Timber Merchants and Sawmill reception, glances at the bustle out on Bento Gonçalves, switches on the ceiling fan, sits down in the swivel chair. Her new trousers are tight. That's the price you pay for looking good. Today is going to be quite something. On the radio she heard them saying it would be one of the hottest days of the year. She unlocks the drawer, takes out her hand cream. She examines her nails, the polish has started peeling. Pretty soon she's going to call up the manicurist and schedule an appointment for about half twelve. Guto hasn't called to say whether or not he's going to the opening of the GIG music festival. She has sworn it a thousand times: she isn't going to the party on her own. Standing there, matching them soft drink for soft drink, watching Celsinho 'Bunny' Coelho hitting on the other girls. Masochism has its limits. They're out of plastic cups in the water-cooler. She gets up, walks over to the next room, the office storeroom, gets enough for two days. When she comes back, she is surprised to find Donato standing at the reception desk. 'Hello,' he begins the conversation. 'Oh man, you startled me . . . How can I help?' She almost drops the cups. 'You stock balsa wood, don't you?' he asks. 'Balsa? . . . I'll need to check with the boss.' Donato comes closer. 'Tell him I need a block.' She smiles in an attempt to convey to him that there are lots of types of block. 'And what dimensions would that be?' trying to be pleasant. 'A hundred by sixty, a hundred by forty,' he says confidently. 'Millimetres?' He folds his arms, with a sigh. 'No. Centimetres.' She can't help smiling. 'Centimetres? Of balsa wood?' She writes the measurements down on a notepad on her desk. Normally at this point she would place a call on her internal line to senhor Deus, but the voice of caution tells her that she should discreetly lock the desk and the door to the storeroom, and go straight out to the warehouse, where the boss is usually to be found. 'Just a moment,' she says. He thanks her with a nod. 'Want to sit down?' she asks. He looks around at the room. 'I'm fine, I'll stand and wait.' She narrows her eyes, reprimanding him (somehow). 'I'll just be a minute, then, I'll be right back.' She goes out into the corridor that leads to the yard and the warehouses. (When she started working there she used to feel invaded by the stares of the other employees, so much so that she had considered going to work in an overcoat and floor-length skirt, but after a few weeks she relaxed, started to enjoy the frisson that she caused; now it's more to do with her actual self-esteem, and with Celsinho – that's Bunny – and one other guy there, who also walks all over her) and as soon as she goes past Wing, senhor Deus's right-hand man, she starts to move more provocatively as she walks. There's no doubt about it, these new trousers are quite something. Then she walks through the area where the other employees are, still showing herself off, approaches the boss, who is busy with the repair of one of the planers. She says excuse me, says there's an Indian at reception, but he's not one of those ones from around Lomba do Pinheiro. And how does she know? She knows that senhor Deus wants to know. It's because of his clothes and the way he talks. He's after some balsa wood, and he hasn't come for sticks or planks, he wants a block, a big block, she says, and hands him what she's written down. Senhor Deus says nothing, he's concentrated on trying to sort out the planer, he just raises his hand in a stop-the-universe-now gesture and, in a way that couldn't be ruder, shoos her with his fingers to give her to understand that he'll come out front soon. Docinho goes back to the office. When she walks into reception she gets another shock. The damned Indian has rearranged all the furniture (the only thing he hasn't moved is the table where she sits). 'You're crazy. You must be. My boss is going to fire me when he sees this . . . What am I supposed to tell him? He's going to have you out on your ear,' she complains. 'It's good to mix things up some-times, to look at things differently,' he replies. 'I don't want to know. Come on, help me put this back in place.' He smiles. 'I like the band,' he says. 'What band?' she asks, annoyed. 'The one on your t-shirt.' He's flirting with her. 'Sinatra?' She's surprised. 'Who else?' he asks. 'This is a joke, right?' She puts her hands on her head. 'I saw them playing a gig when I was a teenager,' he replies. 'Where?' she asks, her hands still on her head. 'In Curitiba.' 'They never played in Curitiba . . . ' She's unnerved. 'You must be mistaken.' And Docinho's boss walks into reception. 'What on earth have you done with this room, Docinho?' Time for some quick thinking. 'Senhor Deus, sir, I . . . I saw, I decided . . . That is, I thought it would look better like this – don't you agree?' He appears satisfied. 'We'll see about that later . . . How can I help you, kid?' turning his back on the receptionist. 'I'm after some balsa wood,' Donato says. 'I've got some cedar, some really light cedar,' he tells him. 'That won't work,' Donato retorts. 'Look, a block in those dimensions is really hard to get hold of, even in cedar.' I read on your webpage that you're the only people who work with it here in the city.' 'To tell the truth, we're the only people in the state,' Senhor Deus says proudly. 'On your page you say you supply materials to the most important sculptors in the south,' he insists.

'None of them works in balsa wood . . . ' and, getting impatient, 'look here, I've got some excellent cedar, I can get that cut to the proportions you're after. If you'd like to wait a few days I can get you mahogany, but I don't think that would be a better option,' he muses. 'It's not going to work, then . . . ' says Donato, firmly. 'Don't you at least want to take a look at the cedar?' 'I don't think so.' Donato is resolute. Then senhor Deus approaches him and takes his shoulder. 'Come on, son, I insist on showing it to you,' and leads him down the narrow corridor. 'Why exactly do you need a block of balsa wood in those dimensions?' 'Building model boats,' Donato plays along. 'Are you going to build a Noah's Ark?' 'To be honest, I was thinking about a Viking ship with rowing traction.' 'There aren't any motors that can simulate rowing traction.' The boy is good. 'That's just the thing,' Donato replies. 'What is?' He doesn't say any more. Senhor Deus doesn't want to lose his cool, he hasn't got to where he is by trading insults. 'You aren't going to say what you want the wood for, are you?' 'Is it a condition of sale?' Donato asks. 'Yes, right . . . no, it isn't.' He looks at his watch. It's starting to get dark suddenly, a storm is gathering. 'Let's go look at the cedar – come, it's over that way.' Senhor Deus does not need to work with valuable woods, it brings him more headaches than profit, but there's a prestige he likes to cultivate, especially in the local boatbuilding industry and among artists, who are the most demanding customers;

that's why he's used to their peculiar ways. He even starts
to miss them, they amuse him so much. This young man
seems to be on a level with his most annoying customers,
and he finds this invigorating. 'Will you have a coffee?'
'No, thank you.' 'Tell, me, how much do you know about
balsa?' Senhor Deus asks. 'Is this a test?' Donato asks. 'I
just want to know whether what you know measures up
to your requirements.' 'And this would help me to order
a block?' 'That's just the thing,' and he smiles. 'Right . . .
ok . . . ' and an animated expression comes over his face.
'If I could choose, I'd ask for balsa from Ecuador, which
to my mind is much better than what you get from Costa
Rica. I know Brazil imports a lot of wood from abroad, I
know a lot of it comes in illegally . . . Like everyone else,
I know that balsa is the lightest wood and, of the light
ones, it's the most resistant of all, which is why it's perfect
for what I need . . . I won't lie to you, the ideal would be
to get hold of a block that's as white as possible, with no
pink in it, and that doesn't weigh more than fifty kilos
per cubic metre, but I know that's asking too much, you'd
only get material like that from a tree more than eleven
years old that hasn't had too much sun; it would cost a
fortune here or anywhere in the world.' 'Fine, ok, kid, I'm
sold. I see you know the business.' They go into the warehouse. A few metres from the door there are four blocks,
each of them two metres high. 'Seriously, I think one of
these might really help you.' He takes a torch the better

to light up the detail in the wood. 'How much does it weigh, this cedar?' He hits the torch hard to get it to come on. 'Going by your spec, I'd say about two hundred and thirty, no more than two-sixty kilos per cubic metre.' 'That's not bad . . . ' Senhor Deus knows the boy is not going to take the cedar (he knows that this is not a transaction of any consequence); he changes his strategy. 'I'm going out back . . . ' 'What?' Donato doesn't understand. 'I'm going to make some calls, try and get two blocks of a hundred by thirty . . . And you'll have to make do with that. I've got good glue for it, I'll throw that in. Not least because . . . this whim of yours is really going to cost you.' 'Oh, I do think I'm going to need a little cedar . . . there are a few of the details that do need to be in a more resistant wood.' 'Just tell me how much you need . . . ' He turns off the torch. 'And about the balsa,' he goes on, 'give me a call tomorrow, towards the end of the afternoon . . . I'd estimate it'll be a week, if we're lucky,' already heading out. 'Now you mention it, how expensive exactly?' says Donato, not moving from the spot. 'Much more expensive than one of those Ecuadorian surfboards you can get at the little shops in Iguatemi or Barra Sul malls . . . You know what I mean, right?' he says, looking back over his shoulder and making a 'hang loose' with his hand. 'I . . . I d-don't surf,' Donato stammers. Senhor Deus opens the door to the yard (it has got completely dark, it's going to rain) and says, looking at the sky in surprise: 'I guessed.'

Catarina

In place of the fabrics, Donato used natural-coloured beach mats made from the filaments and fibres of flexible reeds. He cut them to size, he connected the pieces using gauze, wood glue, cobblers' glue, he made the trousers and then a jacket that closed in front with sticky tape. His hands and feet were left uncovered. Only after he has put on the fibre clothing (he doesn't know how painful it will be) will he put on the wooden mask. Almost every morning he looks at the Polaroid photograph. Luisa keeps calling, every day, and he doesn't answer. He only replied to one of the emails, a reply that said '*I'm alive and well*'. He thinks about identifying which tree Maína hanged herself from; according to his research, it is the place where her soul entered the earth. Thinking about this is hard. He looks at the photo, the masks made of paper and card, the paints whose colours he tries to make out under the sepia of the image's natural chemical decay; it's almost impossible to make out anything black or brown, the frames around the eyes of the masks, the eyes. Today would not be easy, because soon he has to make a decision about which chants he is going to use (the secret of what he's planning is in the chants, in the songs, even those that have been lost for generations can return in dreams; he doesn't need to be asleep to dream, any shaman knows that, any Indian, even a half-caste Indian, can be a shaman if he is alone). He sees no harm in being one of those Indians who prefer to think they are at war with the non-Indians, because the non-Indians all seem to want them kept at a distance. He has discovered that walking alone helps him to find the chant. If it does not come in a dream, an Indian can invent his own song. Donato is angry; when he's angry like this he shouldn't leave the house. Today Donato needs to leave the house. The chants help you to find someone who is far away and someone who is dead. He will get Maína's name right in the chant, he will stretch out the letter *i* in the middle of the name, the *i* is the most vertical of the letters. He was absolutely certain when he saw the owl flying over the water-tower of the DMAE, the municipal department responsible for water and sewage, in the neighbourhood called Moinhos de Ventos, on one of his walks. DMAE . . . Moinhos . . . *mãe* . . . Maína. For years the voice of the wooden owl has been in thought. Someone who dies does not speak, but invents his hearing. Maína will hear him. The spirit must know that it is still loved. Donato is confused, he is making things up. It's necessary to sing for a certain number of days. He still doesn't know how many. He's making things up. Even lost songs can come back. Donato looks at the Polaroid photograph. It is nearly two in the afternoon. He will sing to find the way back. The mask will connect their two souls. Donato puts on the straw clothes and then the mask. He opens the front door. It's one of those seemingly perfect days. It will take him almost an hour to get where he means to go.

Catarina emphasises what she has already said at the start of the interview. 'What matters is that I got together with my two best friends and set up this Foundation to bring music and dance to the busiest public spaces in Porto Alegre,' she says, looking across at the newspaper reporter from *Jornal Zero Hora*. 'We are giving people the chance to take possession of a ludic moment,' and she takes another sip of her orange juice. The journalist asks something else. She replies. 'It's a complex game that deeply touches the population who move around public spaces and touches those of us who carry out the project . . . I found myself facing more fear than willingness to get involved . . . I've also had to face my own reflection, and I think I have been a mirror to a lot of people.' She breathes in, straightens her posture, breathes out. 'Sometimes I get the impression that we're fated to a morbid narcissism and we aren't able to relate to the openness that we need, without making judgments, without prejudice . . . ' The two of them look at each other with the kind of complicity possible in interviews. 'Anything else, Catarina?' he asks with a smile. She has another sip of juice. 'You know something, Daniel? In the intervention in Praça XV, which is what those photos were that I was showing you, the street pedlars were aggressive. It was a natural sort of reaction to the sudden invasion of their space . . . We started slowly because we could sense that the atmosphere was tense . . . Things were actually going well . . . With each minute that passed I could feel their acceptance of us growing, their tolerance, their interest . . . then I noticed a black boy, strong, handsome, a bit crazy . . . The boy came over . . . He stood right in front of me, wanting to take part . . . I touched him, we began a choreography, he took control, he moved aggressively towards me, wanting to be in charge, he wanted to speak,' she says, and gestures quote marks in the air with her index and middle fingers. 'He wanted to express himself . . . and if I'd tried to speak, too, to speak just as forcefully, there might have been a confrontation . . . ' She stops for a moment, breathes. 'It wasn't an easy experience. As I said, there was a lot of aggression in the air . . . But that's the way it is; it's the price you have to pay . . . The poetic mustn't be a privilege, a hermetically sealed container, it has to be out on the streets, in everyday life, even if it isn't reflecting what is beautiful, what is pleasant . . . It's a part of it . . . ' She takes her glass of juice, puts it down in the centre of the table. 'Anything else?' the reporter asks again. 'I've already talked too much. I have to tell you, today hasn't been an easy day for me. I almost phoned to tell you I wasn't coming . . . It was better to come, to speak.' He confides to her that it has been a wonderful conversation and that he's going to fight to get a full page in the paper. He tells her a second time how much he admires her, she thanks him and gets up, he offers to take care of the bill. She thanks him with a nod. They walk over to the entrance of the Café do Porto and say goodbye. She leaves, distracted, down Padre Chagas (she's in the part of town where she was born, the part where things work, where it's possible just to wander at random), then turns left onto Fernando Gomes and walks as far as Rua 24 de Outubro. She is intending to go a few metres further down the pavement in front of the DMAE gardens and then take Miguel Tostes, then after that Vasco da Gama till she reaches the book-shop just before the corner with Fernandes Vieira, and there to check whether the book about popular dances from the twenties has arrived from the distributors yet. But a surprising figure, the figure standing outside the gate to the DMAE garden, catches her eye. It doesn't look like anything she has ever seen before. Someone is wearing a kind of wooden mask-cum-body armour that goes down as far as the pelvis, covering most of the torso, the neck, the face. A single piece attached to the shoulders and round the neck by leather straps and opaque, light gold buckles in the same shade as the wood. Underneath he is wearing a piece of clothing made of straw that must be hellish in this heat. The back of the head is visible, where it isn't crossed by the leather straps, you can see the brown hair in the gaps. Judging by the bearing, she has no doubt it's a man. He is holding himself very straight. It's quite clear he is not comfortable wearing that gear: his hands are still, close to his hips, holding the lower part of the mask-cum-body armour from which two wooden sticks the size of motorcycle handlebars are poking out, as though he were pushing a shopping trolley. Catarina wonders how strange it would be to see him in motion. She takes the phone out of her pocket, films for two, three minutes. Zooming in, zooming out. She walks closer to him. She stops less than two metres away, films a little more, she's careful not to stand within his field of vision, she just watches. People walk past not hiding their disgust at what they're seeing; there are not many who smile, even fewer who remain impassive. She tries to understand this. And she registers the chant, the low, almost inaudible sound that emerges muffled from behind the mask. It is a sad song, sung in a language she does not recognise. The funereal tone of it overwhelms her, breaks her, pulls her away from the errand she had given herself. Catarina closes her eyes, just stands where she is, listening. The two of them: the strangest couple. A few minutes go by before he stops singing. It takes her a little time to react, to open her eyes and see him (with a huge shock) standing right in front of her, face to face. 'I didn't mean to bother you,' she says. He doesn't reply, he just turns to the side, walks a few metres away (her suspicion is confirmed: the way he moves is startling). She is embarrassed, yet she still walks over to him, turns till they are face to face. 'Hi, I'm Catarina . . . The music you were singing . . . it's sad, and . . . and it's very beautiful,' and then she moves closer to the face of the mask to see whether she can see his eyes. 'Do we know each other?' The wrong question, Catarina. 'It can't be easy, being here . . . ' Another wrong question, Catarina. He takes half a step back. From close up, the mask is not so odd, even though the upper part of the chest is smudged with whitewash, sawdust and a yellow powder. 'Look,' she surprises herself at the liberty she is taking, 'I've just had this idea that you're going to find a bit nuts . . . but it's just that your silence is making me nervous . . . I do performances in public spaces . . . it's a piece of experimental work . . . and I really was interested in that . . . in your . . . ' this was not what she had meant to say. 'So . . . so that we can talk one day when you're free, I'll write my phone number very faintly here on the wood . . . ' She takes a pen from her bag. 'I'll do it in tiny little writing . . . ' She shows him the pen. 'May I?' He does not react. She reaches her right hand out to the body of the mask (her fingers are stained with something that looks like powdered baby milk; she thinks about asking him what that is, but doesn't). 'I'll jot it down here, where it isn't stained.' She starts to scribble. 'I'll write it very faint so you only need to sand it over to make it disappear again.' This takes more than a minute. 'It's come out very well. If you want . . . ' and she stops talking, she lets a few more minutes pass. 'Do you need any help?' she asks, her tone now less effusive. 'To be honest there is something else I want to write . . . ' He starts up his singing again (so quietly that she is not sure) and turns his back. She's awkward now. 'Well, I guess that's my cue to leave.' She walks around and faces him one final time. 'I won't bother you any more. I'll see you. You can find me easily if you look on the internet.' She goes off towards Praça Júlio de Castilhos. This guy is doing something worthwhile, people might not stop to look at him in the way they stop to watch her dance, but she is sure: everyone who walks past and glances at him, singing like that, even those who are scared, are not left indifferent. And she puts the pen back in her bag telling herself not to look back.

two sounds

That second time, Spectre would have to be something he's not been up to now: attentive, patient. 'So, you're the guy in the mask? Your father would be proud,' he said with irony. 'You think so?' the Guy retorted. 'This little spectacle of yours is ridiculous . . . I hope it's worth it.' Spectre knew what to do to provoke the Guy. 'And do you have the diary of the Indian who killed herself to hand?' he asked. 'In this folder here on the table . . . ' was the Guy's response. 'You still don't understand,' Spectre was trying to be friendly. 'All there is in the exercise book are the scrawls of a brainless girl who fell in love with a coward . . . I'm not even sure how to describe a cretin who gets a fifteen-year-old Indian girl pregnant then vanishes into thin air . . . ' The Guy sat down next to him. 'His name's written there. You can see the Indian girl crossed out his name wherever it appears,' said the Guy, and he put his arm round Spectre's shoulders. Spectre took a note out of his pocket and handed it to the Guy, saying: 'Just don't read it now. Wait till you're a long way from me before reading this crap.'

Ten to eleven at night. Donato wakes up. The experience has drained him.

The straw has chafed his skin and, in some places, rubbed it raw. Right, so now he is an ailing kind of superhero. Fine. He turns on his computer, still unsure whether he found what the girl wrote on the mask funny. PROPERTY OF CIRCUS CATARINA. He types what she wrote into Google, follows the link to a blog, but not hers, hers is a different one that's called just Catarina; he finds this only after he has typed the same search terms into Google using the Images category. A lot of photos of her. The girl is a local celebrity, the youngest in a family that created and *exported* ballerinas all over the world. There is a recent post on the blog under the title FRIEND with the word 'watch' linking to a page on YouTube: *http://www.youtube.com/watch?v=1EYmwfoa1mE*. She had filmed him on the pavement at DMAE. At the end of the video there is a telephone number. He gets his phone, then pauses, wondering whether he really ought to call.

Catarina gets onto the social networks, the chat functions of her email providers, the instant audio and video message programs to see which of her contacts are online, hoping to find one in particular, one whose status has shown 'offline' for a while. She has created the world around her with no great difficulty, she has been doing this for years, but right now, on this really strange day, she doesn't know what to do. Eleven-thirty at night. She gets up from her desk, takes off her clothes, goes to the bathroom, puts on the shower cap, she takes care to cover her ears, steps into the cubicle, turns on the shower, closes her eyes, lets the water splash onto her forehead. She hears her phone ringing. She finishes showering. Five to midnight. Phone in her hand. A missed call from an unfamiliar number. She calls back. 'Hello? Someone called my phone from this number,' she says. There is no answer. 'Look, I'm not in the mood. Tell me who this is, or I'm hanging up,' irritated. 'You are almost weirder than I am,' comes the voice from the other end. Catarina hangs up, throws her phone onto the bed. She puts on her nightie. She thinks a moment. She picks up her phone. Calls again. 'Hello,' the voice replies. 'You got one extra chance, asshole, this is your last shot, are you going to tell me who you are or aren't you?' 'I'm the guy in the wooden mask you wrote your little funnies on.'

'I never expected you to call so quickly, I didn't even expect you to look me up at all.' She's all set to explain herself. 'Look, I wanted . . . ' He interrupts her. 'To say you're sorry for your joke?' She goes on. 'I was going to write down the phone number and then . . . well, ok, I admit it: it was just me wanting to be annoying. Today wasn't one of my best days, I got some news yesterday that unsettled me. But I don't know why I'm telling this to a complete stranger.' Another silence. 'I'm not usually a joker . . . ' and she feels the conversation is about to go off the rails. 'I called to say that tomorrow I'm going to be outside the Sheraton Hotel. At three in the afternoon,' he says. 'Anything else?' she asks. 'I wanted to thank you for your attention this after-noon. You were generous. Today was the first time I've worn the mask. I thought it would be easier.' Catarina is disarmed. 'What you're doing is very brave . . . ' He interrupts her. 'The mask scared me just as much as it scares everyone else . . . You arrived in time for me to understand that I shouldn't give up.' She had meant to conclude her question about what that was all about, then, about what he meant by *generous*, where he got that chant from that had reached right into her soul and petrified her, but she stayed silent for a moment, and he hung up.

*

One in the morning. Donato connects to Skype. It's the first time he's done so since arriving in Porto Alegre. Luisa is away. Less than twenty minutes later, the call comes. Typical time for her. He accepts. Hi, Luisa. He turns on the camera. She turns hers on, too. The two of them look at each other: framed faces in different sizes on the screen. Noises from the two environments crackle through the speakers built into his laptop. Well? she asks. Both of them know they should not talk about the days that have already gone by. He says that being on his own has done him good. She says she understands what he means. He comments on the house and then says he has begun to suspect that this really is the place for him. Then she asks whether he's had a look at all the stuff she left. Many times, he says. He knows now that she was only fulfilling Maína's request. He asks whether she and Maína had been friends. Luisa says yes, that there had been an incredible empathy between them, but that Maína ended up becoming closer to Henrique, perhaps because Henrique had been so attached to her son. Donato lets her talk about it and, as he looks at her on the monitor, he realises that she is not the same woman who left the city more than a month ago saying she would be back in forty days. He knows that she's doing well without him. Luisa did as much as she could, there's no reason to condemn her. And she says that at first she thought the whole business of Henrique adopting him was lunacy, but they were not together at that point, there was no way she could have persuaded him against it. Luisa and her candour. Then they were left once again with no idea what to talk about and, out of the blue, Luisa says she's got herself a boyfriend, a guy her age. Donato just tells her he's been sleeping on her mattress, and she smiles (which he captures with a Skype screenshot) and then, herself again, Luisa replies that they can talk about that properly tomorrow.

liquidisers

Catarina arrived before him, sat down at one of the tables in the ice cream parlour on the other side of Barreto Viana, strategically positioned behind the tower of potted Swiss cheese plants that adorn the outside, she asked for the menu, put her video camera down on the table and waited. Here he comes, from Praça Maurício Cardoso. She starts filming. He stops outside the hotel. She keeps filming from a distance for a few minutes longer. Time to get up and meet him. She crosses the street and, still filming, walks over to him. 'Hi.' He's singing (and he doesn't stop to greet her). 'Can I film for a bit? This is a great camera, the sound quality is nearly perfect. I want to have some record.' He keeps singing, she goes on filming. Never crossing the boundaries of the public pavement, he walks close to hotel entrance. The take there lasts a minute. Eyes squeezed in between the fixed slits in the direction of the lens. She cuts to his whole body, which is now maybe some four metres away. Two security guards in black jackets enter the frame, approach the masked man, try to talk to him, but he does not interrupt his singing. The taller of the security guards waves his arms in annoyance, he's telling him to keep moving, to leave, get out of there. Catarina shouts: 'Hey, you can't force him to leave, the pavement's public space, didn't you know?' The guard turns to the camera and orders Catarina to switch it off. She cuts to the back of the man in costume. The security guard is yelling that the police will be here in a few minutes, that you can't be filming the front of the hotel without permission and that they are embarrassing their clientele. Catarina tells the guard he's acting out his role as the Wicked Witch of the West beautifully. The guard threatens to take her camera, but a group of people who have got involved in the situation stop him. (*What a lovely new opportunity has just presented itself.*) Catarina does not stop filming. The masked man sings more forcefully, louder than he has up till then. The police arrive, but (very much as a consequence of Catarina justifying the beauty of the peaceful performance that is taking place there) there's already a larger group supporting this *pair of performance artists*. The policemen tell them not to dawdle too long, they might get in the way of the traffic. Catarina keeps filming. The police leave. The security guards keep their hands off, but standing a little under two metres away from the man in the mask, they realise there is not much they can do. The masked man seems to be in a trance. She doesn't disturb him for nearly half an hour, she doesn't turn the camera off for a single second. But the time comes for her to say: 'Man, this isn't the right place for you, there are better places for you to be doing your ritual. Let's get out of here.' He does not move. 'I'm staying,' he says. 'You really are crazy . . . These guys are going to end up giving you a beating,' and she takes his arm. 'Let go,' he warns her. She obeys. 'What do you suggest?' asks Catarina. He doesn't reply, but she can see that he has been worn out by the whole thing. 'We can go to my apartment. I live with my great-aunt, but this is the day she goes out with her friends and she only gets back in the evening. There's the maid, but she's on my side.' Not letting go. 'Come on now, forget all this, for today, at least.' He hesitates. 'Come on, do it for me.' She gets behind him and gives him a push. He starts walking, sluggishly, with dislocated steps. And they have already been walking for more than fifteen minutes. 'Why have we been zigzagging round all these blocks?' he asks. 'Oh, you've discovered my plan at last,' and she laughs. 'You really don't know when to stop,' he says. 'To be honest, I thought you'd complain a lot sooner.' He stops. 'I was waiting till I was sure . . . I can't see very well in the mask.' She gives him an affectionate glance. 'So tell me what you think now? Have we already gone past the building? Are we far? Near?' He turns his back and starts walking. 'Right . . . Back this way, we're nearly there. The building's on this street.' He stops and turns to face Catarina. She's smiling and pointing at a building with a grey and blue frontage, many stories high, a hundred and fifty metres from where they are standing. 'The plan was to get you to break a sweat so you'd have to take that mask off.' She walks over and takes his arm. A police car passes them slowly and the two policemen look at them closely. There's no denying it: he has been gaining some notoriety. 'Seriously, though. Can I ask you something? Would you take off those clothes, and that mask?' He answers, 'That's not going to happen.' She grimaces. 'Have you got some kind of deformity?' she asks, concerned. 'What kind of deformity were you imagining?' he asks. 'On your face?' She adopts a scared expression. But he knows she isn't the type to be scared. 'Perhaps,' he provokes her. They reach the building. 'Shall we?' The gate opens (the man on the front desk has already seen her). They go in, she with her arms folded, cool. 'Hi, senhor Carlos,' she greets him with a wave and heads for the lifts. She presses the button, they wait. 'Do you like heights?' she asks. The lift arrives. She presses the button for the fifteenth floor, then reaches out her right arm to touch the surface of the mask, scratching it lightly with the nails of her middle and index fingers. He doesn't wait for her to ask: 'Balsa wood.' 'A custom-made life-vest,' she teases. They step out of the lift, walk over to 1502, Catarina rings the doorbell. The maid answers it, a girl of eighteen at most. 'Thank you, Fátima.' Catarina kisses the girl on the cheek. 'This is a friend of mine. You don't need to worry about serving anything because he has made a promise to one of the saints and he isn't going to drink, eat or take off the mask until Easter next year. You can make a green tea for me, leave it on the coffee table and get on with your own things without worrying about us . . . ok?' The maid excuses herself and leaves. 'Want to listen to some music?' Catarina asks. 'No. I just want to understand why we're here,' he says, looking through the windowpane at the privileged view of the inside of the DMAE water treatment plant. 'And I'd like to believe that the fact we're here started with a good coincidence,' she says, animated. 'A coincidence? I see . . . ' he replies. 'I try not to be afraid of good things,' and she positions herself in front of him (between him and the window). 'And how do you know I'm a good thing?' he says. 'I'm in a hurry to get to know you . . . And because I'm in this hurry, that's how I know. And when I know, I know right away.' She is touching the mask. 'And what if I'm violent, the kind of guy who might, say, cruelly take advantage of a situation like this?' She makes an angry face. 'Like in that Prince song?' He doesn't reply. 'In that case I'd use one of the dozens of protections that right now are scattered strategically about the house. All of them within reach, all of them very well hidden. Besides which, as you can see, I'm a strong woman . . . ' She shows off the strength in her biceps. He steps to one side and keeps looking out of the window. 'You like taking risks, Catarina, don't you? And completely gratuitously.' She shakes her head. 'I don't think the fact I want to get to know you is gratuitous at all.' The two of them stand in silence until the maid comes back in with a pot of tea and a cup. 'Thanks, *negra*,' says Catarina, looking him straight in the eye. 'I'm going to my room to get changed, to put on something lighter so I can dance a bit here in the living room . . . When I come back, will you do that chant for me?' He sighs. 'I will, then I'll go . . . ' She leaves the room, but comes back at once. 'And do you mind if I get the camera to do some filming?' she asks. 'No,' comes his reply. 'Great. I was going to say make yourself comfortable, like you could possibly make yourself comfortable wearing that thing.'

Catarina goes into what is supposed to be a bedroom, her bedroom. The nails and drawing-pins from her last street intervention have been on the bed for more than a week along with scraps of green plastic and two kinds of sticky tape: masking and double-sided. (She sleeps on the leather sofa in the library, and the bedroom is a mix of bedroom, walk-in closet, study, meeting room, video-editing room and office for her Foundation, especially when she needs to use the Mac to write up projects with other partners; the cleaner is allowed to gather up whatever's on the floor, hoover, tidy the clothes in the wardrobe, but never to touch the bed, the bookshelves or the desk.) She undresses, puts on an oversized jumper that goes all the way down to her knees. She takes the burgundy-coloured bag hanging on the clothes rail. She scatters berets, wigs and masks across the bed, picks out one of the masks, a kind of Spirit mask, puts it on. She looks at the disarray. It's the first time in weeks that she has been able to go in there without being overtaken by a mad desire to turn back the hours, the days. She gets the digital video camera that happens by good fortune to be in plain view. As soon as she can, she will ask the cleaner to clean everything and change the sheets and the curtains and leave the windows open and allow the sun, which is strong there in the mornings, come in. She runs to the living room. 'Sing for me,' and she takes off the jumper. He begins his chant, and she dances dressed only in the mask and her underwear.

With some effort Catarina's great-aunt is overcoming the restrictions imposed on her knees and ankles by osteoarthritis. She puts her key in the lock with care so as not to disturb whatever Catarina is up to this time (it's always easy to tell whether her great-niece is in the house or not), she turns it, opens, enters. 'What on earth are you doing, Catarina?' she shrieks. Seventy-two years on one side; twenty-one on the other. Catarina is losing the thread, she no longer understands the importance of the basic principles, she thinks she has mastered them already, she thinks that positioning herself critically against the canons of dance will make her somebody in the history of dance. She does not suspect how foolish she will feel a few years from now for having failed to tackle this most basic of disciplines like any other, for not having examined its technique exhaustively. The prizes that this great-niece won so young have done her harm. Catarina is pure impulse. Catarina is naked in the living room. And who is that thing in the terrible mask? 'I can explain,' says Catarina. 'Who is this pervert?' The old woman puts her bag down on the table by the door. 'He's . . .' Catarina hesitates. 'Get out of my apartment, you animal . . . What's that smell, have you been smoking pot?' 'Bettina, look, the smell is from the wood, the wood of the mask.' Catarina gets dressed. 'I don't want to know.' And looking at him, 'And you, I've already told you to get out of my sight.' He doesn't move, just watches her. 'Look here, you . . . you . . . whoever you are . . . Take off that thing . . .' She takes the glass ashtray from the coffee table like someone who means to hurl it if necessary. 'No,' he replies. 'My name is Bettina de Alencar Macedo, you scoundrel, and I am the owner of this apartment.' The maid comes into the living room, Bettina immediately turns to her. 'And you . . . I begged you not to let strangers set foot in here . . . You . . . you're fired.' Catarina goes over to him. 'Look, I'm sorry . . .' Bettina still is not satisfied. 'What's your name?' She gets between them. 'You don't have to answer.' Catarina takes his arm so they can leave the apartment together, but he doesn't move. Bettina addresses the maid. 'Bring me a pen and paper, quickly.' Catarina is trying to drag him out, but he is too strong for her. 'But madam, you've just fired me' (surprising Bettina with a cynicism that has not been apparent before now). 'Don't play smart with me, my girl . . . Go fetch what I've asked you to.' The maid does as she's told. 'And where do you live?' Bettina keeps going. 'That's enough, Bettina,' Catarina steps in. 'Why?' Donato asks. 'Because I'm going to report you to the police,' says Bettina, threatening him. The maid hands her employer a pencil and a sheet of paper. 'That's going too far . . . ' Catarina objects. 'You can find me on Avenida Cristovão Colombo, madam, number eight hundred and thirty-nine . . . It's a house.' Bettina is panting. 'You still haven't said your name.' The great-aunt is nervous, shaking. 'You've got the address now . . . I'm not going to go anywhere . . . ' Bettina puts a hand on her chest. 'You don't want to give your name? Fine, you'll be answering to the law all the same . . . And now, for the last time, remove that monstrous costume.' He moves towards the door. Catarina opens it. 'My name is Donato, and it wasn't a pleasure to meet you, madam.' Both of them go out into the hall. She won't go down with him, because she has to go back in and confront Bettina. She will tell Bettina that she has finally managed to embarrass her in front of a friend – one of the most polite ever to have been in that apartment. Her great-aunt will allow her to speak, and then she will say a dozen sentences that will demonstrate just how shaken she was by what she witnessed, sentences that will make Catarina understand that, this time, she is not joking.

insomnia

Spectre asked whether the Guy had heard of the Indian Poxi, or Guaraci, a mythological figure, a monstrous being capable of witch-craft, spells and dreadful deeds, less good at being understood by the other Indians. The Guy says it would be best if Spectre stopped his research now, he was getting sick. Spectre paid him no attention and told him that after a number of conflicts and misfortunes, Poxi transformed himself into the sun. They walked over to the window and looked at the day. As they shared the sunlight flooding in, the Guy said that he had kept the note Spectre had given him, he said he got nightmares from the drawing that was on it. Spectre gave a frightening laugh and said that soon the newspapers were going to report on the measures that certain bodies and the government were going to take against him. He assured the Guy that he'd be prosecuted as a threat to public order, for slander and defamation, but that it wouldn't make any difference, because ultimately they were never going to wake up again. And now it was the Guy's turn to laugh.

Catarina does not give up on Donato; in the space of two weeks she has made the masked man an internet hit, his public appearances attract more and more people, radio and tv programmes have already included him in their news broadcasts, a young musician from the city has recorded his chants and – using a backing track (and videos edited by Catarina) – is planning a performance accompanied by the Teatro São Pedro Chamber Orchestra for the end of the year, a performance which, he has promised, will be broadcast online. Donato's intentions remain unclear, however, to Catarina and everyone else. She needs to make him adopt a position (this is undoubtedly the next step), she tells herself as she drinks an Old Engine Oil beer at the Etiquetaria, looking at those walls covered with dark wood panelling and made even gloomier by the very weak light coming from the lamps and the chandeliers that give the bar a hazy texture. An oppressive place, but she likes it. They still have the spaceships, trains, racing cars, crazy buggies and assorted wind-up toys from the sixties and seventies, all of them incredibly well preserved, scattered in every corner and on the dusty surface of the coffee table in front of her. She always discovers some new toy when her drunkenness hits a certain point. She finishes her beer. She has given up waiting for the friend who was coming to meet her to hand over the items that were in the house of a mutual friend, a friend Catarina doesn't want to speak to any more. She gets up, pays for what she had and walks out of that darkness. It would have been good, actually, to have met the friend who didn't show up, to have a chat, but it's no use, there are some things she can't share with anyone. She walks down Protásio Alves. It's a lovely day. She comes to the little amusement park outside Santa Teresinha Church, buys twelve tickets, heads straight for the big wheel. She hands the bundle of tickets to the man operating it, telling him not to disturb her because she isn't getting off the ride till she feels like it. She gets into pod number six. The wheel starts to rotate; after a while she loses track of how many circuits she has done and it's then that she starts paying attention to the landscape. She looks at the crowds below her, recognising the lad in the blue cap she walked past earlier today on the street where her building is, then at the Bordini supermarket, and she gets the impression that he has been standing there watching her now for some time. He seems to have realised that she's spotted him (though she still cannot see his eyes), he turns, he walks away. There is nothing Catarina can do. There is no way of escaping from the pod without throwing herself out; it will be several minutes before she puts her feet on solid ground. Let him go. Poor thing (the best of them all).

Days later. Today Catarina has understood the reason for his fixation with the Sheraton. His target is actually the Sheraton restaurant: the president of the National Indian Foundation has lunch there when he comes to Porto Alegre to visit his girlfriend.

When he received the medical diagnosis the day before yesterday confirming that the youngest of his three daughters, the one aged a little over one and a half, has hearing problems – 'She suffers from severe auditory deficiency,' the doctor reported – what the employee who looks after the swimming pool at the Nautical Union Guild club felt was self-hatred, a hatred at having no way of meeting the costs of the surgery and the other hugely expensive treatments they had ahead of them. He tried in vain to sleep, and in the morning he couldn't look at his wife, he couldn't eat his breakfast. He needs a loan because he has no more time to lose; he went to his parish church to speak to the priest, but it was too early, he knew it was too early, the priest only arrives around ten. He wasn't able to wait, the bus took longer than usual. He lives a long way from the club. He arrived at the Nautical Union Guild to explain his absence from work the previous night and attempt to get his manager to excuse it. He had to wait for the meeting that the manager was attending to come to an end. His colleagues told him about a madman who was causing absolute mayhem outside the Moinhos shopping mall, which is the one at the Sheraton Hotel. At the time he attached no particular significance to this, but when he left the club, dazed, even with his manager having signed off his absence, the club employee thought it would not be a bad idea to go up to Quintino Bocaiuva towards 24 de Outubro, turn onto Tobias da Silva and walk on as far as Félix da Cunha.

The next thing he knows, the club employee is standing outside the Sheraton Hotel in the middle of a crowd of teenagers and curious bystanders, watching the guy wearing a carved wooden board that looks like nothing else on earth. Two cameramen, and two others who appear to be assisting them, are filming as though there were something important happening. The club employee can't see very well (the young people are all too tall). The man in the mask is talking into the microphone attached to the stand in front of him; his voice is not being amplified, it's only there to capture audio for what is being filmed. The club employee feels comfortable in the midst of all that pandemonium, he isn't alone. He wants to touch the guy somehow, to listen to him. He approaches. 'I'm not trying to make enemies, I'm not trying to destabilise anyone but, for all the reasons I've explained, I'm not going to leave the government alone, still less the president of FUNAI, this gentleman who spends more time travelling around Europe than signing papers in his office or visiting the indigenous lands occupied by farmers, by employees of the mining firms and all sorts of modern-day prospectors.' He stops for a moment. 'I'm not going to leave this gentleman alone, just as I'm not going to leave the National Health Foundation alone, nor the section of the police and the judiciary that are in hock to the colonels of the North, the Northeast, the Centre-West, dangerous people who at this very moment are with absolute impunity designing a plan to criminalise indigenous leaders using falsified evidence . . . accusations with no legal basis . . . protecting the slaughter of whole tribes . . . ' A very beautiful girl approaches the masked man to tell him that the FUNAI president's girlfriend is arriving in a taxi. The masked man speaks (the club employee is close and can hear): 'I challenge the Ministry of Justice and the President of the Republic to launch a complete review of the processes in which the leaders of the indigenous communities in these three regions have been condemned . . . As of today, I will give the government thirty days to dismiss the president of FUNAI . . . I . . . ', and he pauses. He walks the short distance to where the club employee is standing. 'You ok?' . . . The club employee is startled. 'What?' The masked man goes on. 'You helped me in the pool the other night. I could have drowned . . . ' The club employee is confused. 'You're that kid? Why're you doing this?' he asks. One of the cameramen positions himself beside the club employee so as to better frame his face. The surrounding crowd begins to shout (they cannot know why exactly). 'Isn't it dangerous for you, to be talking about the government like that?' he says, bewildered. 'The people who occupy indigenous lands, they're the dangerous ones.' The club employee tries to speak but cannot. 'All ok with you?' asks Donato. 'Me? I, um . . . I found out . . . ' – he feels worn out – 'that my youngest daughter is deaf.' The masked man tries to comfort him. 'I'm so very sorry for you.' It seems to be an effort for the club employee to speak. 'I'm sorry, but there isn't anything you can do for her, is there?' Donato stammers (when Donato is wearing the mask he never stammers), 'M-m-me? Bu-but what could I do?' The club employee closes his eyes. 'I know you can't . . . I just thought . . . I had to ask . . . because once you've missed your chance . . . I, I . . . don't know . . . We could do a swap . . . I . . . I can't seem to . . . ' The club employee leans on the mask, and even Donato letting go of the handles to try and hold him is not enough to prevent him from fainting and his body hitting the ground.

Lucinho Constante, president of FUNAI, needs another two years to finish creating the plan that he has been presenting at government seminars as 'the brand new, rationalised synthesis of the most successful programmes for the inclusion of indigenous peoples in the western world'. From Canada to New Zealand, he is testing the results (and he is sure he is headed in the right direction). He hates bureaucracy, he hates civil servants, those who have passed the public examinations and those with tenure, he hates the idiocy of the *sertanistas* who claim to be protectors of the forest and are really nothing but loudmouths with no ability to listen to, and support, their own families, who make endless claims about their love for the tribes that continue to hold out against the white man, but who lack the serenity to remain alert to the more fundamental demands of the day-to-day. He hates the alienation of academics, that breed that should be helping to discuss solutions, those fat peacocks; he hates those who don't mind killing and those who don't mind when others kill. He can't bear to hear any more about the Raposa Serra do Sol reserve; he can't bear to hear yet again that in nineteen such-and-such governor so-and-so liberated whatever lands in order to plant rice, soya, to extract timber; he can't bear to hear any more about the Federation of Indigenous Organisations of the Brazilian Amazon, about the Central Coordinating Organisation of Isolated Indians. His trips to Porto Alegre are his way of hanging on to what sanity he has left. Dealing with Indians, defending them while encouraging some willingness to compromise, is a fool's errand. A waste of time, sometimes it's just a waste of time. He didn't want to stop outside the hotel, he thought all the commotion looked unusual. He spotted the man, he was higher up than the others, wearing a kind of wooden armour. He asked the taxi driver to keep going. He called Antônia. They agree to meet in a more discreet restaurant in Menino Deus.

When Antônia leaves the Sheraton she realises at once that someone there knew, probably all of them knew, that she and her boyfriend had arranged to meet in that restaurant. The one in charge (she knows who it is: that brainless Catarina) approaches and tells her it's no use changing restaurant, they'll find out, they'll follow them. At the restaurant in Menino Deus, Antônia describes what happened. The president of FUNAI wants to know whether they were really filming, if it was one of those demonstrations with slogans, because when he'd gone past and been suspicious he hadn't seen anything like that. She tells him it was a group of people standing around a guy wearing a kind of armour made of straw and wood, and that he tried to approach her but hotel security came and she quickly got into a cab.

Lucinho Constante means well, but he is cornered (he can't quite articulate his research and networking strategy to the global authorities making advances in the field of solving indigenous problems). From that day on, he has tried to be more cautious. It is all going well, yet tomorrow, at this same late hour, a foreign journalist will track him down and, right at the beginning of the interview, will ask him why it was that about six months back he'd stated that the Indians in Brazil own too much land.

ready to destroy

'You know something, man? I liked that rumour about you working miracles,' said Spectre. 'The club employee having that fainting fit was perfect, and him reviving like that, telling everyone
you're special – oh go fuck yourself it was pure Hollywood.' The
Guy has already started closing all the windows in the very large
house. 'He was just really tired, worried about his family. I don't
know what more there is to it,' he replied. 'We need to use that
guy again, that guy is awesome.' It had been a while since Spectre
had got this excited. 'We're keeping him out of it,' the Guy replied
firmly. 'We've got everything lined up and ready to go, my friend,'
said Spectre. 'What for?' The Guy was having trouble closing one
of the latches. 'Don't you get it? We've got everything we need to
establish our own church.' The Guy finally managed to turn it and
shut the window. 'I'll give you a few days to think about it, we don't
have to decide anything now. We're doing fine. We're not in any
hurry,' said Spectre. 'I don't need to think about it,' retorted the
Guy. 'If it's up to me, the most you're going to get is a martyr,' the
Guy replied impatiently. Spectre laughed. 'A martyr? Really? Well,
a martyr works for me . . . You see? We work like a Swiss clock.' A

long silence followed. 'You know this isn't going to last,' insisted Spectre. 'But the point is that I'm not going to need much more time,' said the Guy, taking him by surprise. The Guy finished closing the windows. 'Can you tell me what you're planning?' Spectre wanted to know. 'No. You do your part, I'll do mine.'

until

Before dawn. The phone rings just once. 'Hello . . . ' says
Donato. 'Were you asleep?' Luisa asks. 'I slept a bit, but
I'd woken up.' 'Are you the guy in the costume?' 'I am.' 'I
don't know what to say . . . What's going on?' She hears
him yawning down the line. 'I'll start with the latest news.
I've received a summons to attend a Minor Offences Court.'
'What do they want from you?' 'I'm not really sure. There
are a few articles from the Penal Code they refer to in the
summons, but I don't know what they mean.' 'I'm going
to have to stay another month here in Goiânia. Which is
why I want you to come here. I'll buy your ticket as soon
as I get off the phone, and after this hearing we'll stay
here together until the day I go back to Porto Alegre.' 'If
you buy a ticket you'll just be wasting your time, Luisa,
your time and your money, because I'm not leaving Porto
Alegre.' 'You're going mad,' Luisa lets slip. 'Maybe I am.
Let's just check, on the fingers of my hand. One, the only
woman I've ever had in my life is my stepmother; two, to

prove the thesis of free will of the father who raised me I became the most un-Indian Indian you've ever seen; three, I grew up satisfied with the false story that my biological mother abandoned me; four, I have a biological father out there somewhere, someone I'm absolutely terrified of meeting; five, I can't stop thinking about Maína, about the road where she lived . . . I don't even know what right I have to have survived this long . . . ' Luisa will hear the rest of this without saying a word (she will just listen). Tomorrow she has to wake up early because she is on a thesis defence panel and she hasn't even finished reading the thesis, which, by the by, is not very good. Things really are turned upside down. Time is running out, but she's happy in Goiânia and she has absolutely no desire to see him again (she feels free), she has absolutely no desire to come back.

important days

Catarina's friend has incredibly good taste in interior design, a rare skill in making the best use of space. It isn't by chance that Catarina feels so at ease in this apartment, in this kitchen, and always asks her friend if she can borrow it when she needs to be alone with someone without having to resort to the embarrassment of going to a motel or to risk running into her great-aunt (a situation still unresolved). She opens the fridge, takes out the glass bottle of water, goes back to the living room and stands face to face with him. (She doesn't know that in the masked man's pocket is a poem he wrote for her less than four hours ago.) 'You all right?' Donato asks. 'I don't know . . . I did something really stupid a while back . . . ' Catarina says. 'Welcome to the Circus Catarina,' he tries to put her at ease. 'I'm not kidding . . . I did something wrong . . . Or not something wrong, but something that went wrong . . . It was just before I met you, and . . . it's ridiculous . . . because I swore to him, to this guy I like a lot or . . . it's just I swore to him I wouldn't tell anyone . . . but I can't do it, I'm up to my neck in this . . . ' He interrupts her. 'What are we talking about, Catarina?' She takes a few steps back and sits down. 'About a guy . . . a guy I still love . . . ' It was supposed to be the most important day. 'Who you love? . . . And do I know him?' he asks. 'No. I'd rather you didn't even know who he is.' She starts to cry. 'He hurt you.' Donato tries to keep his cool. 'Worse . . . He forced me to . . . ' She falls silent. 'Forced you to?' he ventures. 'An abortion . . . ' she says, sobbing. 'He was violent, is that it?' Donato asks sympathetically. 'He convinced me, he persuaded me, he blackmailed me . . . I thought I would get over it, but it wasn't like that . . . I wanted the baby, I really wanted a child, because it was this guy's child . . . you understand?' He has to interrupt her. 'And you're telling me this because . . . ?' She lies down on the sofa. 'The chant from that day outside the DMAE water-tower . . . it . . . after I heard it, in some way I can't explain . . . it helped me understand how much I regretted having got rid of the baby . . . When I closed my eyes and just tried listening to you . . . For those minutes I felt like the baby I got rid of was still with me . . . I mean, inside me . . . except it wasn't going to grow, wasn't going to come out, be born – oh, I don't know . . . But at the same time, and this is the crazy thing, it was comforting to admit what I was feeling,' she says, and dries her tears. 'You know it isn't really like that. It wasn't a baby yet.' She sits up again. She's looking better. 'I know that, I'm not a complete idiot.' She takes a deep breath. 'What matters is that . . . finding you, a faceless stranger, doing something I respected from the very first moment . . . in a way it made me stop and admit that I'd made a mistake . . . and it's nothing to do with morality . . . it's just that I wanted,' she starts crying again, 'I really wanted . . . ' Donato tries to make her see reason. 'A child isn't a toy, Catarina . . . and at this point in your life, you know . . . You're still so young . . . ' She gives him a crazy smile. 'I bother everyone so much already . . . a child wasn't going to make a difference . . . know what I mean?' Not letting him go on, 'He made . . . the bastard made me swear that I'd keep it secret . . . It's awful, it's an awful feeling . . . And the son of a bitch . . . he won't even speak to me any more . . . he just cut me off . . . I've been feeling so weird . . . a stranger when I'm around other people . . . ' and she looks at him. 'Except me . . . Am I right?' She lowers her gaze. 'Almost,' she says, awkwardly. 'That chant . . . ' she starts speaking again. 'If I were to choreograph it . . . and if I got into it . . . I thought it would help me face up to the situation . . . that we could be partners and we'd fall in love with a shared piece of work . . . and we'd fall in love . . . but you're so different, you aren't all jumbled up with the others . . . with the string of idiots I've known . . . the idiot I am . . . you're not jumbled up with anything.' He considers saying that she isn't being clear, but he doesn't. 'I think you're idealising me, Catarina,' is what he says. 'You idealise me, too,' she murmurs. 'I'm sorry. All along I've tried hard to understand you, not as an artist or . . . but for God's sake, if you'd just take that mask off at least . . . You can't even come out from inside this bizarre character you've created, this messiah figure I invented and you joined in . . . Know what I mean? I've tried to imagine what you must be running away from to get you to a point where you put on that mask and bury yourself so deeply in all this madness,' she complains. 'I have a purpose,' he says. 'A purpose,' mimicking him, his serious tone of voice and São Paulo accent. 'Catarina,' and Donato's voice comes out even more serious than usual. 'What?' she softens. And he says: 'I don't want to live any more.'

poem written not long ago

to drive out the mornings
to stand the past to attention
to cry in front of you
to have imaginary children
and put up with them
when they are more savage

and above all
when they sleep with no clothes on
during those fatal fights
in the damp chambers of the prison
built by your own hands
(at my wakes)

where there are no longer
any coincidences
nor the limestone shadows
from that dead day
on the dead pavement
outside that square

the day before the hearing

The president of FUNAI tendered his resignation, but the resignation has not yet been officially accepted. The number of the undersigned multiplies online, analysts are saying the masked man inspires people to pay attention, he is undoubtedly an unpredictable provocateur. At eleven in the morning he will speak at a small press conference called by Catarina (the first offline interview to have a wide reach) to talk about the meaning of his appearances and about the hearing at tomorrow's Minor Offences Court.

'What's the mask for?'

'The mask is an allegory, it has a personal purpose.'

'What would that be?'

'To reclaim my identity, my dignity as an Indian.'

'Reclaim your identity by hiding?'

'. . .'

'You've threatened the government. Am I right in saying that?'

'If talking about the dignity of indigenous people is

threatening,' he pauses deliberately, 'then I'm delighted to be the cause of such a threat.'

'Is there any way you could clarify a bit what you mean by dignity?'

'It's about returning the lands that have been usurped . . . When I was younger I thought the only solution was to take all the Indians and civilise them in the non-Indian way once and for all, but I was wrong.'

'Is it true you've done a deal with a toy company to produce a doll wearing a mask just like yours?'

' . . .'

'And that the toy mask will be removable?'

'That's absurd. It's never going to happen.'

'But if it did, do you think any child would want it?'

'Children aren't usually scared of things that are real.'

'Are you real?'

' . . .'

'Is it true that people have been mobilising and encouraging donations to your cause right across Brazil?'

'No.'

'What about this hearing tomorrow?'

'Justice wears a blindfold . . . A blindfold? I won't be going that far myself.'

Then, deliberately disturbing the rhythm of the interview (to tell the truth, this was the only reason he agreed to do it), Donato says he would like to read out two very short stories written by his mother, a young Guarani Indian called Maína who lived on the side of the BR-116 and who, like hundreds of other Indians all over Brazil, precisely because she was unable to see any sign of a possible future, committed suicide in nineteen ninety-three. After this, and as though it would be impossible to go back to answering questions, he volunteers to talk about the meaning of his chanting. He confirms that, yes, the straw and wood do hurt a little, and the interview comes to an end.

An hour and a half later, Donato arrives home. He turns on his computer, checks the messages. Another one from Rener. She has been sending messages for more than two weeks. They always say the same thing, to add her on Skype or make a reverse-charge call to the number of the house where she's living now. (If not today, then when?) He opens Skype, calls the number she has given him. 'Who is it?' the voice asks in French. It isn't a good connection, there's some hissing, but all the same he's so pleased to hear her. 'Curumim here, Brown Sugar.' She laughs. (How he has missed that laugh.) 'You told me to forget you, but I couldn't do it,' she says. 'I can see that.' 'I'm never going to forget you, my shy little thing . . . ' He says nothing. 'I wanted to give you a bit of news, and ask you for something,' she says. 'Just like that, after all this time? Ok. You've managed to scare me, Rener,' he stutters a little but it's barely noticeable. 'I'm moving in with a guy . . . ' she says. 'He's French?' She takes a moment to answer. 'Yes.' He leans on the table with the computer on it. 'And is he cool?' he asks. 'I think he's really cool.' He can tell she is happy. 'You're still very young for this, Sugar . . . You sure?' 'I love him, that's all . . . I got tired of changing boyfriends every week . . . and, another thing, I'm pregnant . . . ' This did shake him. 'You're going to be a mother? Really?' She lets out a shriek (one of those genuine Rener shrieks). 'I'm seven months gone already. So isn't that Proper News?' she asks. 'I . . . yes, of course, it's a huge piece of news. I'm very happy,' he says, unnerved. 'And now the request . . . drumroll . . . I want you to be the baby's godfather . . . You know how my family's Catholic . . . ' She is preparing the ground. 'I know . . . and Catholics . . . ' 'You know I'm crazy, right? And this guy, though I really do like him very very very much, well he's a lot crazier than me . . . ' Still preparing him. 'What does he do?' He takes on a paternal tone that makes no sense. 'He works in the circus, he's a clown . . . ' Coincidences. 'Now I can see our childhood games have gone too far.' She burst out laughing, she's jubilant. 'Things are coming full circle, Curumim. For better or worse, there's no way out. Accept it.' 'The godfather of a child, a child with two irresponsible parents?' he says happily. 'Right! The child of your best friend, almost the love of your life,' she says and laughs. 'Listen – you really love this guy?' Silence. 'I'd like to think so . . . He loves me very much, I'm sure of that.' 'Everyone loves you, Rener.' 'That time is over, Curumim, I'm no longer that revolutionary . . . Listen. I've already spoken to my parents, they're going to pay for the flight . . . and you'll stay here at mine.' He says nothing. 'I need to think. It's quite a hard decision . . . ' 'I know you'll accept . . . Paris will be good for you . . . I'll leave it to you to choose a name for her,' she says. 'Her?' and he can't contain himself. And Rener starts telling him everything that has happened to her in these past years and makes him laugh a lot. The Skype credits are running out. He will let them run out and then he will call her back.

When he came back to Brazil in nineteen ninety-five with only the clothes on his back and a law trainee's rucksack, the first thing Paulo did on walking out of the arrivals area at Salgado Filho Airport was get into a taxi and ask the driver to take him to Barra do Ribeiro (he didn't stop to think about whether the money he had changed in São Paulo would be enough for the whole fare). They passed the last of the three bridges that come after the Casa das Cucas, asked the driver to clock exactly six kilometres, and stopped nowhere at all. There was no more encampment. He made the driver pull over. He walked between the low shrubs, a sign that there once used to be a clearing here, a little open space, came to the foundations of the white house. Nothing left. He returned to the taxi, asked them to drive on a bit further south. He managed to find another three encampments; he stopped at all three and asked after the Indian women. They told him that they'd moved to a village in the north of the state, and that was it. Seeing that the driver was starting to lose his temper, he asked if they could keep trying just a little longer, the driver refused, they had gone much further than they'd agreed, and Paulo threatened to stay right where they were and not pay the fare, and the taxi-driver gave him another twenty minutes. They arrived at what seemed to be the last encampment. A well-spoken Indian who was very insistent on selling his handicrafts gave him the news of Maína's death. Paulo asked how it had happened and he said it would be best for Paulo not to know. Paulo grabbed hold of his arm hard, said the information was very important to him. The driver got out of the cab, telling Paulo to let go of the Indian. Paulo stopped short, apologised to the Indian and (in front of the Indian) thanked the taxi driver for his intervention (sometimes Paulo needs them). He looked up at that sky, the landscape that had acquired a threatening horizon. Time to return to Porto Alegre. On the way back, he couldn't look at the road. The first days flew by. A week, a week in his parents' house was enough for him to have his first crisis. He no longer needed the superhuman self-control that he had learned in London, in his homeland some kind of relief ought to be possible (relief that no longer existed anywhere), but no. Thinking that it will get better. Allowing himself to feel hope. This is the fatal symptom of a moment when you are no longer able to find peace. He started to medicate himself, fixed up some job or other to keep himself busy, went back to studying law to keep himself busy; he couldn't get seriously involved with anybody. One day he started teaching at a social awareness programme in Vila Cruzeiro. It was this that kept him going. And so the years went by. Trying not to succumb once more to the confusion of thoughts, trying not to give in to panic and to the growing fragility of his emotions. He met new people, had girlfriends, watched his friends get poorer, get richer, marry, separate, people who had been alienated going into politics, people bursting with ideas getting tired of politics. There was no place to hide: his friends are the new impresarios, the judges who will soon become High Court judges, High Court judges who will soon be serving on the Supreme Court, coordinators of the most important government programmes, actors, writers, state police chiefs, heads of the Federal Police, members of the Public Ministry, academics, newspaper editors, owners of high-traffic blogs, tweeters with many followers, advertisers, diplomats. Life goes on. He enrolled in the master's programme to keep himself busy and completed it with honours to keep himself busy, he started teaching on a law course, one of those really crappy ones in a far-flung corner of Rio Grande do Sul just to keep himself busy. Paulo saved up money and bought himself an apartment in the centre of Porto Alegre when it wasn't yet fashionable to live in the centre of Porto Alegre. His parents still keep up a crazy pace of trips with married friends of theirs. His sister has married a Canadian and had four children, she isn't planning to come back to Brazil. A lot has happened in the world. He never heard from Rener again, or the Lebanese men. Two years ago, Leonardo, who is today one of the country's District Prosecutors, invited him to be his chief of staff, Paulo did not want to accept (working with a friend, as his subordinate, is one of the hardest things), but he accepted. Today is the graduation day of the girl who is working as an intern in Leonardo's office. The Ceremonial Hall at the state university is packed. Paulo hasn't the patience to watch guys his age showing off long-legged twenty-year-olds with highlights in their hair, each one more Miss Brazil than the last, the keys to their imported cars, their thousand-*real* suits, their anabolic workout. The intern is a sweet girl but she isn't worth the sacrifice. Paulo leaves at the beginning of the guest of honour's speech. He leaves the building, crosses Avenida Osvaldo Aranha heading towards Independência. He's hungry, he decides to have dinner in a restaurant in Barros Cassal, where the food is good and cheap. He sits at a table in front of the television because it's the furthest from the table where the members of a crummy local band are sitting, yet another crummy band trying to relive a great moment in the world history of rock music, with their stereotypical clothes and a breed of dog in their name. Right in time for the news. He asks for a steak with a fried egg, listens to the story about that Indian in the mask who is going to have a hearing tomorrow afternoon at the Central Forum. Yet another dickhead doing whatever he can to draw attention to himself. He is being accused of theft, but there are many other accusations. The man gives laconic answers to a few questions and then asks if he can tell some stories by his mother, an Indian woman called Maína. Paulo gets up, walks straight over to the volume button, turns it up to maximum. The guys from the appalling band protest. He shrugs, tells them to go suck Bob Dylan's greasy dick. The story told by the man in the mask is about an old Indian woman who spent her days by the side of the road gathering up loose pages from newspapers and magazines carried there on the wind, and Paulo begins to shake, he is shaking from his head down to his feet, and one day, the masked man continues, the old Indian woman was bitten by a lizard and before fainting from the poison that was circulating round her body she made a bonfire of the paper she had gathered and when the flames began to imitate a sacred song of return the Indian woman dressed herself in them and disappeared. Paulo turns, takes his blazer off the back of the chair and leaves the restaurant. He doesn't even look at the guys from the band gesturing for him to go fuck himself.

palindromes (second part)

Paulo steps out of the lift, turns right and sees that he has arrived on time. Lawyers, interns, curious bystanders, litigants, civil servants, security guards; apart from the journalists almost everyone is troubled by the presence of the man in the mask. Paulo approaches. 'You're a very brave lad,' he says. Donato turns. 'Sorry, senhor, I'm not in the mood to talk.' Though the sound that comes out from behind the mask is muffled, it's possible to hear that he is apprehensive (over the years Paulo has become good at detecting apprehensiveness). 'And your followers?' Paulo asks. 'I'm on my own,' says Donato. 'Don't you get cramps standing in the same position for such a long time?' He ventures this other question. 'Sorry if I wasn't clear, senhor, I don't want to talk,' he replies. 'Wouldn't it have been better to call for a lawyer to go with you? I can offer my services for free. It would be a pleasure to go into that hall with you,' and he gestures towards the hearing room. 'Let the world adapt,' Donato says and moves away from him. 'They're going to make you take off that mask . . . ' Paulo follows him. 'I've stuck my forehead to the mask with superglue.' Donato does not stop walking. 'I knew Maína, your mother . . . ' Paulo says. Donato stops. 'What's your name?' 'Paulo.' 'I was planning to hang myself tomorrow, Paulo.' And Catarina runs over. 'I'm sorry, I'm so late, aren't I?' and hugs Donato. 'Catarina, I'd like to introduce you to my biological father: Paulo.' Paulo moves away and, pathetic as always, seeks support from the wall. 'Are you kidding?' she says. 'Can you give us a moment, Catarina?' Paulo is looking down at the floor as if the floor might suddenly disappear. Catarina leaves. And Donato, understanding what it is to be two dead men (in Maína's final breath), wants to hear a little more of the voice that till this moment he has only heard in the hissing of the recording that dribbled out of one of the audio cassettes that Luisa kept.

For Maina

And for Donato

Rener

I got up at five in the morning, turned off my computer, went into the living room, picked up the mask that was still on the floor, tore off the leather straps, leaving just the wood, I sawed it in half. I looked out the window, it was still raining. After so many years, it was still raining. Sometimes, in secret, I would drive to Pelotas trying randomly to find Angélica and return her exercise book. I would order a coffee at Aquários and then I'd return to Porto Alegre. Luisa never knew about my return trips Pelotas. Luisa doesn't know I used her in the story. She doesn't know about the times I stopped the car by the roadside and made a huge mental effort to get time to turn back. Luisa is going to hate the way I decided to depict her, she'll hate where I've put her. Luisa has been the only important person in my life these past few years, but I can tell how tired she is. They say it's normal to be demanding and take advantage of those we like most. It was you, Luisa, who suggested I write this story, after all. Perhaps I'll replace your name with another, with Carla Cecília, perhaps. I don't know. I keep wondering what people who know me are going to say. Will it give my political enemies new arguments to use? Is it a completely ridiculous idea that – when I drove back those few kilometres, unable to go very fast because of the storm – I found the Indian girl dead? Would that revelation be too absurd? Now here comes the difficult part of this whole epic play, Luisa. Nobody knows that I tried to revive her, nobody reported that her body rolled over, and she was lying face up on the ground, and her pregnancy was visible. There was no sign of life. I touched her – understand? I touched her and I didn't have the courage to put her in the Beetle. I will never be able to save the country or the world, Luisa, writing plays doesn't have that sort of power. I know it's not wise, the idea of seeing a life within the dream of a dead person. I'm sorry, Luisa. But I think that's what it's like when you can't see a way out: nothing is apart, life is what it is, engagement, defeated generations, and we get used to the pain, the pain that will, finally, do the rest.

author's
acknowledgments

Besides the advice and invaluable friendship of Isa Pessoa, I am immensely grateful for the partial readings undertaken by Anna Dantes, Antônio Xerxenesky, Beto Brant, Camila Dalbem, Daniel Galera, Fernanda D'Umbra, Maína Mello and Olavo Amaral, and for the extremely pertinent suggestions they made. Likewise the reading of two thirds of the second version out loud (so that I could get a sense of the way it sounded) by the actress Glauce Guima. In addition: the bibliographic references furnished by Ana Elisa de Castro Freitas, Alberto Mussa and Marta Machado, and the advice of Gilson Vargas, Joca Reiners Terron, Ronaldo Bressane and Simone Campos. Finally, to Marcelo Ferroni and André Marinho and their respective editorial teams, as well as to the staff of Petrobras and the Ministry of Culture.

There were two days, when I was still living in the Jardim Botânico neighbourhood of Rio de Janeiro, when

I read the first version of the novel to Marlene Iara Rocha Scott and Elói Rodrigues Scott, ever-present parents; besides the fun of it, there were little suggestions I did not follow, valuable though these suggestions were.

The titles of the first two chapters and the fourth were taken, with the poet's permission, from *Fragma* (Expressão Gráfica e Editora Ltd. – Fortaleza, 2007) by Cândido Rolim – my way of paying tribute to this remarkable writer.

Part of the interview given by Catarina to the reporter in the final chapter was adapted, with permission, from the interview I carried out with Thais Petzhold, who with Laura Leiner and Fernanda Chemale ran the Projeto Transeuntes (the Travellers' Project).

Dear readers,

We rely on subscriptions from people like you to tell these other stories – the types of stories most publishers consider too risky to take on.

Our subscribers don't just make the books physically happen. They also help us approach booksellers, because we can demonstrate that our books already have readers and fans. And they give us the security to publish in line with our values, which are collaborative, imaginative and 'shamelessly literary'.

All of our subscribers:

- receive a first-edition copy of each of the books they subscribe to
- are thanked by name at the end of these books
- are warmly invited to contribute to our plans and choice of future books

BECOME A SUBSCRIBER, OR GIVE A SUBSCRIPTION TO A FRIEND

Visit andotherstories.org/subscribe to become part of an alternative approach to publishing.

Subscriptions are:

£20 for two books per year

£35 for four books per year

£50 for six books per year

OTHER WAYS TO GET INVOLVED

If you'd like to know about upcoming events and reading groups (our foreign-language reading groups help us choose books to publish, for example) you can:

- join the mailing list at: andotherstories.org/join-us
- follow us on Twitter: @andothertweets
- join us on Facebook: facebook.com/AndOtherStoriesBooks
- follow our blog: Ampersand

This book was made possible thanks to the support of:

AG Hughes
Adam Butler
Adam Lenson
Adrian May
Aidan Cottrell-Boyce
Aine Bourke
Ajay Sharma
Alan Ramsey
Alastair Dickson
Alastair Gillespie
Alastair Laing
Alec Begley
Alex Martin
Alex Ramsey
Alex Webber &
    Andy Weir
Alexandra Buchler
Alexandra de
    Verseg-Roesch
Ali Conway
Ali Smith
Alice Nightingale
Alisa Brookes
Alison Hughes
Alison Winston
Allison Graham
Alyse Ceirante
Amanda Anderson
Amanda Banham
Amanda Dalton
Amanda Love
    Darragh
Amelia Ashton

Amy Capelin
Amy Sharrocks
Amy Webster
Ana Amália Alves
Andrea Davis
Andrew Marston
Andrew McCafferty
Andrew Nairn
Andrew Pattison
Andy Burfield
Andy Paterson
Angela Creed
Angela Thirlwell
Angharad Eyre
Angus MacDonald
Angus Walker
Ann McAllister
Ann Van Dyck
Anna Britten
Anna Milsom
Anna Vinegrad
Anna-Karin Palm
Annabel Gaskell
Annalise Pippard
Anne Carus
Anne
    Claydon-Wallace
Anne Maguire
Anne Waugh
Anne Claire Le Reste
Anne Marie Jackson
Annette Nugent
Annie McDermott

Anonymous
Anthony Quinn
Antony Pearce
Archie Davies
Asher Norris
Averill Buchanan
Ayca Turkoglu

Barbara Adair
Barbara Latham
Barbara Mellor
Barbara Thanni
Barbara Zybutz
Barry Norton
Bartolomiej Tyszka
Belinda Farrell
Ben Schofield
Ben Smith
Ben Thornton
Benjamin Judge
Bettina Debon
Bianca Jackson
Blanka Stoltz
Brenda Scott
Brendan McIntyre
Briallen Hopper
Bruce Ackers
Bruce & Maggie
    Holmes
Bruce Millar

C Baker
C Mieville

Calum Colley
Candy Says Juju
    Sophie
Cara & Bali Haque
Caroline Adie
Caroline Perry
Caroline Rigby
Carolyn A Schroeder
Carrie
    Dunham-LaGree
Cath Drummond
Cecily Maude
Charles Beckett
Charles Fernyhough
Charles Lambert
Charles Rowley
Charlotte Baines
Charlotte Holtam
Charlotte Middleton
Charlotte Ryland
Charlotte Whittle
Chris Day
Chris Gribble
Chris Lintott
Chris Radley
Chris Stevenson
Chris Wood
Christina Baum
Christina
    MacSweeney
Christina Scholz
Christine Lovell
Christine Luker
Christopher Allen
Christopher Marlow

Ciara Ní Riain
Ciarán Oman
Claire Brooksby
Claire Mitchell
Claire Tranah
Clare Fisher
Clare Keates
Clare Lucas
Clarissa Botsford
Claudio Guerri
Clifford Posner
Clive Bellingham
Colin Burrow
Collette Eales
Courtney Lilly
Craig Barney

Damien Tuffnell
Dan Pope
Daniel Barley
Daniel Carpenter
Daniel Gillespie
Daniel Hahn
Daniel Hugill
Daniel Lipscombe
Daniel Ng
Daniel Sheldrake
Daniel Venn
Daniel James Fraser
Daniela Steierberg
Dave Lander
David Archer
David Breuer
David Craig Hall
David Eales

David Gould
David Hebblethwaite
David Hedges
David Higgins
David
    Johnson-Davies
David Roberts
David Smith
Dawn Mazarakis
Debbie Pinfold
Deborah Bygrave
Deborah Smith
Delia Cowley
Denise Jones
Denise Sewell
Diana Brighouse
DW Wilson &
    A Howard

E Jarnes
Eddie Dick
Edward Baggs
Eileen Buttle
EJ Baker
Elaine Martel
Elaine Rassaby
Eleanor Maier
Elina Zicmane
Eliza O'Toole
Elizabeth Cochrane
Elizabeth Draper
Elizabeth Polonsky
Emily Jeremiah
Emily Rhodes
Emily Taylor

Emily Williams
Emily Yaewon Lee &
   Gregory Limpens
Emma Bielecki
Emma Kenneally
Emma Teale
Emma Timpany
Eric Langley
Erin Louttit
Eva Tobler-Zumstein
Ewan Tant

Fawzia Kane
Federay Holmes
Ferdinand Craig Hall
Fiona Doepel
Fiona Malby
Fiona Powlett Smith
Fiona Quinn
Florian Andrews
Fran Sanderson
Frances Chapman
Frances Perston
Francesca Bray
Francis Taylor
Francisco Vilhena
Freya Carr

G Thrower
Gale Pryor
Garry Wilson
Gavin Collins
Gawain Espley
Genevra Richardson
George McCaig

George Sandison &
   Daniela Laterza
George Savona
George Wilkinson
Georgia Panteli
Geraldine Brodie
Gill Boag-Munroe
Gillian Cameron
Gillian Doherty
Gillian Jondorf
Gillian Spencer
Gina Dark

Giselle Maynard
Gloria Sully
Glyn Ridgley
Gordon Cameron
Gordon Campbell
Gordon Mackechnie
Graham R Foster
Graham Hardwick
Graham & Steph
   Parslow
Guy Haslam
Gwyn Wallace

Hannah Perret
Hanne Larsson
Hannes Heise
Harriet Gamper
Harriet Mossop
Harriet Sayer
Harriet Spencer
Harrison Young
Helen Asquith
Helen Bailey

Helen Buck
Helen Collins
Helen Weir
Helen Wormald
Helena Taylor
Helene Walters
Henrike
   Laehnemann
Hilary McPhee
Howdy Reisdorf
Hugh Buckingham

Ian Barnett
Ian McMillan
Inna Carson
Irene Mansfield
Isabel Costello
Isabella Garment
Isobel Dixon
Isobel Staniland

J Collins
Jack Brown
Jacky Oughton
Jacqueline Crooks
Jacqueline & Alistair
   Douglas
Jacqueline Haskell
Jacqueline
   Lademann
Jacqueline Taylor
Jacquie Goacher
Jade Maitre
Jade Yap
James Clark

James Cubbon
James Huddie
James Portlock
James Scudamore
James Tierney
James Upton
James & Mapi
Jane Brandon
Jane Whiteley
Jane Woollard
Janet Bolam
Janet Mullarney
Janette Ryan
Jasmine Dee Cooper
Jasmine Gideon
Jason Spencer
JC Sutcliffe
Jen Grainger
Jen Hamilton-Emery
Jenifer Logie
Jennifer Higgins
Jennifer Hurstfield
Jennifer O'Brien
Jennifer Watson
Jenny Diski
Jenny Newton
Jeremy Weinstock
Jerry Lynch
Jess Wood
Jethro Soutar
Jillian Jones
Jim Boucherat
Jo Elvery
Jo Harding
Jo Hope

Joan Clinch
Joanna Ellis
Joanne Hart
Jocelyn English
Joel Love
Johan Forsell
Johannes Georg Zipp
John Allison
John Conway
John Fisher
John Gent
John Stephen
    Grainger
John Griffiths
John Hodgson
John Kelly
John Nicholson
Jon Iglesias
Jon Lindsay Miles
Jon Riches
Jonathan Evans
Jonathan Shipley
Jonathan Watkiss
Joseph Cooney
Josephine Burton &
    Jeremy Gordon
Joy Tobler
JP Sanders
Judith Norton
Judy Kendall
Julian Duplain
Julian Lomas
Julian I Phillippi
Juliane Jarke
Julie Freeborn

Julie Gibson
Julie Van Pelt
Juliet Swann

Kaarina Hollo
Kaitlin Olson
Kalbinder Dayal
Kapka Kassabova
Karan Deep Singh
Kari Dickson
Karla Fonesca
Katarina Trodden
Kate Gardner
Kate Griffin
Kate Leigh
Kate Rhind
Kate Waugh
Kate Young
Katharina Liehr
Katharine Freeman
Katharine Robbins
Katherine Jacomb
Katherine Wootton
    Joyce
Kathryn Lewis
Kathy Owles
Katia Leloutre
Katie Martin
Katie Smith
Kay Elmy
Keith Alldritt
Keith Dunnett
Ken Walsh
Kevin Acott
Kevin Brockmeier

Kevin Pino
KL Ee
Koen Van Bockstal
Kristin Djuve
Krystalli Glyniadakis

Lana Selby
Larry Colbeck
Laura Bennett
Laura Jenkins
Laura Solon
Laura Woods
Lauren Ellemore
Lauren Kassell
Leanne Bass
Leni Shilton
Lesley Lawn
Lesley Watters
Leslie Leuck
Leslie Rose
Linda Harte
Lindsay Brammer
Lindsey Ford
Liz Clifford
Liz Ketch
Liz Tunnicliffe
Liz Wilding
Loretta Platts
Lorna Bleach
Louise
    Bongiovanni
Louise Rogers
Lucie Donahue
Lucy Luke
Lynn Martin

M Manfre
Madeleine
    Kleinworth
Maggie Peel
Maisie & Nick Carter
Malcolm Bourne
Mandy Boles
Mansur Quraishi
Marella Oppenheim
Mareta & Conor
    Doyle
Margaret Jull Costa
Maria Pelletta
Marina Castledine
Marina Lomunno
Marion Cole
Marion Tricoire
Mark Ainsbury
Mark Howdle
Mark Richards
Mark Stevenson
Mark Waters
Marta Muntasell
Martha Gifford
Martha Nicholson
Martin Brampton
Martin Conneely
Martin Hollywood
Mary Hall
Mary Wang
Mary Ann Horgan
Mathias Enard
Matt Oldfield
Matt Riggott
Matthew Bates

Matthew Francis
Matthew Lawrence
Matthew Steventon
Matthew Todd
Maureen Cooper
Maureen Freely
Maxime
    Dargaud-Fons
Melissa da Silveira
    Serpa
Michael Harrison
Michael Johnston
Michael Kitto
Michael & Christine
    Thompson
Michelle Bailat-Jones
Michelle Purnell
Michelle Roberts
Miles Visman
Milo Waterfield
Monika Olsen
Morgan Lyons
Moshi Moshi
    Records
Murali Menon

N Jabinh
Nadine El-Hadi
Nan Craig
Nan Haberman
Nancy Pile
Naomi Frisby
Nasser Hashmi
Natalie Smith
Natalie Wardle

Natasha
    Soobramanien
Nathaniel Barber
Nia Emlyn-Jones
Nicci Rodie
Nick Chapman
Nick James
Nick Judd
Nick Nelson &
    Rachel Eley
Nick Williams
Nicola Balkind
Nicola Cowan
Nicola Hart
Nina Alexandersen
Nina Power
Noah Birksted-Breen
Nora Gombos
Nuala Watt

Olga Zilberbourg
Owen Booth

PM Goodman
Pamela Ritchie
Pat Crowe
Patricia Appleyard
Patrick Owen
Paul Bailey
Paul Dettman
Paul Gamble
Paul Hannon
Paul Hollands
Paul Jones
Paul Miller

Paul Munday
Paul Myatt
Paul Sullivan
Paulo Santos Pinto
Penelope Price
Peter Law
Peter Lawton
Peter Murray
Peter Rowland
Peter Vos
Philip Warren
Philippe Royer
Phyllis Reeve
Piet Van Bockstal
Pipa Clements
Polly McLean

Rachael Williams
Rachel Bailey
Rachel Henderson
Rachel Kennedy
Rachel Van Riel
Rachel Watkins
Read MAW Books
Rebecca Atkinson
Rebecca Braun
Rebecca Moss
Rebecca Rosenthal
Regina Liebl
Renata Larkin
Rhian Jones
Richard Ellis
Richard Jackson
Richard Martin
Richard Smith

Richard Wales
Rishi Dastidar
Rob Jefferson-Brown
Robert Gillett
Robert Saunders
Robin Patterson
Robin Woodburn
Rodolfo Barradas
Rory Sullivan
Ros Schwartz
Rose Cole
Rose Skelton
Rosemary Rodwell
Rosie Hedger
Rosie Pinhorn
Ross Macpherson
Rossana
Russell Logan
Ruth F Hunt
Ruth Stokes

SE Guine
SJ Bradley
SJ Naude
Sabine Griffiths
Sally Baker
Sam Ruddock
Samantha
    Sabbarton-Wright
Samantha Sawers
Sandra de Monte
Sandra Hall
Sandy Derbyshire
Sara D'Arcy
Sarah Benson

Sarah Bourne
Sarah Butler
Sarah Fakray
Sarah Pybus
Sarah Salmon
Sarah Salway
Saskia Restorick
Scott Morris
Sean Malone
Sean McGivern
Seini O'Connor
Selin Kocagoz
Sharon Evans
Shazea Quraishi
Sheridan Marshall
Sherine El-Sayed
Shirley Harwood
Sigrun Hodne
Simon Armstrong
Simon M Garrett
Simon John
   Harvey
Simon Okotie
Simon Pare
Simon Pennington
Simon Thomson
Sinead Rippington
Siobhan Higgins
Sonia McLintock
Sophie Eustace
Sophie North
Stef Kennedy
Steph Morris
Stephanie Brada
Stephen Abbott

Stephen Pearsall
Stephen H Oakey
Stewart McAbney
Stuart Condie
Sue & Ed Aldred
Sue Doyle
Sunil Samani
Susan Tomaselli
Susie Roberson
Suzanne White
Sylvie Zannier-Betts

Tammy Watchorn
Tamsin Ballard
Tania Hershman
Tasmin Maitland
Thomas Bell
Thomas Bourke
Thomas Fritz
Thomas JD Gray
Tien Do
Tim Gray
Tim Robins
Tim Theroux
Tim Warren
Timothy Harris
Tina Andrews
Tina Rotherham-
   Winqvist
Todd Greenwood
Tom Bowden
Tom Darby
Tom Emmett
Tom Franklin
Tony Messenger

Tony & Joy
   Molyneaux
Tony Roa
Torna Russel-Hills
Tracey Martin
Tracy Northup
Trevor Lewis
Trevor Wald
Trilby Humphryes
Tristan Burke

Val Challen
Vanessa Garden
Vanessa Nolan
Vasco Dones
Venetia Welby
Victoria Adams
Victoria Walker
Visaly Muthusamy
Viviane D'Souza

Walter Prando
Wendy Langridge
Wendy Toole
Wenna Price
William G Dennehy

Yukiko Hiranuma

Zoe Brasier
Zoë Perry

Current & Upcoming Books

Title: *Nowhere People*
Author: Paulo Scott
Translator: Daniel Hahn
Editor: Ana Fletcher
Copy-editor: Sophie Lewis
Proofreader: Sarah Terry
Typesetter: Tetragon
Series & Cover Design: Hannah Naughton
Format: Trade paperback with French flaps
Paper: Munken LP Opaque 70/15 FSC
Printer: T J International Ltd, Padstow, Cornwall, UK